DIRTY LITTLE SECRETS

A J.J. GRAVES MYSTERY (BOOK 1)

LILIANA HART

ALSO BY LILIANA HART

JJ Graves Mystery Series

Dirty Little Secrets

A Dirty Shame

Dirty Rotten Scoundrel

Down and Dirty

Dirty Deeds

Dirty Laundry

Dirty Money

A Dirty Job

Dirty Devil

Playing Dirty

Dirty Martini

Dirty Dozen

Dirty Minds

Dirty Weekend

Dirty Looks

Dirty Liars

Dirty Valentine

Addison Holmes Mystery Series

Whiskey Rebellion

Whiskey Sour

Whiskey For Breakfast

Whiskey, You're The Devil

Whiskey on the Rocks

Whiskey Tango Foxtrot

Whiskey and Gunpowder

Whiskey Lullaby

The Scarlet Chronicles

Bouncing Betty

Hand Grenade Helen

Front Line Francis

The Harley and Davidson Mystery Series

The Farmer's Slaughter

A Tisket a Casket

I Saw Mommy Killing Santa Claus

Get Your Murder Running

Deceased and Desist

Malice in Wonderland

Tequila Mockingbird

Gone With the Sin

Grime and Punishment

Blazing Rattles

A Salt and Battery

Curl Up and Dye

First Comes Death Then Comes Marriage

Box Set 1

Box Set 2

Box Set 3

The Gravediggers

The Darkest Corner

Gone to Dust

Say No More

Laurel Valley

Tribulation Pass

Redemption Road

Midnight Clear

Forgiveness River

Atonement Trail

*My childhood did not prepare me for the fact
that the world is full of cruel and bitter
things.*

—J. Robert Oppenheimer

To Scott, Ava, Ellie, Max, Jamie, and Graham—
Because you are the most amazing people I could ever hope
to know and love. Thank you of giving me the privilege of
being a wife and mom.

ONE

Fourth-generation mortician. That's a lot of
dead bodies.

I thought I'd be proud to carry on the family legacy, but that was before I knew the job would be hell on my social life. I mean, who wanted to date a woman who drained blood on a regular basis and whose scent of choice was embalming fluid?

Sure, I got a little lonely sometimes. It mostly happened when I was preparing a body in the middle of the night instead of snuggled up next to someone warm with a pulse. But dead bodies were my business. And I hated every minute of it. I never wanted to take over the family funeral parlor. I wanted to be a doctor. Well, technically, I *was* a doctor, but I preferred to be one for the living.

My parents had died early last year, and the gossip and scandal involved would have broken someone with a lesser constitution, but I'd managed to hold my head up. Mostly. It was because of my parents that I'd had an impromptu career change. The only thing I had left of them was the crumbling old Victorian I grew up in and Graves Funeral Home—believe me, it was a hell of a legacy.

I had little choice but to resign my job at the hospital, pack my bags, and move back to Bloody Mary, Virginia— population 2,902. The good thing about owning a funeral home in Bloody Mary was that hardly anyone ever died, despite the rather macabre name. The bad thing about it was I had a ton of student loans to pay back and not a lot of income.

Did I mention the budget cuts?

Ahh, my life was simple before the budget cuts. The mayor's decision to be more fiscally conservative left King George County without a coroner. So, I, J.J. Graves, in a moment of temporary insanity, volunteered for the job. In all actuality, I was strong-armed into taking the position out of a sense of duty to the community and the guilt of tarnishing my family's good name. Well, tarnishing it any more than it already was.

Which brought me here. Alone in my bed in the middle of the night. My bedroom so cold white puffs of breath clouded above my face every time I exhaled because I couldn't afford to crank the heater above sixty-five degrees. My toes wiggled and fought for release beneath the nubby covers I'd tucked under the mattress too snugly, and goose bumps spread across the top of my skull and tightened the skin so much that it felt as if the follicles might snap off.

I'd been wide awake for more than an hour, thinking of my family, what was left of my legacy, and how much my life in general sucked. Not for the first time, the thought entered my mind that it wouldn't be so terrible if I just packed a bag and left everything behind me without a word to anyone. I didn't have any family to worry over my disap-pearance. No children to leave belongings to. Sure, my friends would miss me for a while. But eventually the people who'd watched me grow up would only have passing thoughts about that Graves girl whose parents killed themselves. All the while I would be starting a new life. Hopefully someplace warm.

But like I always did, I immediately dismissed the thought. It took more courage than I had to start over and leave everything familiar behind. I needed something in my life besides a lackluster career and a mountain of debt. A man would be nice. But chances of that happening were somewhere between negative four and zero. Not because Bloody Mary didn't have its fair share of men, but because I was just picky. Bloody Mary wasn't exactly teeming with single males under the age of forty who had health insurance and all their own teeth.

I huffed out another white puff of breath and rolled over, punching my pillow and clearing my mind of all thoughts that didn't involve counting sheep. I'd had trouble sleeping since I'd moved home. Maybe it was because the house was empty and made weird noises and my imagination assumed the cold blasts of air and the rattling pipes were the haunts of all my ancestors shaking their heads in pity. Or maybe it was because the mattress was old and lumpy. Who knew? But I'd learned to function on just a few hours of sleep when I was in medical school, so I was used to having bags under my eyes and skin that looked like it never saw the light of day.

The silence of the house smothered me—a heap of decaying wood and rotting shingles that crushed me with the weight of neglect and responsibility—so I burrowed under the covers, searching for peace of mind and the comfortable spot on the mattress that always seemed to elude me. I'd almost talked myself into getting up and starting a pot of coffee when the phone warbled on the bedside table.

I cursed under my breath and flailed under the covers so my sheets resembled something along the lines of a straitjacket. My pulse jumped and throbbed in the side of my neck, and each pounding beat marched through the synapses of my brain until I became lightheaded with something I recognized as fear. I closed my eyes and let out a slow breath.

The only time I got calls in the middle of the night was when someone died. I hated death. I hated that my parents had left such a massive responsibility on my shoulders. And most of all I hated that I was the only one the dead could turn to. I missed the living. The dead made me think of too many things I wasn't quite ready to face.

Against my better judgment, I answered the phone.

"Who died?"

"Very professional, Dr. Graves," said Sheriff Jack Lawson. "You always assume the worst. What if I was calling to invite you to poker tonight at my place?"

"At five o'clock in the morning? Who died?" I asked again. Jack had been my best friend since we'd been in diapers, and I knew without a doubt he'd be the one person who'd search for me if I just disappeared one day. I squeezed the phone in a white-knuckled grasp as silence reigned on the other end of the line. I prepared myself for the worst.

"It's Fiona Murphy," he finally said.

"Oh God," I whispered, untangling the covers and sitting up on the side of the bed. The wood floor felt like a sheet of ice under my feet, and I drew them up quickly so they were back under the covers.

"To say the least." Sirens and muted voices came across the line, and I knew Jack must be at the crime scene.

My teeth chattered—I couldn't tell if it was from the news or the cold—and I gritted them in determination so my words came out clearly. "Where's George?"

George was Fiona's husband. He was the meanest man I'd ever met, and Fiona had a new bruise every time I saw her. George was a gifted mechanic and owned the only garage in town, so despite people disapproving of the way he treated his wife, he had a large customer base and enough money to build a house that was one of the nicest in the county. He also had big hands and a wicked temper, and there wasn't a doubt in my mind he was the reason Fiona was dead at age thirty.

"George has already been picked up and booked on a first-degree murder charge. We need you down at the site. The crime scene guys are almost finished. I'm warning you, Jaye, she doesn't look good. Johnny Duggan found her in the ditch just off Canterbury Street on his way to work."

I swallowed the lump in my throat and prayed to a God I'd stopped believing in for strength. "I can handle it, Jack. I'm all she's got." It was the least I could do for a dead friend.

Bloody Mary—population 2,901.

TWO

I SHOVED MYSELF INTO LONG JOHNS AND A PAIR OF GRAY
sweats, pulled a black ski cap over my head and buttoned
the black down parka I'd gotten on sale at Eddie Bauer a
couple of years ago up to my chin. I put on two pairs of
thick socks and my all-weather boots. It was freezing
outside, and I hated being cold. Only the dead were cold.

I grabbed my medical bag and the expensive digital
camera I'd bought when I still had a well-paying job,
glanced longingly at the coffeepot, and slammed the front
door behind me without locking it.

My Suburban was parked on the graveled driveway, the
dull sheen of the black paint making it look a little worse for
wear. Not to mention the huge dent over the back left
wheel where a deer had decided it wanted to commit
suicide.

Suburban? you're probably thinking. I'd put my foot
down about the hearse my parents had kept in the garage. It
had worked for them, but I was satisfied with hauling bodies
in a Suburban. I was a twenty-first-century mortician, and
despite what the gossipers had said, I very seriously doubted

my parents were rolling in their graves because I'd had the audacity to sell their hearse on eBay. They were too busy hauling coal in hell to worry about what I was doing.

It took a few minutes to scrape ice off the windows and let the defroster work. Despite the fur lining my gloves, I couldn't feel my fingers. I looked for any sign of life as I backed out of the drive, but the yellow glow of my headlights touched on nothing but solitude. The trees were naked and brittle—the limbs twisted, as if they were hugging for their own warmth—and the sky was a dark navy spackled with the fading light of stars as it edged closer to daylight.

I lived at the end of a county lane called Heresy Road—where rocky land sloped until it met nothing but the frigid water of the Potomac. The road was a mixture of gravel and potholes—it was private, dreary, and I hardly ever got trick-or-treaters, vacuum cleaner salesmen, or Jehovah's Witnesses. My closest neighbor was a mile down the road.

The town was still tucked into sleep for the most part, and I maneuvered the roads quickly—my headlights glancing off quaint houses, a red-bricked schoolhouse, and a library with a clock tower that drove me crazy because it always struck the hour seven minutes too late.

There hadn't been enough moisture left over from the rain the day before to cause the roads to ice over, so I pressed harder on the accelerator. I turned onto Queen Mary and noticed the lights were on in St. Paul's Cathedral, which meant Reverend Thomas had already been notified of Fiona's death. A smattering of people would be in throughout the morning to pray for Fiona's departed soul.

When I got to Canterbury Street, it was crowded with vehicles and people, some curious, some weeping, but all had the glassy-eyed stare of shock. Things like this never happened in Bloody Mary. I beeped my horn to get through and parked by Jack's cruiser. His lights flashed a disorienting red and blue.

"Nice outfit," he said by way of greeting. I wasn't normally a vain person, so Jack's comment didn't really bother me all that much. He'd seen me at my worst—hangovers, cramps, bleached hair that turned orange, and crying jags—and he was still my best friend, so I wasn't really worried about trying to impress him.

I caught sight of myself in the reflection of the tinted windows of his car and grimaced. Just because Jack was used to seeing me at my worst didn't mean others were. It wasn't a pretty sight. On the positive side, I was relatively tall and had an athletic build, which was just good genes because I hated doing anything remotely athletic and I loved carbohydrates. My eyes were gray, my hair was black and swung just below my jawline, and if you looked really close before I got a chance to buy a box of Clairol, you'd see the occasional strand of silver. The women in my family had a tendency to go gray early. They also had a tendency to die young and tragically, but I was keeping my fingers crossed on that end of things.

All in all, I was pretty average, despite my sarcastic wit and inventive use of the English language, which I had to admit was pretty exceptional. But dressed from head to toe in my winter paraphernalia, with no makeup and the dead-eyed stare of someone who'd had a very small amount of sleep, I looked like the love child of Sporty Spice and the Stay-Puft Marshmallow Man.

Jack grew up the rich and privileged son of a tobacco farmer, and now he was the youngest elected official in the whole county. He skimmed just over six feet tall and he kept his dark hair cut close to the scalp. A thin slash above his right eyebrow made him look like a pirate, and I'd told him more than once he should thank me for giving him a little extra character, considering it was my cleat that collided with his face during a baseball game when we were kids. He was blocking the plate, I swear.

The more I looked around at the crowd, the more I realized it was mostly women who lined the streets, probably wanting to catch an early morning glimpse of Jack Lawson. Between his looks and his money, there weren't many women in the county who would turn down an opportunity to become his wife. Jack wasn't really interested in a wife, but between you and me, he'd auditioned about 80 percent of the women in Virginia for the job.

"I see you brought your fan club with you," I said in retaliation for the outfit remark.

He winced and rubbed his fingers along the short growth of his beard. "That's not funny. I almost didn't respond to Johnny's 911 this morning."

Jack had the unfortunate pleasure of being manipulated by many well-meaning parents who were desperate to marry their daughters off. He'd had thirty-two false alarm 911 calls this year where he was either met at the door by a naked woman or parents who just happened to have a home-cooked meal served with a side of their single daughter.

Johnny Duggan was the latest conspirator in the plot to snag the sheriff for his daughter. Stella was a middle-aged third grade teacher who had a pair of shoulders the New York Jets could put to good use and who always wore her underwear a size too small. Johnny Duggan was down to his last chance of getting her out of his house.

Johnny was currently huddled in the back of a police cruiser, sipping coffee with shaking hands and giving a statement to one of Jack's officers. He was a small man and had worked as the groundskeeper for the county for as long as I could remember, which was why he'd stumbled across Fiona's body at such an ungodly hour of the morning. His skin was toffee brown and wrinkled from the sun and age, but when he smiled his whole face lit up and it was easy to ignore the fact that he sometimes looked like a dried raisin.

"He still trying to set you up with Stella?" I asked.

"Yeah, poor bastard." Jack said with a tight-lipped smile. "But I won't be the sacrificial lamb to save that man's sanity." Jack handed me a cup of coffee in a Styrofoam cup. "I had to tell him that I was having a wild and crazy affair with you to get him off my back."

"I haven't had one of those in a while. Was it good?"

"The best I've ever had," he said soberly.

"Good to know I haven't lost my technique."

We stood in silence for a couple of minutes. I drank my coffee and warmed my insides, while Jack observed the crowd. I noticed Floyd Parker from the *Gazette* talking to anyone who might have any interesting gossip to spread around. He wrote frantically in the little red notebook he habitually carried, his eyes shrewd and calculating. The jerk.

Floyd was huge. Like, the Rock huge. But he wore wire-framed glasses to break away from the jock image. Really, he looked like the love child of Clark Kent and the Incredible Hulk—minus the green. Floyd had played some college ball at Virginia Tech, but I think his grades were too good to keep him from being anything other than second string. He was a handsome man and could almost give Jack a run for his money in the women department.

And yes, I can admit to one night of frenzied passion

with him when I was away at med school and incredibly lonely. It was a moment of pure insanity. Not one I'm proud of, and he never lets me forget it. But even if I didn't hate him for seeing me naked, I'd still hate him for what he'd done after my parents had died. Floyd Parker was lucky I didn't run him down with my Suburban every time I saw him in the street.

Floyd caught my gaze, looked me over from head to toe, and smirked. I restrained myself from grabbing the gun Jack had strapped in his shoulder holster and pumping Floyd full of lead. I compromised by shooting him the bird instead. Jack smothered his laugh with a cough, and my mood lightened for a brief moment until I thought about the body I was about to see.

"All right. I'm ready," I said, tossing my cup in a plastic sack. I put my hand on Jack's arm and gave it a comforting squeeze. "Thanks, Jack, for giving me a minute. This is harder than I thought it would be."

Jack nodded and we walked over to the crime scene together. Fiona's gunmetal-gray Ford Taurus sat on the side of the road and faced in the opposite direction of her house. The Taurus had to be at least ten years old, but it still looked new. George was meticulous about things being in order and tidy in appearance, which was probably the only reason he never put marks on Fiona's face.

"She finally decided to leave him, huh?" I asked.

"Looks like it," Jack said. "I spoke with the sister this morning. She said Fiona talked to her last night about eight o'clock. Said she was ready to get out, leave for good. They had an appointment this afternoon to meet with an attorney to file for divorce."

I looked inside the open trunk and noticed the neatly lined suitcases.

"The sister lives in Florida, so she wasn't expecting her until sometime this morning," Jack said.

"Did she have car trouble?" I asked.

"Ran out of gas. We haven't gotten a confession out of George yet. He's still busy playing the grieving husband, so he hasn't told us yet if the empty gas tank was his idea. My thoughts are that this was very well planned out, to the last detail, just the way he likes it."

I followed the tread of another set of tires behind Fiona's car and watched the last of the crime scene guys take more photos.

Jack pointed to the deep treads in the mud. "Her killer pulled in right behind her. He knew she wasn't going to try and hike her way into town in freezing temperatures, and chances were less than slim that someone would drive by and see her that late at night. She had the standard blankets in her back seat like anyone else with a brain in this area. We found a cell phone in the bottom of her purse, fully charged, but instead of staying inside out of the wind and calling for help, she gets out. Why?"

"Panic, maybe?" I said and shrugged my shoulders. "If she thought her husband was going to come after her maybe she decided she'd take her chances with the elements instead of staying in one place where he could find her."

"Yeah, that was my first thought, but look at her footprints. The ground was soft after yesterday's rain. She steps out of her car and goes around the back to meet whoever pulled in behind her. There's no indication she was trying to run away. Her trunk was closed when we found her this morning, so she wasn't trying to get anything and get back inside. I'd thought at first she might have been getting another jacket. There's one back there."

I looked at Jack in confusion, knowing I was missing something important, and then the lightbulb went on.

"You don't think it was George?" I hissed in a shocked whisper. It wasn't an opinion I wanted anyone else to hear. In a small town like Bloody Mary, the citizens had a tendency to declare guilt first and ask questions later. I knew this from experience. And they wouldn't care for their sheriff to have a different opinion. It sure wouldn't help him win the next election.

"That's for you to help me find out," he answered, his teeth gritted in a smile so hard I was surprised they didn't turn to dust.

Jack ran his hands through his hair in a gesture I recognized as frustration. He knew how small towns worked, and he knew he was walking a fine line. He'd forgotten his hat again, so I pulled the spare I always kept out of my pocket and handed it to him. Jack was good at his job. He was way overqualified to be the sheriff of a podunk town, and no matter how unpopular his theories, I would always back him 100 percent.

I squeezed his arm in support. "I'll look into it," I assured him.

He nodded in gratitude and pulled the ski cap down low over his ears. "This is how I see it. She runs out of gas and realizes she's still too close to home. Not too much time passes before someone else pulls up behind her, and by the size of the tire treads, it looks to be some kind of truck."

"George has a truck," I said, playing devil's advocate. "And who else would be traveling this road that late at night?"

"I know, and we'll test the treads and take samples from the bottom of his tires, but don't you think that if Fiona recognized her husband's truck behind her, she'd dig out the cell phone from the bottom of her purse?"

"What if his lights kept her from seeing who it really was?"

"Listen, Jaye, I know you want it to be George. Even *I* want it to be George. There's not a man in this county who deserves to be in jail more than he does, but we have to look at every possibility. My gut is screaming over this."

The last time Jack's gut had screamed over anything, he'd been shot three times and forced to retire from a job he'd loved.

He pointed to the clearly imprinted treads in the now-frozen mud. "He pulls up behind her, and let's say she doesn't recognize the vehicle. She feels relief, maybe gratitude that luck should be on her side tonight. She's invincible and has just taken the biggest step of her life. She gets out of the car calmly and takes four steps toward him. Have you noticed that as clear as the tire treads are in the mud, there are no footprints from him that show us the initial meeting?"

I had noticed, but I wasn't entirely sure what that meant, so I let Jack continue to paint his picture.

"That tells me he deliberately kept to the pavement. He probably got out on the passenger side."

"So maybe he just didn't want to get muddy."

"Maybe. So he comes up to her, talks to her a bit. Maybe he tells her to grab her purse, that he'll take her into town. I don't know. But for some reason she turns and he strikes a blow to the back of her head. You'll have to tell me once you get her in if it was multiple times, but my gut says once. He just wanted to incapacitate."

There was a small amount of blood on the ground near

the trunk, and the crime scene team had already numbered and photographed it for their report.

"Then what?" I asked.

"We found more blood in the back seat of the car. The blankets were shoved to the floorboard. That's where he raped her. He tied her up and waited until she was coherent before the rape, then left the rope on the seat. Didn't tidy up after himself."

I shivered as we made our way to the other side of the car. To Fiona. Jack had painted a clear picture in my mind, and after I got her on the table, I'd be able to tell him for sure if his theories were correct.

The December air was brittle with cold, and the wind chill was several degrees below freezing. The sun peeked through the bare trees and cast everything in a pinkish hue. The only good thing about the temperature was that Fiona Murphy was well preserved.

Fiona hadn't died with dignity. Her naked body was sprawled facedown, her arms and legs at abnormal angles. I ignored the yellow spray paint the crime scene unit had used to trace her and moved so I could snap pictures from different angles. When I was through, I squatted down beside her to get a closer look.

"God, she's a mess. Some of these bruises look weeks old," I said as I ran my gloved finger down her back and around to the side of her ribs. "The ones along the spine look fresh. And I'll make sure when I get her back to the lab, but by the coloring I'd say they've been there no more than a day."

There was blood matted to the back of her blond hair where the initial blow had been struck. It had turned black and flaky overnight.

"He posed her here," Jack said. "Everything about this scene is deliberate. Look at the footprints."

I looked down at three precise footprints labeled with a yellow tag. I stood and moved back so I could take a look at my own. My footprints were visible, but they were smeared. The killer's were a different story.

"They're perfect."

"I know. He places her body here, poses her arms and legs, and then plants three perfect footprints next to the body. Look how close together they are. He either has extremely short legs or was trying to shuffle slowly with the body in his arms."

"And if he was shuffling slowly, there would be smears," I finished for him.

"What do you want to bet that those perfect footprints are the same size as George Murphy wears?"

"You think someone deliberately set up George? Who would do such a thing?

"I don't know. Maybe one of the hundreds of people in this town he's managed to piss off."

When put that way, the list of suspects could go on forever. I flexed my leather gloves that were tightening with the cold, took a deep breath, and turned the body over. A long red silk scarf was wrapped around Fiona's throat and mud was caked on the side of her face. I tried to look at the scene dispassionately through the lens of my camera, documenting the broken capillaries in the eyes due to the strangulation and the swollen tissues around the neck. Her face was the palest marble, and the hopelessness that had been imprinted on her face over the years had vanished in death.

"There's no facial bruising," I said. "George has always been careful about that for the most part, but there are bruises on almost every other surface of her body. Apparent cause of death appears to be strangulation. And I'll definitely rule it as a homicide. After everything she's been through, someone chokes her to death. I'd say she's been dead no longer than six or seven hours, but it's hard to tell. I can't gauge the time of death accurately by body temperature because of the weather, so I won't be able to give you a firmer TOD until I get her on my table. The sister's story about the phone call helps narrow it down a little, but that's the best I can do right now."

Jack squatted next to me and his every breath sent cold puffs of white into the air. He put a comforting hand on my shoulder.

"I'm sorry, Jaye. I know you were friends."

"It's been a long time. George didn't let her have any close friends." Guilt ate at my insides despite the fact that it had been out of my control. I remembered a skinny, pale-haired girl built like a dancer with laughter in her eyes. A girl who'd grown into a quiet young woman stuck like so many others in a town that offered little. A woman who George Murphy had taken one look at and decided to claim for his own. She hadn't had any better offers.

"I'm sorry for you too, Jack. I know you were close once."

"Yeah, well, that was in high school. Like you said, it's been a long time."

"He didn't bother to condomize for the rape, so we'll be able to nail him with DNA. Let's get her back to the lab, and I'll get started. It's the weekend, so you know everything's going to be slower. I'll have to send the DNA to Richmond as soon as you get a sample from George. It'll probably be the end of next week before the results come back."

"We're already on it," Jack said. "Let's get her loaded up and I'll follow you back."

I looked into Fiona Murphy's open, empty eyes, and brushed the matted hair back from her face. I couldn't give her dignity. But I could bring her justice.

THREE

The drive through town was slow due to the fact that everyone recognized my vehicle, and word had obviously spread about Fiona's death. Cars slowed almost to a stop and gawkers on the sidewalk made the sign of the cross as I led the procession back to the funeral home.

"You've got to be kidding me," I murmured. I wasn't expecting Fiona to sit up in the back and answer me, so I took the time to swear as I saw a pear-shaped, elderly woman in a peacock-blue wool coat and yellow snow boots. Mrs. Meador was flagging me down with the precision of a traffic cop, and there's no way I'd stop to give her the time of day. Fiona would thaw before I was able to make an escape. So I gave a polite beep of my horn and a little wave as the Suburban came close enough to touch the sleeve of her flailing arms. She pursed her lips in disapproval, narrowed her eyes, and I knew I was going to get a tongue lashing from the old bat the next time I saw her. Very few people thwarted Mrs. Meador and survived to tell the tale. I looked in my rearview mirror and saw Jack shaking with laughter as he turned his sirens on to move traffic along a little faster.

It took almost half an hour to make it back to my lab, which wasn't good considering it usually took about twelve minutes to drive from one side of Bloody Mary to the other. The funeral home parking lot was blessedly empty, and I pulled the Suburban under the attached carport nearest to my lab.

Don't let my cloak-and-dagger-like references to my place of business confuse you. The "lab" is little more than a refurbished basement at the funeral parlor, but it's top of the line and as nice as any you'd find in a bigger city. My parents had been meticulous about every aspect of their business. It was their personal lives they hadn't had very good control of.

Graves Funeral Home was on the corner of Catherine of Aragon and Anne Boleyn, close enough so people wouldn't have to go out of their way to find it, but far enough away that I was afforded a little privacy. There was a strip mall across the street that housed an attorney, a laundromat, and a veterinarian who moonlighted as a bookie out of his back room when he wasn't castrating steers or selling discounted drugs to anyone who didn't have good medical insurance.

I waved to Denny Kasowski, the vet, as he watched us unload Fiona from the back of my Suburban with slack-jawed fascination.

"Geez, Jaye, don't encourage him. I've been trying to bust him for the last eight months. He's got his fingers in so many illegal pies that the cage is going to eventually close on him for a long time."

I started to whistle as I followed Jack into the side door of the funeral home. I didn't figure it was a good time to mention that I'd bought a case of penicillin and a year's supply of birth control pills out of the back of Denny's trunk.

We rolled Fiona down the ramp into the basement lab area, and he helped me get her moved onto a sterile metal table that had a deep indention around the entire perimeter to catch any stray body fluids. I flipped the ventilator on, stripped off the mountain of cold-weather clothes I was wearing, and snapped a pair of latex gloves on my hands. Jack, bless his heart, was kind enough to offer to stay with me, but it usually took him less than ten minutes to get sick from the smell. The man could look at crime scenes and blood all day, but being closed in a room with a dead body and embalming fluid was just too much.

"Jack, you're looking a little green," I said, my grin evil. "Let me get her set up and get the samples, and I'll meet you upstairs for breakfast. Jasper Bridges slaughtered a pig a couple of days ago and brought me some fresh sausage to help pay for his mama's interment."

Jack went pale. He turned and ran up the stairs gagging. I laughed a little to myself. It was a cruel thing to do, but it wasn't funny every time.

I turned the stereo on so it blared classic rock and took a deep breath. When I turned to face Fiona, I gave her an apology before I got to work. She was only the second homicide I'd worked on since I'd taken the job as coroner. Like I said before, hardly anyone ever died in Bloody Mary.

And the last murder I'd dealt with hadn't exactly been something that had the potential to cause an avalanche of trouble if handled the wrong way. Bobby Gentry had been my first murder. His brother Billy had gotten back early from a hunting trip and caught him climbing out of his bedroom window naked. Billy's wife, Loretta, had only been wearing

Bobby's cowboy hat at the time, so I could understand how Billy had jumped to the right conclusion. Billy had left a hole in his brother's chest big enough that cause of death wasn't too difficult to determine. And there hadn't exactly been a lot of internal organs left to remove during the autopsy. It had been an open-and-shut case considering there'd been a witness and Billy had been more than happy to confess to the deed.

It wasn't like this time. I already felt the pressure to do right by Fiona, and I'd barely started. I'd been at the top of my class at Columbia Medical School and worked for two years as an ER doctor at Augusta General, so I could at least tell the difference between an anus and an aneurism, but I was only a coroner because I wasn't board certified to be a pathologist. I'd had to take a board examination to get my mortician's license, but I'd had the advantage of growing up in a funeral home on top of my medical background, so it hadn't been difficult.

A coroner wasn't unusual in small towns. Usually the town doctor took on the position, but Doc Randall hadn't wanted the job—smart man—so I'd been the next best thing. Considering Doc Randall had already seen the early side of eighty, I was thinking I might eventually get to take over his job and do what I was trained for. Since all the women in my family had died before the age of fifty, I wasn't holding out too much hope.

Jack would take a little while to turn back to his normal color, so I set to work on preparing Fiona's body. I gathered a blood and semen sample to send to Richmond, and then switched on my black light to look for fibers. I bagged what I found, cleaned her body with strong-smelling disinfectant, then took out my recorder to officially document my findings.

I flipped the stereo off so there would be no questions if

the tapes needed to be heard at a trial. "Fiona Murphy. Caucasian female. Age thirty. Victim has shoulder-length blond hair and blue eyes. Small crescent-shaped birthmark on right thigh, and small tattoo of what seems to be a dragon on left buttock."

I couldn't imagine what Fiona had been thinking when she'd picked a dragon for her symbol. Actually, I couldn't believe she'd gotten a tattoo at all. I looked her over once more before I started listing the other marks that marred her skin. Her body had enough damage to fill up every official document I had.

"Swollen tissue around neck due to strangulation. Multiple hemorrhages in neck muscles and broken blood vessels between the head and shoulders are also indicative of strangulation. Multiple contusions on both right and left arms and abrasions on wrists indicate she was restrained."

I looked closer at her wrists, turning them over slowly in my hands, and then moved down the table to look at her ankles. There were old burn marks. Fiona had been tied up before. Interesting.

"Evidence shows signs of old ligature abrasions around both wrists. Deep bite marks found on both left and right breast, probably more than a week old by discoloration around area. Bruising around ribs one, five, six, and seven. Contusions and slight abrasions on hipbones. Secondary set of bite marks found on both thighs. There are abrasions on both knees, and again, old ligature marks on ankles."

I took measurements of the bite marks on her breasts and thighs. And then I did it again.

The marks belonged to two different people. What had George made her participate in? Her feet and face seemed to be the *only* parts of Fiona's body that didn't have a mark of some kind. Not even her murderer had tortured her as much as her own husband.

I stopped my train of thought. Jack's impression of the murder scene already had me declaring George's innocence. I flipped Fiona over and went through the same routine as quickly as possible. I almost felt guilty for working on her. Fiona needed some peace in death.

What made it worse was she'd been killed just as she'd found the courage to escape a life of misery. I shook my head and covered her body in one of the white sheets I kept folded on the shelf. I rolled her into the refrigeration unit, washed up at the sink by the stairs, and headed up the stairs to meet Jack. I closed the reinforced steel door that protected the dead while I was away and locked it behind me.

Jack sat at the small table in the kitchenette that had been added on to the downstairs of the funeral parlor when my parents had first married. I looked at the clock, surprised that I'd been at it almost an hour.

"You are a horrible, vengeful woman," he said.

"Yeah, isn't it great?" The green tinge had left his cheeks, but he was still pale. "Here are your samples," I said as I handed him a small paper bag. I tossed the file of notes I'd taken on her body in front of him, and he gave me a curious look before he picked up the file and began to read. Looking at the torture Fiona's body had been through had affected me more than I'd expected.

His mouth tightened as he saw the extensiveness of the damage to Fiona's body. And then he stiffened. "Two sets of bite marks? You're sure?"

"I measured them twice. But who knows who the second set belongs to."

"I'll get someone to take an imprint of George's mouth

so we can compare. I have no idea who else is going to come up in this investigation, but things could get sticky."

"I really hope you're wrong, Jack. I want it to be George."

"There's all kinds of justice, Jaye. If George is responsible then he'll pay."

I nodded and wrapped myself back up in my coat and gloves. "Let's grab some breakfast. I've been up for hours and I'm starving."

"Are you still having problems sleeping? You should have bought illegal sleeping pills from Denny instead of those birth control pills. It's not like you have to worry about getting pregnant wearing outfits like that."

I narrowed my eyes, but my lips twitched before I could help it. It was hard to argue with the truth.

"Jerk."

"But you love me," he said, pulling my hat down low so it covered half my face. "Let's go. I want to stop by the Murphys' and see what my boys have found before we get breakfast. I'll drive the sample into Richmond myself so it gets there before they close for the day."

Jack looked toward the basement stairs and back at me. I saw the conflict and indecision on his face on whether or not he could eat breakfast with me and keep it down. I had a tendency to talk shop at the dinner table.

"You owe me for that stunt you pulled earlier. If I wasn't such a gentleman I'd make you buy breakfast."

It *was* a good thing Jack was a gentleman because I only had about four dollars and seventy-three cents in my wallet.

Fiona's car was being towed away as we passed by the scene of the murder. An officer stood in the middle of the road, flagging us down as we made our way toward the Murphys'.

"What's up, Riley?" Jack asked.

"I just thought I should give you this, Sheriff," he said, handing Jack a small key. "I found it in a second search of the car. It had fallen between the seats, so I had a little trouble getting it out."

"It's a safe-deposit box key," Jack said, holding it out to me so I could study it. "I've got one just like it for First National here in town. Good work, Riley." Jack put the car in gear and headed to the end of the street.

The crowd had dispersed to go back to their homes or jobs, and there were only two police cars parked in front of the Murphy house when we got there. A pair of scuffed boots stuck out from underneath George's truck, so Jack and I headed in that direction to see if anything of consequence had been found.

"Officer Mooney?" Jack asked. "Is that you under there?"

"Yes, sir," Mooney answered. He scooted out on his back and then stood slowly, working the kinks out. He held a plastic bag in his hand, but I couldn't really see what was inside.

Jeremy Mooney had been two years behind me in school, but his sister Alice was my age. Alice had barely gotten her cap and gown untangled and thrown on the floor before she'd headed out to the nearest big city. Jeremy had decided to do two years of junior college in Nottingham and join the force. He was the kind of guy who'd live in Bloody Mary forever, marry a local girl and breed a fifth generation of Bloody Mary Mooneys. He was twenty-eight years old and still carried the pudgy baby fat of adolescence and a light sprinkling of peach fuzz on his upper lip. He always looked like a kid playing dress-up in his patrolman uniform.

"What have you found?" Jack asked.

Jeremy held up the little plastic bag so we could see what looked like a tiny sliver of mud. "I've found next to nothing," he said. "And I had to work to scrape this much off the tires. If he'd left prints with this vehicle in the mud down yonder then there would be splatters up under the wheel wells and the undercarriage, but I haven't found anything. It's clean as a whistle."

Jeremy chewed a wad of pink bubble gum and had a thoughtful look on his face. "George is one of those people who's blessed with having both balls and brains. Pardon me again," he apologized, face turning red.

I just rolled my eyes because being irritated at Jeremy was like being irritated with a homeless puppy. It just wasn't possible.

"I'd agree with that statement," Jack said patiently.

Jeremy scratched the top of his sandy head. "Well, it just seems to me that George wouldn't be one to kill his wife and then go into town, plain as day, for a car wash to get rid of the evidence."

I hoped I'd concealed the surprise on my face that Jeremy was able to come to that conclusion by himself. He'd never struck me as the sharpest knife in the drawer, but I was sure Jack had hired him for some reason or other.

"People who commit murder do all kinds of crazy things," Jack said. "Why don't you head into town and start talking to people at the diner and at the places across from the car wash. Maybe we'll get lucky and someone will have seen him around town."

"Yessir, I'll get right on it," he said, leaving the bag with us.

"He surprises me sometimes too," Jack said, reading my mind. "Behind the naïvety is a pretty sharp brain."

We headed inside the house just in time to hear the commotion. Detectives Colburn and Nash had identical grins on their faces. Both detectives were about a decade older than Jack and had been part of the department before Jack had been elected. I didn't know either of them well, but they gave Jack the respect he deserved and didn't try to cause trouble for him like a couple of the other older officers.

"We found the mother lode," Colburn said. "Would you like door number one or door number two?"

"Just give it to me in order," Jack said. "Tell me what you found first."

"There was a hidden panel inside the closet," Nash said, taking over. "Let's just say that George's tastes in erotica run to the exotic. And some of it looked painful."

I thought of Fiona's battered body and shuddered.

"You okay?" Jack asked.

"Yeah," I said. "Just remembering."

Colburn and Nash looked at me oddly, and Jack squeezed the back of my neck in warning not to say too much, even in front of other cops, so I shut my mouth and gave them a blank-eyed stare. I wasn't a good liar on my best day, and it was plainly obvious they wanted to ask more questions, but good manners kept them from doing so.

"What else?" Jack asked to distract them.

"We found a piece of paper with several sets of numbers printed on it in a box of Playtex hidden under the sink. They look like bank account numbers."

"Nice work, detectives." Jack had a grim smile as he held up the piece of paper. "We'll take a look. Finish up here and then close it down," he said, slapping Colburn on the shoulder. "Make sure everyone has their report on my desk before they go off duty. We don't want anything to slip by us."

We headed back to the Suburban in silence. I couldn't think of very many situations where an abused woman would have the courage to keep multiple bank accounts and get herself a safety deposit box. And what could she possibly have of any worth to hide in them?

"Would you look through a box of Playtex if you thought a woman was hiding something important in there?" I asked Jack.

"I wouldn't look through a box of Playtex if there was gold bullion in there," Jack said. "There are just some places a man should never go."

That's what I'd thought he'd say. Fiona had obviously still had some wits about her. But why hadn't she taken the account numbers with her if she was really leaving her husband? It seemed to me a woman starting a new life would need something to start it with. If Fiona had money saved, then she'd definitely be taking it with her.

I thought of my own scenario of picking up and starting over, and I wondered how I'd make it without leaving any electronic tracks behind and with enough cash so I wouldn't have to sleep under a bridge or beg for food. There would be no possible way to get that kind of startup cash without delving into the darker side of life. It left me asking the question again of what Fiona had been mixed up in.

Only this time I wasn't so sure that George had anything to do with it.

FOUR

SLAUGHTER'S CAFÉ WAS THE ONLY PLACE IN TOWN TO have a sit-down breakfast in the mornings. It consisted of one tiny room with tables crammed into every available space, a kitchen that I never tried to look into because I didn't *really* want to know what was going into my stomach, and a long cracked linoleum counter with a hand crank cash register on top. The walls were painted the color of egg yolks and the floor was covered in twenty years of bacon grease. Despite the potential for ptomaine poisoning, it did a brisk business because the food was outstanding.

"When is Fiona's family set to arrive?" I asked over a steaming plateful of eggs, bacon, and pancakes. Jack had offered to pay, so I was able to get more than the measly eggs and toast my four dollars and seventy-three cents would have bought. I shot Jack's own bowl of lumpy oatmeal a look of disgust. The man might be fine to look at, but he had no taste in food.

"Her sister's the only family she's got left. Phyllis is her name. She was several grades ahead of us in school, so I don't really remember her. She and her husband will be in this afternoon to help make arrangements for the body."

Jake spooned up a glop of oatmeal onto dry whole-wheat toast and took a satisfied bite. "You know," he said. "You're going to keel over with a heart attack if you keep eating like that. Think what a bind that's going to put us in if our only coroner dies. We'll have to give your body to John Luke Stranton over at the Here and Gone Funeral Parlor, and he'll use too much rouge like he always does and you'll look like a hooker. I hear he doesn't put underwear on the bodies either."

"I've heard that too. Cheapskate. And his prices are outrageous. I can't afford him. You'll just have to bury me in my backyard."

"We could just weigh your body down with rocks and throw you off the cliffs by your house. There's always room for one more body in the Potomac."

"That's not a bad idea. You know, I had no idea how much it cost to bury a loved one until I took over the business. Mom and Dad had left instructions to be cremated, and they'd already taken care of the cost, so even then I didn't realize how exorbitant it all was."

Jack squeezed my hand and looked at me steadily, but I focused my attention on my food and pretended the tears pricking at the corners of my eyes weren't there. My parents had left me in a real fix financially, but they'd also left me in a fix emotionally. Jack was probably the only person who really understood how much it had hurt me to not be able to say goodbye to anything but their ashes. They'd already been cremated by the time I'd been notified of their deaths. And there was a rage inside me that was festering into something I wasn't ready to face. It was so much easier to just put one foot in front of the other and try to tackle the other problems they'd left me with.

"If you feel so guilty you could always lower your prices."

"No way. If I go any lower I'll be able to qualify for food stamps. If more people died in this stupid town it wouldn't be a problem."

"Bite your tongue. Life makes my job a lot easier."

"Well, then, as long as your life is easier then I'm fine with being destitute. The house is falling down around my ears, I have student loans to pay off, and Mom and Dad took out a second mortgage on the funeral home." I still didn't know what that money had been used for. I couldn't find any record of it being spent, and just the thought of it made my stomach cramp. My parents couldn't be criminals. Not on top of everything else.

I drizzled more syrup on my pancakes and took joy where I could find it in the pained look on Jack's face.

"That's disgusting, Jaye."

"You know, a lesser woman would probably be huddled on the floor in the fetal position crying her eyes out after everything that's happened to me in the last year. But nothing can get me down. Things might look bad now, but in another twenty years, my education will be mine free and clear. And then I can start shoveling my way out of the rest of it. My attitude is so positive that I could give Oprah lessons."

Jack grinned a lopsided smile and spooned up another bite oatmeal. "I was just thinking the other day that there was something different about you. You know, all that good fortune that's coming your way is a reason to eat better and live to see the day. Or I could give your stubborn behind a loan."

"No thanks, Jack. It's my problem. I'll deal with it my way." It was the same thing I told him every time he offered. I'd feel like I was taking advantage of our friendship if I took his money, and that friendship was pretty much the only solid thing I had left in my life.

I cleared my plate with a satisfied grunt, thankful I'd worn sweats with an elastic waist, and licked the last bite of syrup off my fork. "I've got to take off. I have a few errands to do in town before I get back to Fiona. Are you going to stop by the bank on your way back from Richmond?"

"I wouldn't miss it," Jack said. "Don't forget poker tonight. I'll let you know what I find out then."

"Thanks for breakfast." I eyed Jack's oatmeal and an idea popped into my head. "You know, that oatmeal looks a little like..."

"Don't even think about saying it, or I'm going to arrest you."

"Sounds kinky," I said. "I'll see you tonight."

<hr>

Bloody Mary was like most small towns. It had all the usual fixtures—a bank, a post office, a grocery store, a gas station, a funeral parlor, and a smattering of independent businesses that barely scraped by from one month to the next. We had a mix of the very wealthy—usually tobacco farmers like Jack's family—and the very poor. The town was more than two hundred years old, and the historical society didn't approve of anything modern built between the crumbling brick buildings and the preserved wooden structures. But we did have two brand-new stoplights that had been put up last spring when Mrs. Meador and Old Lady Barlow got into a fistfight over who had the right-of-way. The police and fire stations were right next to city hall, and all three structures sat smack dab in the center of King George County, since they served all four cities in the county.

And like most small towns, any event that occurred, big or small, was going to be discussed and speculated over everyone's morning coffee. And this morning, the death of Fiona Murphy was the biggest event to happen in Bloody Mary in quite some time.

I parked the Suburban in two of the tiny parking spots in front of the post office. It was a perfectly square, red-bricked building with a flat roof and two small windows in the front. It sat on the corner of Henry VIII and Tudor, and thanks to its strategic location, it ran a close second to Martha's Diner as the center of gossip.

As soon as I walked through the doors to check my post office box, I knew I'd made a mistake.

"Well, Dr. Graves, I didn't expect to see you in today," Carlton Fisk said.

Carlton had been the postmaster for fifty-two years and he knew everything. And I really do mean *everything*. I'd been scared spitless of Carlton Fisk my whole life. The man was creepy. He could predict what the weather was going to be on Tuesday of next week, he'd picked the winning lottery numbers twice, and he knew when every woman in town was ovulating.

Like I said. Creepy.

The fact that he was about six feet eight and as old as Methuselah didn't help matters any. His skin stretched taut over his bones, and thin white hair fell in strings down to his shoulders. His eyes were milky blue, and he drove a 1925 Studebaker Phaeton. Oddly enough, he'd decided to sell his house and move into one of the new condos that overlooked the county square. He said it was better for his social life.

He'd been married once upon a time, but his wife had died before I'd been born. Probably before my mother had been born.

"Good morning, Mr. Fisk," I sang cheerfully as I headed toward my mailbox as fast as I could go.

The few people who were inside the post office stopped what they were doing to listen, just in case there was something new to discover.

"I hear you've had a busy morning," he continued. "Poor Fiona. That girl never stood a chance against George. We all knew what he was doing to her, could see the bruises plain as day, but she wouldn't accept any help."

Carlton shook his head at the pity of it, while I dug around frantically in the bottom of my purse for my mailbox key. Why was it that I could never find what I was looking for when I was in a hurry?

"Aha!" I said after unearthing it. But since I was an equal opportunist when Murphy's Law was involved, I dropped it on the ground.

"I heard from someone over at the police station that the size of those footprints they found matched George's shoe size," Carlton went on. "But they said there were no shoes in his closet that matched the tread. They also said the tires were the same as on his truck, but there was no mud on the wheels of George's tires like there should have been. I've always thought that George was a lot smarter than he let on. Though I probably should have guessed it. He is a good mechanic."

Someone at the police station had been busy gossiping. And if I had to hazard a guess I'd say it was Barbara Blanton, the dispatch operator. The woman had a mouth the size of Kentucky and a finger on speed dial at all times. We'd barely left the Murphy house ourselves more than an hour before.

What if George hadn't killed Fiona? What if it was only made to look that way? I kept coming back to that thought. Something felt off. But no one would know for sure until the DNA test came back for the sperm sample I'd sent off with Jack.

"That's interesting, Mr. Fisk, but we won't know anything for sure until later next week."

"I know, I know, but I've got a feeling that this is more than it seems," he said. "I surely do. And you know how accurate my feelings are."

I knew all too well. Mr. Fisk was the one who'd told my parents it wasn't a good weekend to go to their cabin in the mountains only a few hours before they drove their car over a two-hundred-foot cliff. The police report mentioned that the steering on the car had seized up, but a witness had come forward saying it looked like there was a struggle going on inside the car and that they'd driven over that cliff on purpose. All I knew for sure was the insurance company still hadn't made up their mind, so I couldn't collect their life insurance policy.

"Oh, by the way," Carlton said. "There was a young man in here earlier looking for you. Nice-looking fellow. An out-of-towner. And he had a nice set of teeth. I know how picky you are about that. This is opportunity knocking on your door. I can feel it."

"Thanks, Mr. Fisk," I said, my teeth clenched so hard I was giving myself a headache. Whenever there was someone new in town, I got phone calls to let me know that I was more than welcome to call dibs, since I was one of the oldest unattached females in the county. It seemed there were a lot of people in Bloody Mary looking out for me.

Whoever this man was, asking where to find me had just opened a whole can of worms that he was liable to regret. But like Mr. Fisk said, I wasn't going to be one of those people to let an opportunity pass me by. I wasn't stupid. I hadn't had a date in eight months and twelve days. Not that I was counting.

I stopped by Martin's Grocery to pick up a few necessities and heard about the mystery man and Fiona's murder once again as I raced my basket up and down the aisles, throwing in only essentials and wincing at the thought of adding to the total on my credit card. But a girl had to eat, and I handed over the plastic to Hilda Martin while calculating how much spending room was left.

"I heard George is so upset by Fiona's death that they had to sedate him at the hospital." Hilda clucked her tongue as she waited for my card to go through. "One of the nurses said he was bawling like a baby, and makin' himself sick with grief. You just never know what's really going on with a person."

I *mmmhmmed* appropriately and signed my name to the credit slip. I grabbed my bags and headed out the door when I heard her call out, "Bring your young man by later and introduce us. He looks like a movie star. And he has very nice teeth."

I grimaced a smile in reply and bulldozed my way to the Suburban, head down, avoiding eye contact with anyone who might try to stop and talk. I breathed a sigh of relief when I was finally inside the safety of my own vehicle. There was a reason I liked living so far away from town.

The road crews had been out salting and sanding, and a mixture of gravel and salt crunched under my tires on my way back to the funeral home. We'd have snow before nightfall. I could smell it in the air. It was a bad time to bury someone in the ground.

I pulled the Suburban under the covered portico attached to the funeral home. My great-grandparents had built the funeral home after World War II. It was a monstrous three-story Colonial with dark red brick and white columns. It was impossible to heat in the winter and even worse to cool in the summer. My grandparents had been short on money after it was built, and they'd turned the top two floors into their living quarters.

And it was my parents, thank the Lord, who'd bought the cliff house where I grew up and currently resided. I wasn't fond of the dead on my best days. I sure as heck wasn't going to live with them. I'd closed the third floor of the funeral home off completely and divided the second level into three large viewing rooms just on the off chance that there was more than one death in a day. Sometimes I was lucky to get one death in a week, so odds were it wouldn't ever be a problem.

I noticed the man who'd been the subject of town gossip for the last half hour sitting on the porch swing under the wide columned front porch. The idiot should have been freezing, but he looked comfortable in his black leather jacket and scarf. Or at least I assumed it was the man from town. It wasn't often I had an incredibly fine specimen of the opposite sex camped out on my doorstep.

I regretted not taking a little time on myself before I'd headed to the murder scene this morning. A little makeup, maybe a slinky dress and heels with matching lingerie would have been along the right lines to make the kind of impression I wanted. Instead I looked like a round, makeup-less meatball in my winter coat. I scowled and wondered not for the first time when Lady Luck was going to give me a little help. Or maybe even a warning. It probably didn't matter anyway. This guy was way out of my league, so I just resigned myself to disappointment.

I pulled grocery bags out of my back seat and watched out of the corner of my eye as he headed my way. His walk was confident. He knew where he was going and what he was doing, and dollars to donuts the man wasn't told no very often.

"Are you Dr. Graves?" he asked, taking a paper sack full of macaroni and cheese, powdered donuts, and Pringles out of my hands. Like I said, I only got the essentials.

He gave me a full wattage smile, and I couldn't help but notice that his teeth were very fine indeed.

"I'm Dr. Graves." I took his offered hand briefly and then grabbed another bag. "You must be the nice-looking fellow who's been asking about me around town."

He laughed with just the right amount of apology and chagrin, and a low throb I hadn't felt in a long time pulsed its way beneath my skin and tingled along my spine. Laugh lines crinkled attractively around his eyes. His hair was dark blond and long over his ears and neck—long enough to pull back in a stubby tail. Some would say he looked shabby or careless, but *sexy* was the only word that came to my mind. His clothes were high quality and his watch was expensive. And everything about him only made me more self-conscious. I broke eye contact and started moving toward the kitchen door. But then I stopped and stared at him again. There was something about him. Something... familiar.

"Do I know you?" I asked, trying to place him.

His moss-green eyes were serious, but there was a sparkle of humor in them. And I could have sworn they'd looked at me exactly that way before.

"Well, I guess that would depend."

I unlocked the side door that led into the kitchen and plopped the groceries on the table. "What should it depend on?"

"On whether or not you've read my books. But don't worry if you haven't. I hardly have any ego at all."

Then it clicked, and I knew who stood in front of me. "Brody Collins."

"Ahh, I was just kidding about the ego. I have an enormous one, so thank you for boosting it a bit."

"You look fairly normal for someone with such a twisted imagination."

"I get that a lot."

I fought the urge to grin and turned my back to put the groceries away. "So what brings you to my doorstep?"

"I hear you're the woman to talk to about dead bodies."

"You could say that." The bitterness in my voice was obvious even to me, but there was nothing I could do to give him a different impression.

"Good. I was hoping you could help me," he said as he leaned against the kitchen counter. A man who looked as if he'd never had a care in the world. "Because I just killed a woman."

FIVE

I had one of those moments where I could literally feel the blood drain from my face, and my life flashed before my eyes. I thought of regrets and things I wanted to do but would never get the chance—like going to Hawaii, having children, and getting revenge on Floyd Parker. Not necessarily in that order.

"Dr. Graves?" Brody asked, a quizzical brow arched. "Are you all right? You're awfully pale."

"This is Virginia in the middle of winter. Everyone's pale." I cleared my throat and edged my way toward the knife block. "I'm sorry, maybe I misheard you. Did you just say you killed a woman?"

"Yeah." His enthusiasm was visible as it changed his entire expression. His eyes darkened to the deepest jade and his cheeks flushed with pleasure. His entire body moved with excitement. I'd never seen someone so happy about death.

"She's the first in my new book, and you always remember the first. It was a real gruesome murder. She was barely recognizable when they found her. But I'll bring her justice in that final chapter. That's the ultimate payback."

"Book?" I asked.

"Yes. I write books," he said patiently, as if he were talking to someone only slightly smarter than a turnip. "I believe you said you've read a few. And if you've read my books, you know I always kill someone. Usually several people."

"I know you write books." Embarrassment tinged my voice.

All I wanted to do was slink down into the basement and finish what I'd started with Fiona. Working with the dead had obviously stunted my social skills. Maybe Jack was right. Maybe when you worked around embalming fluid it started to seep into your skin and eventually you became a perfectly preserved specimen of something not quite normal.

"I was just confused about the killing part. You never know what to expect in my business, and it's been a long morning."

"I've heard, which is why I'd like to work with you while I'm in town. If you don't mind, of course."

He gave me that smile again that made me want to nibble at his lips like candy, and I couldn't help the sigh that escaped. I knew there was no way he could seriously be flirting with me, and I knew for a fact he was trying to charm me into getting his way, but I couldn't control my reaction to it.

He brushed a lock of hair behind my ear like he'd been doing so his whole life, and I froze like a deer in the headlights. He continued his explanation as if he hadn't noticed my reaction to his touch.

"I'd like to see the process of how you, being a small-town coroner, deal with violent postmortems. And then observe how you put the pieces back together, so to speak, for their funeral. You're the whole package. Exactly what I need."

I realized I was still wearing my coat and sweating like a pig, so I yanked off my hat and gloves and stripped out of my coat to reveal my sweats. I decided I needed to do something to keep occupied while all of that testosterone was in the room. My face was hot, and I didn't know if it was from temperature, embarrassment, or because I was turned on. Maybe all three.

"Would you like something to drink?" I asked. I put grounds in the coffee maker and poured in water. I looked longingly at the cupboard where I had a bottle of Jameson Irish Whiskey stored and wished I lived in a culture that found it appropriate to tipple a little before performing an autopsy.

"Coffee's fine," he said.

"How did you find out about this so quickly?" It was still shy of noon. "You can't tell me you had any interest in researching me before this happened. Bloody Mary is barely a speck on the map, and my career as coroner has been less than that."

"You could say it was fate. I happen to live in Richmond and saw the story on the early morning news. And I can also say that I've got friends in the police department who were happy to let a few details slip. After I heard the nature of the crime, I decided it fit perfectly for my newest book. Bloody Mary is the perfect town for these crimes, and you're right in the middle of it all. I think you'd be just the kind of character I could use as a female lead to drive my detective crazy."

I snorted out a laugh before I could help it. "News flash,

Brody Collins. I'm not some simpering fan who can be persuaded to do something foolish because you have an overabundance of charm. Men like you do not flirt with women like me, and I think it undermines both our intelligence to pretend otherwise. I'm a lot easier to impress when honesty is involved."

That had never been truer until after my parents died. That was when I'd realized my entire life had been a lie.

"Honesty then." He nodded soberly. "I'd really like to observe you for a few days."

"I'll give you fair warning, murders are few and far between in Bloody Mary. In the whole county, for that matter. It's going to be a short research session."

"Does that mean you'll let me observe you?" He held out his hand and watched me with patient eyes. I had a feeling they saw more of me than what I was comfortable with.

"I guess so, for what it's worth." I held out my hand for a no-nonsense shake between two business partners.

Awareness flared inside of me just before his hand touched mine. My mind was screaming *mistake!* even as attraction tingled across my skin. My breath caught in my chest and I watched in fascination as his pupils flared and the thin green ring seemed to glow with the heat of his desire. His thumb rubbed over the pulse in my wrist and he took a step closer.

"You're wrong, you know." His breath whispered across my skin, and it took all my willpower to keep from leaning into him.

"About what?"

"A man like me can't help but flirt with a woman like you. I'd be insane not to. That lean, sexy body under layers of clothes is wreaking havoc on my imagination. Full lips that beg to be kissed. And wounded eyes the color of cloudy skies. Your eyes undo me." He leaned closer, his lips barely a whisper from mine, and I knew if I didn't stop things now, he'd find out how his much his words affected me. No one had ever spoken to me as if, in that one moment of time, I was the center of their universe. It had been so long since I'd been held. And my body and my soul thirsted for contact.

I pulled away quickly and wiped my hands on my legs nervously.

He looked at me with a combination of understanding, sympathy, and lust, but he let me escape. "Why don't you give things a chance? You might be surprised to see where it goes. I have a feeling there could be something amazing between us."

"Or it could be a complete disaster," I returned.

I was a complete fraud. I wanted honesty between us, but there was no way I could tell him how afraid I was of the chemistry that had just plastered me against my kitchen counter. I'd never felt anything like it before and I was terrified I'd be the one to screw things up. I had a whole lot of baggage I carried around with me.

He smiled as if he'd heard my thoughts, and the look he gave me was one of fierce determination. "I've been known to be patient."

I nodded and fled toward the basement door. I hated to break it to him, but he was going to need a lot more than patience. Something more concrete—like a good attorney or a private investigator who would keep his mouth shut. In my experience, most people didn't want to associate with anyone whose parents' activities were being investigated by the FBI.

SIX

"That's a pretty high-tech security system for a small-town coroner," Brody said. "The medical examiner in Baltimore has the same system."

I keyed in the code and waited as a series of locks unbolted. The thick metal door opened on silent hinges, and I led the way down metal stairs that echoed loudly with every footstep. The basement room was sterile and white from floor to ceiling. Metal shelves with my equipment lined one wall, four filing cabinets lined another, and a long counter with double sinks lined the third. On the fourth wall was the walk-in refrigeration unit and the metal tables I used for embalming. The fluorescent lights glared blindingly over the metal and white, and the ventilation system whirred softly in the background.

"My parents had the extra security added when I was a teenager," I said. "A few of the high school kids decided it would be fun to break into the funeral home on Halloween, drink beer, look at dead bodies, and generally scare themselves to death. Sheriff Drummond was in charge then, and he showed them what it felt like to sleep inside a cell for a night."

I didn't add that the current sheriff was one of the guilty parties involved. And Jack's mama had put the fear of God into him way more than a jail cell ever could.

"My parents didn't press charges, and those kids are all fine, upstanding citizens of Bloody Mary today. But my parents had to overdo it on the security because the relatives of the deceased weren't too happy about the situation." And in hindsight, the added security had probably been necessary for my parents' extracurricular activities.

"Ahh, to be young and foolish again," Brody said with a wistful smile.

I went to the walk-in refrigeration unit and pulled out Fiona Murphy. The unit was meant to hold three bodies comfortably on gurneys, and I hoped I never saw the day when there were more than three residing there.

"What happened to her?" Brody asked when I pulled the sheet down far enough to show the marks at her throat. Death was always surreal when you looked at a body away from the crime scene—to see one naked and still, slightly blue tinged and somehow peaceful in the aftermath of violence.

"I got called to the crime scene early this morning. She'd been found by a man on his way to work, lying in a ditch at the side of the road."

"Hell of a way to start the day."

"You're telling me." I pulled on my surgical gloves and protective overcoat, strapped on my prescription goggles, and pulled the sheet to the end of the gurney. "Here, put these on," I said, tossing him a pair of gloves. He blew into the end of each glove before sliding his hands inside. It was obvious he'd had practice. Latex gloves were a pain to a novice.

My mouth watered as he pulled a pair of horn-rimmed glasses out of his shirt pocket and slipped them on. I rolled my eyes at my idiocy and rushed to fill the silence before he noticed I'd been staring. "Her body was found near her car. She'd run out of gas on the way to her sister's."

"So do the police think it was a case of being in the wrong place at the wrong time?"

"Nope. She was on her way to her sister's because she was leaving her abusive husband of twelve years."

"Okay," Brody said. He ran his fingers through his hair, and his eyes narrowed in thought. "So she packs her bags and tells him she's going to live with her sister, and he follows her until she runs out of gas. And luck just happens to turn in his favor so he has the opportunity to kill her. That doesn't seem very likely."

"This wasn't a crime of passion. It was premeditated and planned down to the last detail. Bob Shiney owns the gas station here in town and he told the sheriff this morning that she bought a full tank of gas yesterday morning, so someone helped relieve her of a few gallons between ten yesterday morning and nine last night when she left her house."

"What do you mean someone? Don't you think it was the husband?"

"He's the most logical suspect," I said, avoiding the question. I wasn't ready to tell anyone Jack's theory on the murder. Research for a book or not, information like that had a tendency to get out, and I didn't want to make things any harder on Jack than they were going to be. "George had a history of violence with her—of violence period—but she never pressed charges against him."

I rolled Fiona over gently and parted the hair at the back of her head. "The first blow was struck here. There are no fibers, so that tells me it wasn't wood or a synthetic material. It was probably a metal pipe of some kind because the wound is even across the skull."

"What do you mean by that?" he asked.

"I mean that if he'd used something like a hammer or a pipe wrench, the blow would have been deeper in the area originally struck, just from the point of impact. This was not a life-threatening wound. It would have given her a concussion and incapacitated her for a short period of time. Which is exactly what he wanted it to do. But you already knew that, didn't you? You obviously know your way around an autopsy room if you've been observing the Baltimore ME. Are you testing me to make sure the small-town doctor knows what she's doing?"

"No, ma'am," Brody said, coughing to stifle a grin.

I narrowed my eyes, ready to spew fire at the insult. I was one of those people who hated failing at anything, and I had enough insecurities about the job without having others add to the problem.

"But I've found it's never a bad thing to ask questions. I never know what answer might strike a new idea or make me consider a different angle."

"Right. Sorry,' I said, feeling more and more like a fool the longer I was in his presence.

"Was she sexually assaulted?"

"Yes. After he rendered her unconscious with the pipe, he moved her to the back seat of her vehicle and tied her with a natural fiber rope, which can be bought at any hardware store in America."

I pulled her arm up so he could see the slight abrasions and discolorations on her wrist. "I collected fibers from the ligature marks this morning and sent them to the lab just in case there's something unusual that will help us identify where he bought it, but I doubt it.

"She fought him during the rape," I said, laying her arm back down. "There was skin under her nails, and the struggle is what caused the abrasions from the rope. She finally found the courage to fight back and leave, and this is what she got for it."

"And all of this happened on the side of the road, fairly early in the evening, without one person driving by?" he asked skeptically.

"You're saying nine o'clock is fairly early in the evening because you're from Richmond. Time moves slower here. The entire town is shut down by that time of night."

"God, how do you survive the boredom?"

"There's a lot to be said for peaceful towns," I answered primly, even though I'd asked myself the same question after I'd been forced to move back home. "There are only four houses on Canterbury Street where Fiona was found. The lots are large in size and surrounded by trees. Even if she'd screamed, the neighbors probably wouldn't have heard her."

I moved farther down the table to where I'd collected the sample of semen that had been left behind. "He did us a favor by leaving his DNA. I sent the sample to the lab this morning. We should have the results back by next week."

"I'll play devil's advocate and say wouldn't the husband's defense be that they'd made love earlier in the evening? The physical evidence doesn't prove murder."

"There was a reason I went to medical school instead of law school. I've never been a fan of injustice. He tore her up a little, caused some vaginal bleeding. Cause of death was strangulation. You can see the marks around her throat.

Murder weapon was a red silk scarf. If George committed the crime, then the sheriff will find a way to prove it."

"I wouldn't think a town this size would have a police department capable of handling a murder investigation."

I bristled a little at the implication. Jack was always underestimated, even by the people who'd voted him into office. "That might normally be the case, and I'll admit the police here don't have a lot of opportunity to get on-the-job experience, but Jack Lawson, our sheriff, knows what he's doing. He'll get the job done."

"I didn't mean to offend you. It sounds like you're close with the sheriff." It was obvious he was fishing for information about our relationship by the competitive glare that came into his eyes.

"We are. Jack's a good man. He'll see to it that whoever killed Fiona pays." His scowl deepened, and he opened his mouth to say something, but I beat him to the punch. "I hate to cut your research session short, but I can't perform the autopsy with you here without getting permission from Jack first. It's his investigation, and anything I find is sensitive information."

Brody's jaw clenched and jealousy practically oozed from his pores every time I mentioned Jack's name. I realized as I was doing it that I was subconsciously trying to push Brody away. I covered Fiona back up and rolled her back into the cooler.

When I turned back around, Brody's body stood rigid and unmoving, and he blocked my path so I had no choice but to face him head on. I somehow found the courage to meet his stare, and I was surprised at what I saw. It was obvious I hadn't deterred him at all. If anything, he looked more determined to get what he wanted. And apparently, he wanted me.

"I'll leave you to your work. For now. But you'll see me again. I'm sure I'll think of a lot of follow-up questions."

My lips twitched before I could control it, and I shook my head in defeat. "I figured as much."

Brody Collins was going to be a handful.

His body relaxed and he gave me a satisfied grin. We trudged back up the stairs to the main part of the funeral home and I followed him out the kitchen door.

"What happens to her now?" he asked.

"Her sister will be here this afternoon to arrange for the burial. I can't embalm her until the paperwork is filled out and I've finished the autopsy. And then, with luck, I won't have to deal with something like this again. Bloody Mary is a safe place. A good town. Though the people can take getting used to."

"Do you mind if I ask you a question?"

"Isn't that what you've been doing the whole afternoon? What's one more?"

"Why would an ER doctor give up her career to move back home and serve the dead instead of the living?"

I stiffened and took a step in retreat before I could help myself. "You can ask all the questions you want about my business, but my personal life is my own."

"You intrigue me, Dr. Graves. I've never been one to let curiosity sit idle. Like I said before, you'd make a fascinating character. If my Detective Ambrose isn't careful, you're the kind of woman he could definitely fall for."

"Then I hope he doesn't mind being disappointed. My life really isn't all that fascinating."

I could tell by the determined look in his eyes that he'd know everything about me by the time he sat down to dinner. All he'd have to do is ask a few questions around town to learn most of it. There were still a few things about my life that even the people of Bloody Mary didn't know, but if anyone could sniff out the truth, I was betting it was Brody Collins. Maybe it would be best to let him find out as much as he could. The FBI sure wasn't very forthcoming with information, though they seemed to thrive on speculation and the seemingly endless amount of questions they had about my parents. Questions I didn't have answers to.

"Have a safe drive back to Richmond. I'm sorry you weren't able to get any interesting information about the murder." I started to close the door, but he stopped it with his hand.

"Oh, I'm not driving back to Richmond. You've inspired me to stay in Bloody Mary and finish the book right here. I don't suppose you could recommend a place to stay?"

I mumbled something unladylike under my breath, and knew with his declaration that it was destined for our lives to be tangled. There was something about him that drew me in, and I wanted his hands on me more than I'd wanted anything else in a long time. I just hoped I could put the pieces back together again once he decided to untangle himself.

I sighed and pointed down the road. "Baker's Bed and Breakfast is right down the street. It's the slow season so I'm sure she's got room for you. Tell Wanda I sent you."

"I will, thanks." He paused like he wanted to say something else, but he just tucked my hair behind my ear again and skimmed his knuckles across my cheek. "I'll see you around, Dr. Graves."

I didn't find my voice until his SUV disappeared down the road. "That's what I'm afraid of."

SEVEN

THERE WASN'T A WHOLE LOT TO DO IN VIRGINIA IN THE winter. An explosion in the population come September explained what most people were doing with their forced time indoors. But for the rest of us who didn't have someone to keep us warm on a snowy night—there was poker. And boy did we take it seriously. I didn't know anyone between the ages of eighteen and ninety-two who didn't belong to a league. Gambling fueled the souls of the weary and fired the blood of every citizen in town.

And once a year, all the practice paid off. The Knights of Columbus hosted a poker tournament at the civic center every New Year's Eve. The grand prize for the poker champion was ten thousand dollars and a trip to Richmond to compete in the state tournament. I'd never had a chance of claiming the prize, and things weren't looking too different for me this year. It was no one's fault but my own. Hollywood had never been in the cards for me, because no matter how much I tried, I couldn't keep from advertising every thought I possessed across the blank canvas of my face—not a good handicap to have for this particular sport.

But Jack, on the other hand, was a wonder. He'd been the champion for the last two years. No one had a better poker face than Jack. And unlike me, Lady Luck always smiled on him—probably because she was a woman and that's what women did with Jack.

It was his turn to host our weekly addiction, and I decided to get to his place a little early to pump him for news on the murder investigation. I was curious to see what he'd found out at the bank, and I'd bought a six-pack of his favorite beer to offer as a bribe so he'd tell me everything he knew. This was a practice that had worked since high school, so I figured there was no need to change things now.

The snow I'd predicted earlier fell in soft, heavy flakes as I walked out my front door, six-pack in hand. I bypassed the rotted boards of my porch and jumped over the three sagging steps that led to the ground just in case today was the day I finally fell through. If I kept my eyes straight ahead, it was easy to ignore the eyesore that sulked behind me like a decrepit old woman, waiting for the right moment to wrap her arms around me and drag me kicking and screaming into the pit of homeowners' hell—which I'm sure is an actual place.

By the time I maneuvered the Suburban around the metal cans the trash collectors had tossed in the street, the gentle fat flakes had turned into a vicious blizzard. The wind blew with a cutting edge that sliced through the naked trees with a whistle and pushed against the Suburban as if it was waging a war against the Michelin tire company in general.

I flipped on my windshield wipers and crept along the single-lane road, my heart thumping a staccato beat in my chest, and the chili dog I'd eaten for lunch churning in my stomach. It was me against the elements—and I was losing.

Thin sheets of ice formed rapidly on the country road, and I cursed when I realized I hadn't had time to put chains on the tires with all the excitement of the day.

I heaved a sigh of relief as I pulled up in Jack's driveway. At least I hoped it was Jack's driveway. I unclenched my cramped fingers from around the steering wheel and tried to bring some semblance of recognition to the structure in front of me. The lights flashing on and off in quick succession from inside the house was Jack's way of letting me know I was in the right place.

Jack lived in a two-story log cabin that looked as if it had been carved from the forest of trees surrounding it. A wide porch surrounded the entire house and a chimney of gray stone jutted from the steep roof. It had taken him three years to build it exactly as he wanted, and he'd done most of the work himself. The house described Jack to a tee—masculine, rugged, and enduring.

I was more than an hour early, and from the looks of the weather, poker night might be called off completely, but there was no way I was going to turn around and brave the roads just so I could go back to a drafty house and a cold bed. Jack had dependable central heat, food, and booze. I couldn't ask for more.

I sat in my car a few more minutes, hoping there would be a break in the weather long enough that I could get indoors with as little embarrassment as possible. I pushed against the car door until it finally flung open with a gust of wind, and the only thing that kept me in an upright position was the fact that my arm was still caught in the seat belt. I held tight to the beer as horizontal sleet pelted my face until it tingled with the pinpricks of numbness, and I trudged, one foot in front of the other, to Jack's front door.

I didn't bother to knock—neither of us ever did—and I

almost wept in relief as heat cocooned my body the moment I stepped inside. Sharp pins stabbed into my skin, and I moaned in pain as feeling came back to my extremities.

"Are you okay?" Jack asked.

"Do I look okay to you?"

"Nope, but I thought it would be polite to ask." He pulled the cap from my head and rubbed my arms briskly to get the circulation moving. "You know, anyone with half a lick of sense would have stayed home tonight."

"Yeah, but then I'd have to wait until tomorrow to get any information from you. I figure it was worth the risk. And your house is better equipped to ride out the storm. We're not just friends because you're pretty."

"I feel so used," Jack said. "What am I getting out of this relationship?"

"Just the pleasure of knowing me," I said. "I am a doctor, after all."

"It's hard to argue with that logic," he said. "Come on in the kitchen. I'll put a pot of coffee on while we wait to see if the others are as reckless as you are."

"I'll ignore that since you're making me coffee. And I'll even share the beer I brought. Did you get the sample to Richmond? Sometimes they leave early on Fridays."

"Oh, I got the sample to the lab. And we'll have the complete analysis by Monday," he said with a smile I recognized, though I'd never been on the receiving end of it.

"How, I'm afraid to ask, did you manage to work that minor miracle?"

"Let's just say that the lab tech was very grateful. She doesn't mind working weekends at all."

"You slept with the lab tech?"

"Of course not," he said. "We're going to dinner tonight."

"You should come with a warning label." Jack's powers over the opposite sex never failed to amaze me. I had seen many a woman fall at his feet over the years. It made my heart hurt just a little to think that one of these days Jack would find a woman who would make him do the falling.

I inhaled the aroma of something sinful when he opened the oven door and had to subtly check my chin for drool. "Incredible. Why hasn't some woman snapped you up?"

"God forbid," he said with a mock shudder.

"Good attitude," I said. "That way I can keep you all to myself. I'm starving. I don't think the chilidog did it for me today."

"It looks like it might be only us tonight with the way things are going outside."

"Good, more for me."

Jack put a tray of hors d'oeuvres in front of me and I dug in.

"Did Fiona's sister make it in this afternoon?" Jack asked.

"Yeah," I said. "I recognized her after she told me her name. She'd already graduated and left Bloody Mary by the time we'd gotten to high school, but I remembered seeing her around town sometimes when I was younger. She was shaken up pretty badly. They were close, talked a couple of times a week, she said. She's scheduled the funeral for Sunday afternoon. They have a family plot in the old cemetery where their parents are buried."

Jack came over and put his hands on the back of my shoulders squeezing lightly. "It's always harder on the living," he said. I knew he realized that Fiona's death had hit me harder than I'd let on. She'd been my friend, even if we hadn't kept up the rituals friendship entailed as we grew to adulthood.

"Yeah, well, it helps for justice to be served in cases like this. It'll at least bring a little bit of peace to her sister to know that the crime didn't go unpunished."

"That's all we can do for her," Jack said. The phone rang and his arm left my shoulder to answer. I felt alone without him at my back, and I realized I didn't know what I would do if anything ever happened to Jack. He was my rock, and I was his. His line of work left a lot of variables.

The sound of his voice startled me out of my melancholia.

"That was Eddie," he said as he sat across from me and filled a plate. "He said he was going to stay home with Charlotte and the kids tonight. He doesn't want to leave them alone in case the storm makes the power go out."

"I can't say I blame him."

Our particular poker league consisted of five smartasses with varying levels of poker ability—me being the worst, Jack being the best, and the other three falling somewhere in between. I was the only woman in our merry band, and I wouldn't have it any other way. In my experience, men were a lot easier to get along with than women—they judged you to your face and they were generally honest unless you were sleeping together. I'd never slept with any of the guys, so I didn't have anything to worry about.

Dickey Harlowe, whose real name was something outrageous like Richmond Dexter Harlowe IV, was the hereditary bank president at First National—fifth generation. Banking was what the Harlowes did, even though Dickey had graduated in the top ninetieth percentile of his class from James Madison University and was truly a bum at heart. So mostly Dickey played golf and signed his name to official documents his secretary sent to him—and since he'd been having an affair with his secretary for three years, she usually knew where to find him. The fact that Dickey was married to a plastic surgery-addicted piranha didn't excuse his adulterous behavior, but it certainly added to the sympathy factor. Dickey's poker skills ran toward the spontaneous with bursts of luck that kept him in the running.

Vaughn Raines was another member of the group. I'd dated Vaughn a couple of times my sophomore year of high school, but we'd decided it was just too weird. Vaughn was a nice guy and a hell of a poker player, but he soon discovered after his dates with me that his affections veered more toward the opposite sex. Apparently, I'd opened his eyes to the fact that he was gay. That wasn't a particularly glowing endorsement for my dating resume, so we'd agreed to keep the secret between us. Vaughn owned an antique store/vitamin supercenter over in King George Proper. Despite the weird mix, it seemed to do very well.

And last in our happy but dysfunctional group was Eddie Turner. Eddie was a typical "average Joe," which wasn't exactly hard to be considering the company. Eddie was the nine-to-fiver. He owned a rent-a-car agency in the city and was married to a really nice woman he'd met on a singles cruise to the Bahamas five years ago. They'd had a traditional Episcopalian wedding at St. Paul's, and exactly two years later his wife had given birth to their first child. And then two years after that she'd popped out one more. Eddie's poker skills were slightly higher than mediocre. I liked his wife, and his kids were cute in short increments of time.

"I thought they said on the weather channel that we were only going to get a few flurries."

"Well, technically we did get a few flurries, but then

they morphed into freezing death crystals. I don't think the weathermen are required to be a 100 percent accurate. That's one of those things that appear in fine print at the bottom of the screen. I'm just glad I'm not on call tonight. There's nothing worse than trying to dig some poor shmoe out of the snow before he freezes to death."

"Happy thoughts, Jack."

"Yeah, I'd much rather talk about murder," he said. "I did find out a few things of interest. Did you know that Fiona was seeing a therapist?"

"What?" I asked. "For how long?"

"I found his name and contact information in the appointment book we retrieved from her house this afternoon. Dr. Henry Hides has an office in Nottingham. When I called to deliver the news, he seemed surprised. She'd been his patient for more than four years."

"You'd think someone like her therapist would be able to spot the signs of abuse. I literally found contusions and abrasions on every patch of skin except for her feet and face, but oddly enough I didn't find any scars. And I checked hospital records, but she never went in for treatment. Not once. But you're telling me the therapist wasn't surprised when she supposedly turns up dead by her husband's hand?"

"Yeah, I thought it was rather odd myself. Why don't we go pay the good doctor a visit tomorrow morning? His office happens to be on the bottom floor of his townhouse, and I'd like to get the chance to see the big picture."

"And four eyes are better than two."

"Exactly. And while we're in Nottingham we can stop by the Alexandretta Boutique. I found a label inside the scarf that was used as the murder weapon. The Alexandretta Boutique is very high-quality handmade apparel. And it's less than two blocks from Dr. Hides' office."

"When was Fiona's last appointment?"

"Thursday morning, ten a.m."

"So Fiona goes to see her longtime shrink and then heads over to an exclusive boutique to pick up a scarf that will eventually kill her in the next ten hours? How much did the scarf cost?"

"One hundred and twenty-eight dollars."

I let out a low whistle at the price. I couldn't remember the last time I'd bought an item of clothing that cost more than a hundred dollars.

"And Marie, the manager at the boutique, was sorry to hear about Mrs. Murphy's death. She was one of their best customers. And that is a quote."

"George and Fiona didn't exactly live like they were rolling in money. And I can't recall ever seeing Fiona look anything more than presentable. She was always clean and her clothes were pressed, but they looked like clothes off the rack. You could tell she had pride enough to try to pass off the illusion of her marriage to everyone in town, even if she did always cower away from anyone who wanted to talk to her for more than a few minutes. Like she was afraid word would get back to George that she was actually having a conversation with another adult. What the hell is going on?"

"That's a good question. Maybe we'll get some answers tomorrow. If this weather ever lets up. We should swing by the hospital and see if George is available to be questioned when we're done in Nottingham. The guard on duty tells me every time the drugs wear off he starts moaning and crying and thrashing around, too distraught to be handcuffed."

"Guilty conscience?"

"Maybe. Or maybe he's planning to go to Hollywood. Who knows? But he can't keep it up much longer. Did you finish the autopsy?"

"Yeah, I was able to confirm the time of death. Between nine thirty and ten is as accurate as I can get. If you figure she left the house at nine on the dot and then make a time allowance for the initial blow into unconsciousness and the rape, we're looking at about half an hour to forty-five minutes from the time she walked out the door. She had her last meal a couple of hours prior to death, just some vegetable soup and crackers. I'll be interested to see what the tox screen shows Monday, but my gut says it'll be clean. She had full capabilities when she was killed."

Jack just grunted like that's what he'd expected all along. "Oh, by the way," he said. "Jeremy Mooney called me while I was headed back from Richmond. It seems that several people witnessed George Murphy getting his truck washed yesterday."

"Really?" I asked, surprised.

"Yeah, he went by the car wash right after he shut down the garage last night. A little after six."

"Figures," I said, deflated. "Do you think he did it on purpose? It rained early yesterday afternoon, but the sun was out by three. Do you think he got the car washed knowing it would be muddy, and then after he killed Fiona, he had it rewashed late enough to where there were no witnesses like the first time?" I was grabbing for straws, and I knew it. "It would explain why the truck was so clean."

"Do you think that's what he did?"

"Not really," I said. "It seems like a lot of trouble to go to. Maybe too much planning in advance."

"That's a personality trait that describes George to a tee, though."

"Well, make up your mind, Jack. You either think he's guilty or you don't," I said grumpily. "Did you find out anything at the bank?"

"By the time I got back from Richmond and tracked down the scarf and the therapist, the bank was closed. It's Friday," he said by way of explanation.

"Oh, yeah. I hate that," I said.

Dickey always closed the bank at four o'clock on Fridays. Wife's orders. Fridays belonged to Candy—whether she needed Dickey to cart around shopping bags, drive her home after plastic surgery, or chase her bratty Yorkie around the neighborhood with a pooper-scooper. Candy wasn't going to let a little thing like work interfere with her life.

"I've got a couple of contacts I still have in DC working on tracing those bank account numbers. We might get lucky there if they can find anything."

I just grunted and headed to the nearest window. The snow was falling even harder, if that was possible. Jack's kitchen was at the back of the house and faced the Potomac. He had a view of hundreds of hardwood trees similar to what could be seen from my place. I looked out the bay window and knew I was in trouble when I couldn't see any sign of the trees, much less the river.

"Looks like you're going to have to bunk here tonight," Jack said. I considered giving a token protest but decided against it. Jack's place was warm; he had good food and all the booze I could ask for. Why would I leave just to salvage my pride?

"Did you give the lab tech this afternoon a similarly lame pick-up line so you could get into her pants?" I asked as I headed toward the living room with the beer and sat on the floor in front of the fireplace. The fire was toasty warm and felt good against my still-chilled skin. This was the kind of weather that made you feel like you'd never be warm again.

"Darlin', I don't have to say anything to get into a woman's pants. I just have to be."

That was a sad fact but true. And I was thankful I was immune. "Let's play Go Fish," I said, attempting to change the subject. "For money."

"I hope you play Go Fish better than you play poker. The only reason I still hang out with you is because I feel guilty that I've taken all your money. You can't even afford to hire some poor schmuck to take you out on a date. What are you up to, four years now?" he asked with a smile and a wicked glint in his eyes.

"Shut up and deal the cards," I said. I decided to keep Brody Collins to myself. There were some cards that needed to be held close to the vest.

EIGHT

I WOKE UP WITH THE SMELL OF A LOCKER ROOM permeating the inside of my nostrils, and it wasn't until I felt the cottony softness of a sock caress my cheek that I realized there was a monstrous foot in my face. There was a hole in Jack's sock so large I could see three of his toes. A finger ran down my instep and reflexes took over. The next thing I knew, Jack had rolled to all fours and was wheezing through his teeth.

"What did you do that for?" he asked. His voice was graveled and sounded as if he'd just swallowed shards of glass.

"You tickled my foot."

"Yes, but that is not a crime punishable by kneeing someone in the balls."

"Well, it's a good thing you met the lab tech yesterday instead of today then. It serves you right for taking advantage of one of my weaknesses. They'll bounce back in no time, and I'll buy you lunch to make up for the damage." The quickest way to get Jack to forget about the pain below his belt was to move his interest to something else. And we could both be swayed by a good meal.

"Yeah, fine," he agreed. "Let's see if we can make it out of my driveway and then you can buy me breakfast too."

"Okay, but it has to be fast food. I'm not made of money, you know."

"And it's no wonder. How you managed to lose thirty-seven dollars playing Go Fish last night is beyond me."

He was right. I wasn't a gambler. I mentally scratched Las Vegas off my top ten list of places to travel and followed Jack to the front door.

"Looks like Harvey's had the snowplow out this morning," Jack said.

Harvey Wallace rented cabins on the south side of the county during the tourist season. The other four months of the year he drove a snowplow when we needed one. And year round he held a seat on the King George County Council. It was a thankless job, but somebody had to do it.

"What time is it?" I asked.

"Quarter 'til seven. Let me shower and change then we can head to your place so you can do the same. I want to get to Nottingham as soon as we can. Dr. Hides wasn't exactly cooperative when we spoke on the phone yesterday."

"You afraid he's going to disappear?" I asked.

"No, I think he'll stay around to see what we find, but I don't think he's going to try and do us any favors by pointing us in the right direction."

"I guess we'll find out soon enough. Hurry and get your shower. I want to check out that boutique while you're talking to the manager. It's almost my birthday, you know."

"I already have your gift. I bought you a year's worth of online poker lessons."

"Gee, Jack, you sure know the way to a woman's heart."

Harvey had done a good job with the plow. The roads were clear and Bloody Mary was quiet. Before long there would be children wrapped from head to toe in their snow gear, making snow angels and building snowmen. But for now, it was peaceful and serene, the snow pristine.

We'd decided to take my Suburban to Nottingham instead of Jack's cruiser because it handled the roads better. I'd gladly handed over the keys when he'd asked to drive.

My house came into view, and I was surprised by how beautiful it looked covered in snow. Apparently, it *was* possible to polish a turd. There was no way to tell that the paint was peeling in sections, or that the side steps to the porch needed to be repaired. The roof sagged just a bit over the wide covered front porch, the weather vane was crooked, and the latticework skirting around the bottom of the house was missing a few boards. But it was home.

And then I saw the Cadillac Escalade parked in my driveway and I forgot to breathe.

"Who's that?" Jack asked.

Oh, good, I wasn't imagining things. Jack saw him too.

I didn't answer because I wanted to regulate my breathing in case I started to hyperventilate. Brody Collins had made quite an impression the day before. And once again, I looked like crap.

"Hello? J.J., who's that man?" Jack asked, snapping his fingers in front of my face.

I got out of the car without answering and walked my way across the snow to the front steps as if I were in a trance, and I vaguely heard Jack following behind me. Brody was dressed warmer today in boots and a long wool coat. He had a ski cap pulled down low over his ears, but his hair was long enough to still be seen in the back.

"Hi," I said.

"Hi, yourself," he said back with a smile. "I thought I'd drop back by and pick your brain some more. I was just about to head over to the funeral parlor. I thought I might buy you breakfast."

Jack mumbled something unintelligible under his breath, but I ignored him. It was just my luck that I'd found a man who fried my circuits, and all he wanted to do was pick my brain.

I realized he wasn't looking at me any longer but just over my shoulder. "Last night was poker night," I blurted out. I knew Jack was back there, but I resisted the urge to turn around and look. "I got stuck in the storm and couldn't make it back home."

I'm not sure I could have made it any clearer that Jack and I weren't together other than just saying it straight out. Brody looked back at me and his eyes softened. It wasn't until I saw the change in them that I realized he'd become almost predatory when he'd spotted Jack.

"I'm glad to help you anytime," I said, breaking the awkward silence.

Jack's footsteps crunched in the snow behind me, and I turned around to introduce him. But after I saw the look he was giving Brody I almost chickened out. If Brody had looked predatory, then I don't know what the description would be for Jack. I'd never seen that look before, not even at a crime scene. Jack was downright scary, and I almost took a step back before I stopped myself and remembered he was my oldest friend.

"Jack, I'd like you to meet Brody Collins. I think you've read a few of his books. He's come to Bloody Mary to do some research." Jack relaxed slightly. "Brody, this is Jack Lawson. He's the sheriff for King George County, but he lives here in town. I'm sure he'd be willing to help if you had any questions for him."

Neither one of them said anything, but Brody did nod his head at Jack in acknowledgment. I guess it was too much to hope for that they'd shake hands.

"Are you tied up for the rest of the day, or do you have some free time?" Brody asked, ignoring Jack.

"We're going to Nottingham this morning to interview a few people about the murder, but I'm available this evening."

"How about dinner? There's a nice little Italian place over in Port Royal I'd like to take you to."

"Dinner sounds great," I said. I knew I had a dopey grin on my face, but there was nothing I could do about it. I watched Brody make his way toward the Escalade.

"Six o'clock, Dr. Graves," he called out.

"I'll be ready." I could feel the anger radiating off Jack in waves. I was surprised he wasn't standing in a melted pile of snow his anger was so hot.

"Who is that guy, Jaye? And when did the two of you get so cozy?"

"I introduced you, but you were too busy acting like a jealous lover to take notice. Brody is a very nice man, and yes, I'm attracted to him. But it's none of your business one way or the other."

We were standing toe to toe now, and our voices carried far across the quiet ground.

"The man has *player* written all over him."

"Are you kidding me? I'm thirty years old. I'm not getting any younger. I haven't had a relationship in four years! I'm thrilled to death to meet a player. I don't suppose it's occurred to you that I'd like to do something with my life besides play poker and slice up bodies, or that maybe I'd like to have a family. You have parents and brothers and sisters and uncles and aunts to go home to for the holidays. I get tired of being alone."

Jack brought his hand up and put it gently on the side of my face, but I jerked away before he could make contact. Sympathy would only make the tears that were threatening fall, and I'd embarrassed myself enough for one day.

"And who are you to pass judgment? Have you looked at yourself in the mirror lately? You'd know better than anyone what one looks like. I don't think I passed judgment on your little tryst with the lab tech yesterday. You know why? Because it's not any of my business what happens in your love life.

"Everyone deserves happiness in their life, even me, and I can't remember the last time I was truly happy. My life has spiraled out of control, and I can't seem to stop it. And if I want to have sex with Brody Collins in the middle of the town square, it's nobody's business but my own. You're acting like a jealous lover instead of my best friend."

I could have sworn I saw hurt in his eyes, and I almost apologized, but the look was gone before I could blink. His anger didn't dissipate but grew more intense—colder—a living thing that smoldered just under the surface and contained by ice.

"Go get dressed. We've wasted enough time this morning," he said. I stood on my front stairs and watched him walk inside, and for the first time that morning I didn't notice the cold that surrounded me. But I did feel the emptiness without Jack's presence.

NINE

Jack waited in the kitchen and made a pot of coffee while I went upstairs to shower and change clothes. I dressed in a pair of tan corduroy pants and a thick sweater the color of raspberries, blew my hair dry, and put on the minimum amount of makeup needed for a day out in public. I was the poster child for low-maintenance living.

By the time I'd come downstairs, Jack had slathered a couple of bagels with cream cheese, so I guessed he didn't feel like eating with me after all. And if I had to judge by the surly look on his face, it didn't look like we'd be having lunch together either.

During the ride to Dr. Hides' residence, I mentally went over the items in my closet that would be good enough for dinner with Brody. And by good enough, I meant sexy. He'd only seen me at my worst. The only problem was the freezing temperature, so I obviously had to wear something warm. It probably wouldn't make a good impression if I wore the little cocktail dress I'd bought for my ten-year reunion and then died of hypothermia before we made it to dinner.

I jerked forward when Jack slammed on the brakes and *oomph*ed when my seat belt cut off my air. I looked over to give Jack a dirty look, but he was already out of the car.

Dr. Hides' townhouse was very respectable in a completely boring way. It was a dark, red-bricked three-story building like the others that lined the rest of the street, and identical white painted dormers were lined across the second floor. There was a bronze nameplate to the right side of the door that said *Dr. Henry Hides, PhD. Psychotherapy*. The door to the left of Dr. Hides' house had an identical nameplate, but the name read *Victor Moreno, Attorney at Law*.

"Nice area," I commented. "Expensive."

Jack remained silent so I elbowed him in the ribs just to make sure he was still breathing. Probably not the wisest thing to do considering the kind of mood he was in. I rang the buzzer before he could retaliate.

A man opened the door. He was short—shorter than me—and stocky. He wore a brown cardigan over a white dress shirt and tie, and a pair of black thick-rimmed glasses stuck out of his shirt pocket. He was probably in his late forties if I had to judge by the amount of gray in his hair and the age lines on his face.

"I'm sorry folks, I'm not a marriage counselor," he said and began to shut the door in our faces. I snorted out a laugh before I could help it, and this time it was Jack who elbowed me in the ribs.

"Are you Dr. Hides?" Jack asked.

"Yes, who are you?"

"I'm Sheriff Lawson. We spoke on the phone yesterday about the death of Fiona Murphy. This is Dr. Graves. She's the King George county coroner. We'd like to take a few minutes of your time if you don't mind."

Dr. Hides looked like he wanted to say no and shut the door in our faces, but he obviously thought better of it and invited us inside. The interior of the place was expensive, but dull.

"I have a patient coming in half an hour. I hope this won't take too long."

The warning was clear, and Jack acknowledged that we'd be out of his way shortly. I guessed it wouldn't be good publicity for a client to see the police questioning their therapist. Or maybe he didn't want us to see who was coming in. It made me wonder if Fiona Murphy was the only person in Bloody Mary who used the services of the good doctor.

"I'm sorry to say, Sheriff Lawson, that I don't know how much help I can be. I've reviewed my files and have found nothing that brought out a red flag as to why Mrs. Murphy would be murdered. And there is the problem of patient confidentiality."

"It never hurts to ask questions," Jack said as a response.

Dr. Hides led us past a large cherrywood desk that was obviously where his secretary sat during the normal workweek. There was only a computer on the surface. Everything of importance was locked in the file cabinets that lined the wall behind the desk. Business must have been good for Dr. Hides. A narrow staircase sat to the left of the room and a large balcony overlooked the foyer we were currently standing in.

"Do you usually have weekend appointments?" I asked.

"Only when a patient feels like one is necessary. My secretary, Janette, only comes in Monday through Friday though, if that's what you're wondering."

I was a little disappointed to see his office didn't have the ubiquitous leather couch that I thought existed in every psychologist's office. Instead there were two identical over-stuffed club chairs that sat in front of his desk.

"You told me on the phone yesterday that Fiona had been your patient for four years," Jack said.

"Yes, that's correct."

"And Fiona came twice a week, religiously, over those four years?" Jack asked.

"I'd have to recheck my files just to be certain, but I can't remember Fiona ever cancelling a session."

"How much are your services, Dr. Hides?"

"To my independent clients I have a flat rate of two hundred dollars per fifty-minute session."

I sucked in a wheezing breath through my mouth and tried to do the math in my head of how much Fiona had given this guy over the last four years. The number I came up with wasn't pretty.

"What do you mean, independent clients?" I asked after my shock wore off.

"Some of my patients are either court or hospital appointed. Those clients are paid for by the state of Virginia, so obviously the rate is quite significantly lowered."

It made sense to me. The state screwed Dr. Hides, so Dr. Hides screwed his patients in return by charging astronomical fees.

"We'd like to collect any files you have on Fiona while we're here," Jack said, taking a seat next to me in one of the chairs.

Dr. Hides took his place behind the desk, and I wondered if he noticed that Jack was doing everything in his power to pretend I wasn't even in the room. I sure as hell noticed, and that brought my simmering anger at our argument back up to a boil. I was the one who should be mad, not Jack.

"I'm sorry, Sheriff Lawson, but for my protection and my client's, I'm not allowed to give you access."

"That's fine, I can have a warrant delivered this afternoon," Jack said blandly.

"That may be, but until you have one in your hand I will not allow you to see any patient's files. Murder or no. And quite frankly, I'd prefer if only *you* took responsibility for transporting and then keeping the files confidential," he said. "Even the police departments like to gossip in a small town." His smile was thin and insulting, and I could feel Jack bristle beside me at the implication.

"Is there a reason you'd like to impede this investigation, Dr. Hides?"

"I'll help you any way I can, but my patients' privacy is of the utmost importance."

"It seems to me that as a doctor you'd want the victim to have justice. That makes all kinds of alarms go off inside my head when I find someone who doesn't. I might feel the need to take a closer look at exactly what kind of therapy you're providing."

"Is that a threat?" Dr. Hides asked, coming to his feet.

"No, sir," Jack said. "Just an observation."

I thought the doctor was trying to do everything he could to be an inconvenience, and I was angry on behalf of Fiona. That a man she paid thousands of dollars to for years didn't seem to want to help find her killer. But Jack was as calm as he ever was.

"You seemed surprised when I called you to tell you about Fiona's death yesterday, Dr. Hides."

"Of course I was shocked. It's not every day one of my clients is murdered."

"She was your patient for four years, so surely you saw the bruises that decorated her body. You'd be trained to recognize the signs of abuse, wouldn't you?"

Dr. Hides licked his lips nervously and my radar went up at his reluctance to say what he was thinking.

"Yes, I was aware of Fiona's bruises and I tried to get her to tell me what happened to cause them, but the subject was off-limits. She even threatened to not come back if I ever brought it up again, so I left it alone."

He was lying, and he'd obviously taken a few moments to collect himself and decide what story he was going to feed us.

"So you were aware that she was an abused woman, even if she didn't confide in you, but you were still surprised that I called you and told you she'd been murdered, more than likely by her abuser's hands."

Jack made it more of a statement than a question, and the doctor opted to stay silent, which was probably the smartest thing he'd done since we'd walked in the office.

"I'm sorry, Dr. Hides," I said, "but I just find it hard to believe that this woman was your patient for that long and you didn't speak about the most obvious topic. Why was she coming to you at all if it wasn't to help with the abuse?"

"I think Fiona was more lonely than anything," he said carefully. "She'd married young, too young, and found that she didn't love the man she'd made vows to. And the vows were important to Fiona. She didn't want to break them."

"But she did," I interrupted. "She'd gotten the courage to leave him the night she was murdered."

The surprised look on the doctor's face was the first genuine emotion I'd seen.

"I take it by your surprise that she didn't mention at her Thursday morning appointment that she was packing her bags and heading to Florida to live with her sister?" Jack asked.

"No, no, I don't believe you. She'd tell me if she was going to make a change that drastic." The doctor was perspiring just slightly above his upper lip.

"I'm sorry, Dr. Hides, but it's true," Jack said. "Did you have a personal relationship with the victim?"

"Of course not. That wouldn't be ethical."

Dr. Hides' skin held a pallor that hadn't been there a few seconds ago. His mouth was pinched, and his pulse beat rapidly in his neck. Once again, he was lying, I thought. But why? Surely if Fiona had been involved with more than one man sexually, one of those men would have mentioned the bruises.

"What about her moods? Did she exhibit extreme highs or lows in behavior? Depression? Did she feel safe?"

"You're skirting the line, Sheriff. I'm afraid you'll have to wait for that warrant."

"Can you give us your whereabouts for Thursday night between the hours of seven and midnight?"

The shock wore off quickly and Dr. Hides was back to being himself. I was sure the break in his composure wasn't something that happened very often. Dr. Hides was a man of utmost control.

"I resent the implication that I had anything to do with Fiona's death, and I'd like to call my attorney if you keep on with this avenue of questioning."

"You're welcome to call your attorney, Dr. Hides, but the question is just a formality. It will help us move in the right direction if we can clear your name off the list."

"Very well, but I don't think you're going to be able to take me off your list," he said, leaning forward slightly. His hands were clasped in a white-knuckled grip, and it was easy to see the rage that lay just below the surface.

"I was home all evening Thursday night. I saw my last patient from five to six, and then I handed the file to Janette to lock up before she headed home a few minutes after the hour. I had a light dinner, reviewed a few files for my patients the following day, and then went to bed after the evening news at ten thirty."

Jack was writing everything down in the little notebook he habitually carried everywhere, and I wondered if it was difficult to keep all the lies and truths and half-truths straight from one suspect to the next. I knew from experience that no one told the whole truth all the time, myself included.

Dr. Hides stood from behind his desk and walked toward the door. "Now if you folks will excuse me, my patient will be here shortly. And if you have any other questions, please contact my attorney." He handed Jack a business card, but Jack didn't bother looking at it.

"Thanks for your time, Dr. Hides," Jack said. "I'll be back with that warrant for Fiona's files."

Dr. Hides didn't bother to respond to that statement or tell us goodbye, but he showed us out and closed the door behind us with a finality that ran shivers down my spine.

"Dr. Hides is a dirty, rotten liar," I said as I headed toward the passenger side of the Suburban. "Did you notice how he was more upset about Fiona cancelling her sessions with him than her actual murder?"

"Oh, yes. And I think we need to add Janette to our list of people to question. Secretaries are usually a pretty good judge of people in my estimation. I'd think it would be pretty tempting to take a peep at a person's file every so often. We'll check her out after lunch, but for now let's head to the Alexandretta Boutique."

I let out a slow breath and was glad we were at least speaking civilly, if not warmly, to each other again. It was almost a relief that a murder investigation cleared the air, even if it was only short lived.

Jack started the car and turned the heater up to full blast before doing a U-turn in the middle of the fairly empty street and heading two blocks north. All the shops that lined the town square were exclusive and high-end, mostly there to gouge the tourists or women like Candy Harlowe.

The Alexandretta Boutique was the mother of all stores. I looked down at my corduroy pants and hiking boots and hoped they let me in the door. The glass-front display windows had *Alexandretta Boutique* written very tastefully in small gold letters in the bottom corner, and behind the glass were mannequins who wore elegant designer gowns. I guess nothing said Merry Christmas like spending two thousand dollars on yourself for a party dress. I let Jack go in first, sure that he'd draw all female eyes in his direction and take the heat off me.

There were only a handful of women in the store so early in the morning, especially on the morning after one of the biggest storms in years. The tiny blonde behind the counter was cool and professional, and she wore a beautiful turquoise suit with big clunky silver jewelry. Sometimes I wished I could be more like her. Femininely competent. Petite. I could do without the blond hair. I'd tried that fashion statement my sophomore year of college and ended up looking like Ronald McDonald. So the lesson was learned. Never use peroxide on dark hair.

Jack and I stayed toward the back of the shop while she finished ringing up customers and wishing them happy holidays in a husky, slightly accented voice. Great, she was also cultured and well-traveled. Was there anything this woman didn't have going for her?

I was about to make a comment to Jack about ogling potential witnesses when I saw what I wanted on a mannequin. It was exactly what I needed to knock Brody's socks off. The dress was a long sweep of cashmere. It had a cowl neck and flowed all the way to the ankles in a forest green so dark it was almost black. A column of twisted gold draped around the waist and hugged the hips. It skimmed the body enough to reveal a womanly figure without showing everything you had.

My mother had always told me to let a man use his imagination. Of course, I was pretty desperate at this point, so I might have to throw my mother's advice out the window and fend for myself.

I left Jack's side and went over to touch it, to tell myself it wasn't really as spectacular as I'd first thought and that I didn't need to run up my credit card for one date.

"Can I help you, miss?" a tall woman with exotic eyes and skin asked. Before I could stop myself, I told her that I'd take it in a size eight, and that I also needed shoes to complete the ensemble. She said she'd take care of it all, so I handed over my credit card with all the will of a lamb led to slaughter. I thought it would be best if I didn't actually see the total price of things. That way I could live in denial until the bill came.

I walked back over to Jack and ignored his accusing stare. "That dress is indecent," he hissed. "You don't want him to think you're easy."

"It's been four years, Jack. I am easy. And the dress covers every inch of skin."

"That's my point. He's going to be thinking of what's underneath it all night."

"Ooh, thanks for reminding me. I need to tell her to add lingerie to my order. You're such a pal, Jack," I said, patting him lightly on the cheek. It was a good thing Jack would never hurt a woman, because I was pretty sure I'd just pushed too far. I ran over to the saleswoman before he remembered he carried a gun and made the change to my order.

I walked back over to Jack and rolled my eyes as he gave me the silent treatment. The blonde behind the counter was just finishing up with the last sale when she noticed us.

"How'd you know that was our gal?" I asked. He didn't answer, so I stepped on his foot.

"I recognized her accent from the phone," he said. He left me behind and made his way across the store to intercept the woman before she could get caught by another customer.

There was a little irritation at the thought Jack was scoping out the goods only a day after his little tête-à-tête with the lab tech. I totally understood the reaction he'd had to Brody earlier. Sometimes having friends was a pain in the rear, and I wasn't sure I liked the idea of sharing Jack with anyone on a permanent basis, as selfish as that might seem. I'd have to think on it, but for right now there were questions to be answered.

"Marie Petit?" Jack asked.

"*Oui*. How may I help you?" She took an initial look at Jack, and then I guess she decided he was worth another, because the second was a lot more thorough and a good deal slower.

"I'm Sheriff Lawson. We talked on the phone yesterday.

I was wondering if you had a few minutes to speak with us." Jack flashed his badge, and I decided not to be irritated that he forgot to introduce me.

"Sure, we can sit in the office," she said, leading us toward a door that said *Employees Only*. Marie turned to the girl who was currently ringing up my purchases. "Grace, watch the floor for me for a few minutes, *s'il vous plait*."

The office was small and cramped. A desk took up one entire wall and wooden file cabinets lined another like soldiers. Papers were piled in precise stacks and ferns sat on plaster pedestals. Two wingback chairs sat tightly in the corner, and an ergonomic desk chair faced them.

Jack and I sat in the two wingbacks, and I had to restrain myself from rolling my eyes when Marie flashed way more thigh than necessary for Jack's benefit as she sat down.

"Like I told you yesterday," she said, speaking to Jack as if I weren't there, "we're all very distraught at the thought of something happening to Mrs. Murphy. I'll do anything I can to help." She emphasized the word *anything* like the secret to Fiona's death lay somewhere behind Jack's zipper. I felt myself snarl before I could stop it.

"How often did Mrs. Murphy come in?" Jack asked.

"Oh, she came in every Thursday like clockwork. About eleven fifteen or so."

"Did she buy something every week?" he asked.

"Almost always. We get new shipments in every Tuesday. Our designer lives in Fairfax and has a workshop there, so we're always getting in something new and unique. Sometimes I would put things in the back for Mrs. Murphy if I thought it was something she'd like."

"What was Mrs. Murphy like?" I asked. Marie Petit looked at me in surprise, like I'd just materialized out of thin air.

"I'm sorry, who did you say you were?" she asked.

"I'm Dr. Graves," I said. "The coroner for King George County." I was thinking maybe I should just have that tattooed to my forehead so people would stop asking.

"She was a very nice woman," Marie said. "She had great taste and knew what she wanted." Marie eyed my clothing with distaste. "I don't know what she did for a living, but she seemed quite cultured and well-to-do." She said the latter like I wasn't even good enough to be on the same planet, much less achieve the same social status.

"Did she ever mention her husband?" Jack broke in.

"*Non*," Marie said, confused. "It was my understanding that she was a widow. I assumed she inherited her money from her late husband. Are you saying she wasn't a widow?"

"Her husband is very much alive," I said. "Did you ever note any marks on Mrs. Murphy? Maybe notice something out of the ordinary when she was trying on clothes in the dressing rooms?"

"*Oui*, yes, as a matter of fact I did. I saw a large bruise on her collarbone that was all shades of the rainbow. But when I asked her about it she said she'd been in a car accident and it was damage done by the...*courroie*." She motioned her hand across her body.

"Seat belt?" I asked.

"*Oui*, seat belt. I had no reason to doubt her. She was a very nice woman."

Jack thanked the tart—I mean woman—and discreetly put her card in the right pocket of his coat and promised to be in touch soon. I rolled my eyes and grabbed the bags waiting for me on the counter.

How could Jack fall for someone that obvious? Why would he want a woman like that? I'd never understand what went on in the male mind.

Lunch was a casual affair of take-out burritos eaten in the car on the way to see Janette Taylor, Dr. Hides' secretary. I was tired of the sullen silence. I wasn't made for long bouts of anger. I was more of an explode-then-fizzle kind of gal.

"I don't want us to be angry with each other, Jack. I'm sorry if I hurt your feelings."

He was silent for a long while, so I just assumed he wasn't ready to move on yet, but then I heard him exhale a long breath. "I just don't want you to get hurt. I didn't like the way he looked at you."

"And I didn't particularly care for the way the French pastry looked at you either, but we're both grown-ups, and even though we spend most of our time together, we have lives apart."

"I know it, but that doesn't mean I have to like it. Just promise me you'll be careful with this guy."

"I promise." I felt pretty secure in my oath. We were only going to dinner after all. I wasn't exactly a believer in love at first sight. I'd seen too many fairy tales destroyed to go for that nonsense. My parents for one. Fiona Murphy for another.

"What do you think about what she said about Fiona?" I asked Jack as he drove out of Nottingham toward King George Proper to Janette Taylor's home.

"I think Fiona had secrets. And maybe there's more going on here than meets the eye," he said.

That was pretty much my feeling as well, so I just grunted in assent and looked at the neat rows of houses with identical dormers and box windows lining the street. Each one had box hedges and brick mailboxes.

"God, how do people live in places like this? There's no character," I said.

"People often find the ordinary a comfort."

"Not us," I said, thinking of our jobs and the houses we both found solitude in.

"No, not us," he said.

Janette's sporty little Honda Coupe sat in the driveway under a mountain of snow. "I guess she's home," I said with a sigh. I was a little tired of getting in and out of the cold. Plus, I wanted to get home and primp for the evening. My fingernails were a mess and I hadn't exfoliated in over a week.

"Hang in there, tough guy," Jack said, punching me on the arm. "Your date will come soon enough."

Janette Taylor answered the door in baggy gray sweats, a bright pink terry-cloth robe, and she sported a swollen, red nose. She had Kleenex hanging out of both pockets and one held tightly in her fist. I could hear the TV blaring in the background and smell the overwhelming aroma of Vicks. Looking at Janette did wonders for my self-esteem after our short visit with Marie Petit.

"What do you want?" she asked, hiding her face in a tissue and sneezing. "I'm not buying anything. It's too fricking cold." She started to shut the door when Jack flashed his badge.

"Are you Janette Taylor?" he asked.

I got the impression Jack was expecting someone a little more refined to come to the door. I couldn't see Janette Taylor and Dr. Hides meshing on a daily basis.

"Yeah, I'm Janette. Listen, if this is about Robby I want

nothing to do with it. We broke up over a month ago and I'm not bailing him out again."

"Good for you," Jack said. "This is about one of Dr. Hides' patients. Can we come in for a few minutes? Like you said, it's fricking cold out here."

"Yeah, sure, I guess. Sorry about the mess. I haven't exactly felt like cleaning up."

"Don't worry about it," I said as I found my way through the maze of cat toys and empty Kleenex boxes to the sofa. I was going to have to boil my body in rubbing alcohol to get rid of all the germs. "How long have you worked for Dr. Hides?"

"A little more than two years. I was sent over from a temp agency when his old secretary left on maternity. She decided not to come back, so I got the job. It pays okay, and I never have to work weekends. What's all this about? Is Dr. Hides in trouble?"

"Can you tell us about Fiona Murphy? Describe her to us. Give us your impressions." Jack said.

"Sure I can. She was a witch from the depths of hell," she said. "She was so hoity-toity I figured she was giving the doc lessons. He has that same blue blood attitude that she does."

I don't think I concealed the surprise on my face fast enough. Fiona sure did wear a lot of hats.

"Are you sure?" Jack asked. "Fiona was a small woman, slender, with shoulder-length blond hair and blue eyes. About thirty years old?"

"Yeah, that's her. Dressed real fancy, and never bothered to say two words to me, other than to ask for hot tea with lemon and one lump of sugar like I was the maid. I wasn't the one who had need of a therapist, now, was I?"

"Did you ever notice any bruises on Mrs. Murphy?" I asked. Janette didn't answer right away, but her eyes got big and she kept licking her lips.

"No, I never saw any," she finally stammered out. "Are you going to tell me what this is about?"

"Mrs. Murphy was murdered sometime Thursday evening," Jack said. "You say you didn't see the bruises, Janette, but you knew about them, didn't you?"

She averted her eyes and didn't keep eye contact. "I could lose my job if he found out," she whispered.

"We'll keep it to ourselves for right now," he said. "Did you look at Fiona's case files?"

"It's like I couldn't help it," she said as she started to cry. "She was such a hateful woman. I wanted to know something about her just so I could feel like I had the upper hand, even when she was snubbing her nose at me."

"Where'd she get the bruises, Janette?" I asked.

"I don't know who, not exactly," she said. "I only was able to read one of the yearly summary pages the doctor keeps at the front of the file. I didn't want to get caught. But he wrote in his notes that she had a sexual addiction. You know." Janette pleaded with her eyes, hoping we could read her mind so she wouldn't have to say the word out loud. "She was a masochist," she whispered, then promptly turned bright red to match the color of her nose. "And I don't think Dr. Hides really cared about curing her of the addiction, if you know what I mean. Their sessions consistently ran over the hour mark, and I was given explicit instructions to never interrupt, even if there was another patient waiting. Sometimes she'd even pick him up for lunch after his eleven o'clock appointment was finished."

"What kind of car was she driving?" I asked.

"A white Lexus. It looked brand new."

Just one more inconsistency to file away.

I felt a little sorry for Janette Taylor. Nothing could make your working relationship more awkward than knowing your boss was having sex with his patients less than twenty feet away from your desk with his patients. *Gross.*

TEN

JACK SLAMMED HIS FIST AGAINST THE DASHBOARD, shoved his cell phone back in his shirt pocket, and muttered out a curse. "I can't find anyone at the district attorney's office or at the courthouse to get me a warrant."

I didn't bother to remind Jack that it was Saturday and people did actually take the weekend off.

"I'll have to call them at home," he said. "I want to know what's in those files. And I want to know today."

"Me too," I said. "And I bet a peach like Janette Taylor reads all the files, not just the ones of the people she dislikes. It would be tempting to know people's darkest secrets." I knew I would be tempted. I had a few secrets of my own I wouldn't even share with Jack, much less a therapist.

Jack sped through the snowplowed streets toward Augusta General to see George Murphy. I hadn't set foot inside the hospital since I'd turned in my resignation. I wasn't looking forward to the visit.

Jack looked at his watch. "I forgot all about the safe-deposit box. The bank closed at noon. You think we could get Dickey to open it up for us?"

"Probably so." Dickey was pretty laid back. He'd probably think it was cool to be needed during an investigation.

"Well, if he doesn't, I'll make sure that his wife accidentally gets a key to his hotel room when he has his nooner with his secretary."

Jack had a real vengeful streak. I'd always liked that about him.

"So we know that Dr. Hides knew about the bruises and lied to us," I said. "And we know Marie Petit and Janette Taylor are painting a totally different picture of Fiona than the one we knew. I'm starting to believe maybe Dr. Hides might be the one responsible for the bruises after all. He was the one who knew her best. Her desires and needs."

"Yeah, Dr. Hides is going to wish he'd never met me," Jack said.

"If he was the one putting those bruises on Fiona, then he's in a whole lot more trouble than anything you could do to him."

"Don't bet on it," Jack said. "The funny thing is that I thought for sure all the stuff we found in the safe at the Murphy house had to have belonged to George. I'm starting to think it might have been hers all along."

"Well, she's obviously been playing a role. She had all of us fooled. The sinner and the saint, depending on who you talk to. And what's up with the second car? Where's she keeping it?"

"If she's got a second life, then surely she has a second place to live. Maybe she's got multiple personalities. I can't think of any other way to explain all this."

Jack pulled into the emergency entrance of the hospital

and put the *On Duty* sign he'd brought with us onto the dashboard. I felt like I was in a race, Jack was moving so quickly through the corridors. He was a man on a mission and had obviously gotten his second wind after talking with Janette Taylor. I, however, was bushed. I wasn't cut out for police work. It was mostly boring and definitely tedious. I needed variety to spice up my life, something along the lines of Ben & Jerry's.

The guard who was stationed at George's door snapped to attention when he saw Jack coming down the hallway.

"Any trouble, Walters?" Jack asked.

The poor guy was nervous. He couldn't have been much more than twenty. I guess I could see how Jack could be an intimidating force as an employer, but I was used to it. I probably would laugh in Jack's face if he ever gave me one of those looks. But it was probably wise for the kid to be nervous. Laughing would only get him fired.

"Everything's fine, sir. He hasn't been given meds this morning per your orders, and there have been no visitors other than Dr. Givens and a nurse or two."

"Good job. Take a break and go get a cup of coffee," Jack said as he slapped the kid on the shoulder.

Walters heaved a sigh of relief like he'd just obtained a pardon and took off down the hallway.

"You're a good boss, Jack. You old softy. Under that gruff exterior lies a heart of gold."

"Shut up, Jaye."

"Shutting up, Sheriff, sir," I said, clicking my heels together and saluting.

I watched Dr. Givens make his way down the hallway with heavy heels and his military stride. He'd been the bane of my existence during my residency. He was a stickler for details and had a bedside manner like a troll. He was tall and imposing and reminded me a little of the Crypt-Keeper with a bony face and dark soulless eyes. Or maybe that image was just me projecting, since I thought of death every time he was in my presence.

If I was to be completely accurate, he looked more like Mike Wallace off of *Sixty Minutes*. He also believed in the school of thought that only men could be good doctors. Or should be doctors, for that matter. I'd been on a mission to prove him wrong when my parents died.

"Dr. Graves," he said by way of greeting. "How's the mortuary business?" He said it with a smug smile and a little chuckle.

I wanted to ignore the hand Jack placed on my shoulder, but when he started squeezing not so subtly I realized I had my fists clenched and was ready to pop Dr. Givens a good one. He had it coming after all the years of torture he'd put me through, but it would probably make Jack feel bad to have to arrest me for assault, so I stood down.

"Business is great. Thanks for asking," I said, sweet as sugar. I could have said something hateful like I was looking forward to him being one of my patients, but I refrained. I thought of something better instead.

"Make sure you say hi to your wife for me," I said with guileless innocence. It was common knowledge that Dr. Givens' wife had left him Wednesday night to run away with her plastic surgeon. She'd told him she was going to help with the raffle at the Ladies of King George Lodge. I think if I was Dr. Givens I'd take notice if someone I lived with for twenty-five years was walking out the door with a suitcase and her new breasts.

Jack's grip on my shoulder went way past the point of pain, and I got a tiny bit of satisfaction at seeing Dr. Givens take a step forward like he was going to take a swing at me, but much to my disappointment he got control of himself and ignored me.

Dr. Givens had known how much I'd hated giving up my position at the hospital, and the last thing he'd told me was that it was a sign from God that I'd been called to do other work. Meaning that if God wanted women to be doctors, he wouldn't have killed my parents. I personally thought God had bigger things to worry about than me being hired on at Augusta General. Call me crazy.

"I'm sorry, Sheriff. I feel like I need to be present in the room while you question my patient," Dr. Givens explained. "He is under great emotional distress and really shouldn't go too long without being sedated."

"Dr. Givens, George Murphy is the prime suspect in a homicide and I don't particularly care what your recommendations are. As soon as we're done speaking with him, he's going to leave this hospital in handcuffs and sit in a cell like all the other criminals instead of trying to win an Oscar."

Jack left Dr. Givens in the hallway sputtering, and I followed him into George Murphy's room. "That was great, Jack. That man doesn't get put in his place nearly enough."

"Glad I could be of service," he said dryly. "I figured it was a better option than punching him in the face."

So maybe I'd gotten a tiny bit out of control. Nobody's perfect.

George's room was spartan and hospital-disinfectant fresh, and he watched us closely as we came to his bedside. He had the lightest blue eyes I'd ever seen, and I shivered before I could control it. His dark hair made his face seem paler than usual, and his cheeks were gaunt with grief. His large frame dwarfed the hospital bed, and I couldn't remember the last time I'd seen him look defeated. George had always seemed larger than life, and he never liked for anyone to stand in his way.

I'd once seen him flatten the umpire at the Bloody Mary/Nottingham Knights of Columbus baseball tournament for calling him out at home, and I'd seen him curse Hester Thibodeaux up one side and down the other when she'd forgotten to have the oil changed after three thousand miles in her Cadillac. No one went to the Murphys' house for Halloween. George was scary enough the other three hundred and sixty-four days a year. That's why the sight of George pale and shaken took me a little off guard. If he was faking, he'd sure missed his calling.

"We need to talk to you a few minutes, George," Jack said. I guess the sight of George surprised Jack a little too because his voice was gentle.

"You've got to tell us what happened, George. We need the truth," I said.

"She's dead," he said, tears trailing down his cheeks slowly.

"What happened?" Jack repeated.

"She left me. Said she didn't love me anymore. I'm not exciting enough, not like I used to be. She said I wasn't what she needed." George stopped to take a shuddering breath. "We had a fight. It made me angry that she could say those things when I loved her more than I had since the day we met."

"What time did she leave?" Jack asked.

"A few minutes before nine," he said, licking his lips. His voice was flat, and the tears continued to fall silently. "She'd been talking to her sister. She wouldn't even acknowledge that I was yelling at her. She just packed up and walked out. Usually a good fight gets her revved, you know?" he said. "I yell and call her names, throw a few things for good measure. She yells right back, and then we make up and everything's all right."

Jack and I exchanged a look. It looked like Fiona Murphy had been playing all of Bloody Mary for a fool.

"Did you follow her because you were angry?" Jack asked.

"I didn't follow her," he said. His eyes were pleading, begging us to believe him. "I swear. I yelled her name after she walked out and ripped the screen door off its hinges when I slammed it. Then I went and got drunk. What else was there for me to do?"

"Did you abuse your wife, George?" I asked. I was curious if he'd answer such a direct question.

George colored slightly; the embarrassed red on his cheeks was a shocking slash against his pale face. "I don't know what you mean."

"Where did your wife get the bruises?" I asked.

"It's not what you think. I'd never hurt Fiona out of temper. I loved her."

"You hurt her out of love then?" I insisted.

"Fiona was just unique," he said. He put his head in his hands, his whole body shaking with grief.

"Did your wife get the bruises during sex?" Jack asked.

"She wanted me to. Even on our wedding night and she'd never been with anyone before. I'd never hurt Fiona if she didn't tell me to," he said, sobbing.

"Were you aware your wife was seeing a therapist?" Jack asked.

The crying stopped and a pitiful hiccup replaced it. "No, she would have told me if she was going to see a shrink. We were close. We told each other everything."

"Didn't you notice all the trips she was taking into Nottingham?" I asked.

"She had a job. Had it almost five years now. She said she wanted to work, and I've got no problem with that. She worked evenings four nights a week. She seemed to enjoy it, even if we didn't get to see each other as much. Sometimes the garage keeps me at work pretty late too," he said. "But I thought things were still good between us. I didn't see that she wasn't happy," He started to cry again.

"George," Jack said. "Was Fiona having an affair?"

George looked up at us with devastated eyes, but I caught a sliver of anger before he concealed it. "Fiona wouldn't cheat on me. I gave her everything she wanted." Even he didn't look so convinced after he said that.

"Didn't you ever find bruises on her body that you didn't put there?" Jack insisted.

George didn't meet Jack's eyes when he answered. "I didn't really pay attention," he lied. "You don't notice stuff like that in the heat of the moment. Fiona wouldn't cheat on me."

"Where'd she work?" I asked, switching topics. We weren't going to be able to go on too much longer. George was breaking down in front of my eyes. He was choked up on leftover antidepressants and grief, but pretty soon the real George would come back to the surface, and I wanted to be far away when the explosions started. I was also scared to think what it meant if George was telling the truth—that he hadn't killed Fiona.

"She was in sales of some kind," he answered. "I'm not sure exactly. All that female stuff gets on my nerves. She said she was glad to have some spending money just for herself, even though I make a good living at the garage. Fiona always has had an independent streak."

You could have fooled me, but I kept the comment to

myself. I obviously knew nothing about Fiona Murphy, old friend or not.

We left George's room, Jack and I both lost in private thoughts.

"In sales of some kind," I said after I climbed into the Suburban and we were on our way back to Jack's place.

"Yeah, I think we can safely assume that Fiona was selling herself. She'd have to have another residence. Some place she could meet clients and hide the Lexus. If George wasn't as exciting as he used to be maybe she was looking for someone more dangerous."

"Looks like she found him," I said.

"I just can't think of anything else she could have been doing to make all of that money," Jack said.

"It would certainly explain all the old ligature marks I found on her wrists and ankles during my examination."

"I need to do a property search and see if anything comes up in her name or a variation of her name. We also need to get financial records for Fiona and George as well as Dr. Hides. We'll see if he had any large withdrawals over the last few years."

"Maybe they traded services so there was no money trail," I said.

Jack parked the Suburban at the front of his house. For some reason, I felt when he got out and went inside things would change between us. He looked at me for a long time before he spoke again.

"I'll keep at it," he said. "It's not like I have a lot of other homicides sitting on my desk. You'd better get out of here so you can get ready for your big date. It might be another four years before you have another one, and your writer friend doesn't strike me as the type to be kept waiting."

"Jack," I began, not really sure what I should say.

"You're the only constant I've had in my whole life. You know that, right?"

"I guess I do," he said, his dark eyes intense and serious.

"I just wanted to make sure you know how important you are to me. I'd never do anything that would endanger that."

He smiled and rubbed his hand on the top of my head like he used to when we were kids.

"I know, Jaye," he said. "Just don't do anything tonight that I wouldn't do."

"That leaves me with a lot of possibilities," I said as I scooted over into the driver's seat.

Jack sighed. "I think I'll head back over to the square and see what time that boutique closes."

I was lighter of heart as I drove away. Jack and I would be fine.

And I'd be even better if I could get my hands on Brody Collins. It had been a long time since I'd felt a man with a pulse.

ELEVEN

I LOOKED LIKE A MILLION BUCKS. I JUST HOPED I wouldn't be paying that much when I got the bill at the end of the month.

Grace, from the Alexandretta Boutique, had exquisite taste. And I only looked at the lacy scraps on my bed with slight trepidation. I was used to my underwear covering my entire behind. I checked the bag to make sure there weren't any how-to instructions, and when I found none I pulled the black lace on slowly to prevent it from tearing. Or disintegrating. Did people really wear underwear like this all the time?

Every tick of the clock on the wall felt like a time bomb. I was running late, as usual. Who knew how long it took to shave legs, wax eyebrows, and slough dead skin? I decided after I put on the dress that it was worth every penny. I felt like a girl. A pretty girl. And because of such I decided to go full out on the makeup and darken my eyes more than usual.

My hands shook as I attached gold hoops to my ears,

and butterflies danced in my stomach when the doorbell rang.

The doorbell had long since lost its pitch and was painful to listen to, somewhere between an augmented fourth and a cat being neutered without anesthesia. It was on my list of things to be fixed.

"Here goes nothing," I said as I gave myself a last look and headed down the stairs.

"Nice doorbell," Brody said when I opened the door.

I blew out a breath and rolled my eyes. It was the bane of my existence that all the men in my life were sarcastic jackholes.

"Thanks." I wasn't really sure what I should do next. He looked pretty amazing. He had on a dark suit and crisp white shirt without a tie, but he didn't look uncomfortable like some men do—the kind of men who only pull their suits out of the closet when their wife's best friend's sister is getting married. He also looked cold.

Should I invite him in? What if he was in the mood right now? He might be out of the mood later. Should I chance it? Or should we just go?

"Well, why don't we get out of here," he said.

I was glad he took the decision out of my hands. I didn't want to start the night with any faux pas.

Dante's was a little family-owned restaurant in Port Royal, which was located in Caroline County. It was also extremely difficult to get a table, and word on the street was you could buy a small country for the same price as a plate of lasagna.

My friend Dickey had once told me that he'd had to make reservations a whole six months before his wedding anniversary to get a table. He put a reservation in for his mistress for the day after because he said he didn't want her to be mad at him while they waited another six months for reservations. How Dickey juggled his love life, I'd never know. But both women ended up satisfied they'd gotten the Dante's dining experience, so he'd managed to dodge another proverbial bullet.

"How'd you get reservations so quickly?" I whispered as we walked in the heavy glass-front doors. Brody just smiled and patted my hand as we made our way to the maitre d'. I guess it was a secret.

"Ah, Mr. Collins," the dark man behind the podium said. His accent was Italian, but I wasn't 100 percent convinced that it was authentic. When I was in medical school, the guy who worked on my car used a similar accent, but he couldn't hide his Bronx origins completely. Though it wasn't exactly his accent that kept me from accepting his indecent proposition, but more of a lack of deodorant use.

"Welcome back," the accent guy said. "Table for two?"

"Yes, please, Giovanni."

We handed our coats to another man who magically materialized. So this was how the other half lived. I could probably become accustomed if I let myself. I wondered if Brody ever had to wait in line at the bank or post office, or if they just ushered him to the front and left the commoners like me to curse him behind his back.

We were led to a secluded corner booth that was in the shape of a semicircle, and Giovanni waited for me to take my seat before slipping a napkin across my lap. A fat white candle sat in the middle of the table and the lights in the restaurant were dim. The only experience I'd had where a restaurant used low lighting was Luigi's Pizza and that was just so you couldn't see the roaches running across the floor.

"Would you care for wine, *signore*? Or perhaps champagne?"

"Would you like champagne, Dr. Graves?" Brody asked.

It was then I realized he'd never called me by name. Maybe I was just a brain to pick for him, and I'd spent all this money to look good for nothing.

"Dr. Graves?" he said, obviously confused by my side trip.

"That would be nice," I said. I waited until Giovanni had gone to complete his task before I brought it up. "You really need to stop calling me Dr. Graves. It makes me feel old."

"I don't know your name. And I refuse to call a beautiful woman by her initials. And it's not my intention to make you feel anything but..." he stopped to kiss my hand and all the spit dried up in my mouth, "...desirable," he whispered.

It was probably a good thing that Giovanni came back with the champagne because I almost made Brody Collins my main course then and there.

"You can call me Jaye," I said instead.

"J is still a letter. What's your real name?"

"Jaye is my real name. Or I guess technically it's my middle name." He still looked confused, so I spelled it out for him. "J-A-Y-E."

"Oh." The tone of his voice was less than thrilled. I got the impression it wasn't romantic enough for him. "What's your first name? Maybe I can call you that."

"Nope, nobody calls me by my first name and lives." Not even Jack knew what the initial stood for in my first name. No way was I about to tell someone I wanted to become involved with.

"Can you tell me about your book?" I asked to change the subject.

"Why? Do you want to know if you're in it?" he asked, smiling.

"Of course not." Okay, yes, I really did want to know, but that wasn't something I was willing to admit to him.

"Well, I hope you're not disappointed, but I decided you were the perfect influence for my heroine. Her name is Aurora, and she's beautiful and intelligent, just as you are. She's leading my Detective Chandler on a merry chase. I just haven't decided if I'm going to kill you off at the end or not. Sometimes the crime supersedes love. Life's not always a fairy tale, you know."

"Isn't that just my luck," I said. Our food was served and the conversation went back to the body currently sitting in a casket, prepared for burial the next day.

"How often do you get bodies across your table?" he asked. I could tell this was information he was tucking away for later use because he got that little crease between his eyebrows like he had when I was explaining the autopsy process to him the day before.

"It depends. I'm never swamped, if that's what you're asking. And deaths like Fiona's don't happen that often. It's only the second homicide I've worked since I took the job. Bloody Mary has only had a handful of murders in the last hundred years. Some weeks I don't get anyone across my table. Others, I'll get two or three from natural causes."

"It must be hard for a woman to run a business that grim by herself and then add the pressures of being coroner. Don't you ever get tired of doing everything on your own?"

Boy, did I ever. But I kept it to myself. My parents had had each other to help shuffle the load and the stress of the job. I had no one.

"I have a couple of college students who help me out a couple of days a week if I need a hand. It's more of an apprenticeship. But really, I'm fine." I was lying through my teeth, and by the skeptical look on Brody's face I could tell he wasn't buying it. I mean really, how desperate did I want to look for this guy? "Let's just say that after my parents died, nothing was more important than carrying on the family tradition. It would have been simpler all around if I'd sold the business, liquidated all their assets, and kept my apartment over by the hospital. But it felt right to come home."

"It was all you had left of them," he said as more of a statement than a question.

"Yeah. I miss them every day. My dad had an old MG that he'd restored, and it was forever having problems of one kind or another. They were driving it up to a cabin they had in the Poconos when the brakes decided to stop working and the steering seized up. The car went over a cliff, and they both died instantly. They would have wanted to go together. They were a team. One of the most solid units I've ever seen."

I took a drink of water to wet my throat that was suddenly dry with grief. I didn't bother to mention that even though their deaths had been ruled accidental, there had been suspicion of it being a double suicide. Floyd Parker had been more than happy to print that little tidbit in his newspaper.

"But it feels good to be back in Bloody Mary," I finally said. "It feels right. I didn't realize how much I missed the subtle nuances of a small town until I moved back."

"Subtle?" Brody asked with a smile. "I wouldn't say subtle was exactly what I was thinking when that woman at the grocery store asked me if I was financially stable enough to support a wife and if I had all my own teeth. I was under the impression she had a single daughter."

"That sounds like Hilda, but you might want to stay clear of her if she's looking for a husband for Cleo. She got her older daughter married off by calling Roy Henderson to come fix a leak in her basement, but as soon as he went down the stairs Hilda threw Georganne down right behind him. She'd planned it all out and left food and water down there for them, and when she let them out a couple of weeks later, Georganne was pregnant, and then they *had* to get married. Of course, it was dark down there, and Roy didn't see what Georganne really looked like until they came out."

Brody was laughing, and I realized this was just what I'd needed. "You're joking," he said.

"Their fifth is due in a couple of weeks," I said, shaking my head. "And Mrs. Martin didn't have to do any time for kidnapping after the charges were dropped. She means well."

"Even so," Brody said. "I think I'll stay away from the grocery store."

"You are wise beyond your years," I said solemnly.

"So tell me," he said. "Do I have reason to be jealous of the sheriff?"

That was a pretty strong declaration as to where he saw this thing between us going as far as I was concerned. "Jack's the best friend I've ever had. But he's like a brother to me."

"Excellent," he said, smiling.

After my initial nervousness wore off things went smoothly. In fact, I couldn't remember the last time I'd felt so comfortable around someone who wasn't Jack. The champagne was gone, and somewhere during dessert we'd scooted closer to each other. My brain was warm and a little fuzzy, so it seemed perfectly natural for Brody to put his arm around me. My body seemed to fit his like a puzzle piece when he pulled me closer against him.

"We should go," he whispered next to my ear. His breath sent shivers down my spine. I looked around the restaurant and realized there were very few people left inside. How long had we sat there talking?

"Are you going to invite me in for a cup of coffee?" he asked.

"It would probably be rude not to," I said.

We were lost only in each other. The quiet voices and clatter from the restaurant disappeared. And when his lips brushed mine ever so gently, I began to feel whole again.

TWELVE

It was still dark out when I woke with the feeling that something was different. An arm wrapped around my waist and pulled me close against a hard-muscled body. My brain finally switched on and the panic receded. Oh yeah. I remembered now. Who knew what inviting a person in for coffee would lead to?

"Go back to sleep," Brody mumbled.

Obviously, Brody wasn't a morning person. He was probably used to calling his own hours, but I was wide awake, and all I could think of was how I'd spent the night. My cashmere dress had ended up somewhere. Maybe the front porch, I couldn't really remember, and I was almost sure my shoes were still in Brody's car. I'd also been right about the underwear. They'd been much too fragile.

But my problems hadn't been solved with one night of passion. I had something new to worry about now: The awkward morning after.

What did I look like first thing in the morning?

Usually I got out of bed wearing only an oversized T-shirt I'd grabbed out of a drawer the night before, poured a cup of coffee, and took it directly into the shower with me, bypassing all mirrors on my way. I was going to have to go to the square and buy some lingerie and nighties if this was going to be a continual thing.

And what was the etiquette on morning breath? Should I get up and brush my teeth before I ravished Brody again?

"I can practically hear the wheels turning in your head," Brody said. "I can't possibly imagine how you'd have enough energy to think after last night."

Before I was able to come up with a solution about my morning dilemmas, Brody rolled me over and was looking down at me.

"You're a lovely sight to see first thing in the morning," he said, running his finger down the side of my face. "Even if it is so god-awful early."

Whew. At least that question was answered. And then he kissed me, and I forgot what I was worrying about to begin with. I'd learned how thorough Brody was the night before. As far as I was concerned, Brody was the Christopher Columbus of sex, discovering new worlds at every turn. Boy, when he set his mind to something, there was no stopping him.

The sky was turning pink when I finally got my breath back. "I think I'm paralyzed," I said.

Brody's snores filled the room in answer. So much for afterglow. I was glad I had the time to myself because I realized Brody Collins was a man who could break my heart. I was already more than half in love with him. And not just because of the sex either.

I slipped out of bed quietly, pulled on a robe, and made my way down the stairs out of habit. I tried to think of something breakfast-like I could eat while the coffee brewed. I found some leftover spaghetti and put it in the microwave, and then I looked at my reflection in the toaster. My hair stuck out in all directions and mascara was smudged under my eyes so I looked like a raccoon.

I needed to get to the funeral home and take care of any additional details for Fiona's funeral. On the Sunday mornings I didn't have to work, I could be found at the sunrise service at St. Paul's. My dad always said church was the perfect place to advertise the business. John Luke Stranton, who owned the other funeral home in the county, went to Our Lady of Mercy Catholic Church, so between the two of us we had our claims staked.

Phyllis had opted to have a graveside service, even though I'd tried to talk her out of it due to the weather. She'd wanted the ceremony to be quick and quiet, and I guess having a funeral service after a night of snow and freezing temperatures would ensure that.

I ate the spaghetti and drank my coffee in the shower and thought life couldn't get much better. By the time I went back to the bedroom to tell Brody goodbye, I was feeling as good as I had in years. I sat a cup of coffee on the nightstand and laughed a little as he rolled over and blindly grabbed for it.

"Whatimsit?" he asked. Or at least I think that's what he said.

"It's still shy of eight. I just wanted to let you know I've got to go into the funeral home."

"Oh, good. I thought you were waking me up to have sex again."

"Nah, you look pretty puny right now. You should prob-ably go back to sleep for a couple of hours and save up your energy. Feel free to help yourself to the shower and whatever's in the kitchen. I'm going to be tied up for most of the day."

"That's okay. I've got some research to do, and then I need to work a few hours this afternoon. Mrs. Baker gave me a suite so I can use one of the rooms as an office."

"Ohmigod. I forgot about Mrs. Baker. She's going to notice you didn't come back last night."

"So what?" he asked, confused.

"Don't you understand?"

"Obviously not."

"Stanley Lipinski saw us last night when you stopped for gas."

"What does that have to do with Mrs. Baker?"

"Everybody knows that Stanley always eats Sunday morning brunch at Mrs. Baker's. And it'll only be a matter of time before she mentions that you never came back last night. And then that's when he'll say he saw us together at the gas station all fancied up. Then one thing will lead to another and they'll put two and two together to figure out you spent last night here."

Brody was laughing by the time I finished explaining. "You're weird," he said. "Is it such a bad thing that people know I stayed the night? King George County doesn't stone women that have premarital sex, do they?"

"Shut up. It's not really a big deal," I said. "It just makes my life more complicated."

He was fully awake now, the coffee and the subject matter having gotten his attention. I'd just gotten off the bed to distance myself and leave for the funeral parlor without saying anything else too embarrassing when he grabbed my hand. "Would you like me to complicate it again tonight?"

I did my best to keep myself from jumping for joy. "That would probably be best," I said. "The damage has already been done."

I left him laughing and realized I couldn't keep the grin off my face. I hoped I could get it under control before the funeral, or I might have some serious explaining to do.

THIRTEEN

"You'd better get that grin off your face or everyone's going to know you slept with the writer," Jack said by way of greeting.

Heat rushed to my face and I ran my fingers through my hair like I usually did when I was embarrassed or nervous. I'd been standing in front of the casket display of flowers for God knows how long.

"I don't know what you're talking about," I said with way more bravado than I was feeling. "What are you doing here?"

"I thought I'd hang around, see if you needed any help. George is going to be police escorted to the grave site in a couple of hours, and I just needed some quiet time after the night I just had."

"Marie Petit?" I asked.

"Unfortunately, no. She didn't close the shop last night until nine, and I had to go on call at ten. Let's just say that last night was a night for the record books. Jenny Negley called to report an intruder, but when I got to her house she answered the door dressed like the porn star version of

Catwoman. She asked me if I was there to declaw her. Whatever that means. Scared the hell out of me."

I couldn't help but laugh. "It's your own fault for being so pretty. What's a girl to do but try to think of inventive ways to catch the most eligible bachelor in town?"

"Well, my night didn't stop there. After I left Jenny mewing after me, I had to head over to the Knights of Columbus hall and break up a fight between Bob Shiney and Harvey Wallace."

I wasn't too surprised to hear this bit of news. Bob and Harvey had been feuding for close to twenty years now, and they were always getting into scuffles. I can't say I could really blame Bob all that much. Harvey had run off and eloped with Bob's daughter as soon as she'd graduated high school, and him being more than twenty-five years older than her at the time. There were a few people in town who'd said the affair had been going on even before she'd graduated, but those folks never said it to Bob's face. And it was kind of self-explanatory since Amanda gave birth seven months after they'd said their vows. But since Harvey and Amanda had been married all this time, it was my personal opinion that it was time for Bob to just let it go.

"And then I got another 911 call from Stella Duggan," Jack continued. "I had to give her a citation for reporting a false crime and tying up the emergency lines. This is the fourth time she's called in a month. Not to mention last night seemed to be the night for stupid kids to play pranks all over town. I can't tell you how many kids I saw with rolls of toilet paper in their arms."

"All in a night's work, Sheriff."

"Yeah," he said, running a hand over his face.

Jack looked tired. He'd been running all over the county yesterday afternoon trying to find a murderer, and then he'd had to work all night because the sheriff's department was understaffed due to budget cuts. He had a secretary and a dispatcher, a handful of detectives, and only slightly more than that to work patrol. And between the two divisions they had to take turns covering the DARE program at the local schools, funeral escorts, parades, or any other event that needed security. They were stretched way too thin, and the extra hours were weighing heavy on Jack.

"Have you had any sleep at all?" I asked.

"Yeah, I grabbed a couple of hours before shift." He looked out the window from my office. "Miserable day for a funeral." The snow was piled high and there were still a few wet flurries falling. "I moved back here so I wouldn't have to do violent crime scenes."

Ah, now we were getting to the crux of the problem. Jack was SWAT in DC, but he'd retired after he'd been the last cop left alive when an op went bad. He'd *barely* been left alive once the smoke had cleared. He'd taken three bullets, had a collapsed lung, a ruptured spleen, and a broken femur. Not to mention the blood loss. By all accounts he should have been dead, but he was here and his friends weren't. He couldn't handle high-pressure situations anymore, so he'd moved back to Bloody Mary and run for sheriff.

Jack's always kind of been my hero, and I believed he could handle more than he thought. He just needed time to heal the inside wounds.

"You're a different person than you were in DC, Jack. A stronger person. A stronger cop."

"It doesn't feel like it, especially when someone gets murdered right under my nose and my gut tells me it's not the most obvious suspect," he said. The frustration and anger were apparent across his face. "And if that DNA sample comes back negative tomorrow it means I've got nothing, and I'm as useless here as I was there."

"That's ridiculous, Jack. What? Are you fishing for compliments? You know you're a good cop. If we hit a snag tomorrow with the DNA, then all we have to do is find another thread to pull."

I could tell the no-pity angle worked because Jack lost the sullen look that was on his face.

"Fine, you're hired as temporary deputy then," he said.

"That's what I get for opening my big mouth and trying to help." I never could get the upper hand on Jack. "Do I at least get to carry a gun?"

Jack looked horrified at the thought. "Umm, no. But I've got a tin badge lying around my office somewhere."

"I guess I'll have to be satisfied with that."

"Let's go to a funeral," he said, tossing me my coat. "And for God's sake, get that grin off your face. It's creeping me out."

Fiona's funeral was everything I'd thought it would be and more. *Miserable* being the word that came to the forefront of my mind.

The men who'd dug the grave had looked cold and worn out when they'd come in to collect their checks. They'd said it had been like digging through ice, and in a sense, that's exactly what they'd been doing.

There was only a smattering of people who'd braved the cold to come say farewell to Fiona. Besides Jack, and me, Phyllis and her husband sat rigid and stoic under the green plastic awning that covered the family plot. Phyllis blotted her tears with a white handkerchief and kept her head held high.

George sat at the opposite end of the row, flanked by two cops and an attending physician, and he wept softly into his hands. Dr. Givens shot me disapproving looks like I was the one who'd caused George so much emotional pain.

Dickey had come without his wife or his secretary. It wasn't often I saw him without one or the other. He was dressed in his banker's clothes, obviously there to represent First National. Which reminded me that we needed to ask Dickey if he would let us in the bank today to collect the contents of the box.

Wanda Baker, of the Baker Bed and Breakfast, sat toward the back, and Stanley Lipinski sat next to her, resting a comforting hand on her shoulder. I always wondered if there was more going on between the two of them than Sunday brunch. They seemed awfully cozy. Wanda kept giving me knowing glances, and I had to turn away before my face flamed any hotter.

I recognized a couple of teachers from James Madison Preparatory where we'd all gone to school, and Floyd Parker from the *King George Gazette* was there because it had been a while since something this newsworthy had happened around here. I shot Floyd a nasty look just out of habit and ignored the smarmy kiss he blew me.

Vaughn and Eddie stood, freezing like the rest of us, but they'd come because they knew Fiona and I had been close once upon a time. But that was the entire list of people who'd come for Fiona. It made me wonder who would come to wish me off into the afterlife when it was my time to go. Was there more than a handful who cared? I didn't have any family to send me off. They were all lying four plots up and two over.

Jack put his arm around me and squeezed gently, like he'd known what was going through my head.

I worked with death on a daily basis and understood better than most how fragile our mortality was. It was funny how some people, like Jack, had gone their whole lives without losing one person who was close to them, while I'd lost everyone. It hardly seemed fair for God to take so much away and not give anything in return.

The Reverend Jonah Thomas spoke words of comfort, but I ignored the content and let the gentle flow of his voice soothe me. I'd heard the words too many times already in my thirty years.

And then the service was over, and Fiona Murphy was lowered into the cold ground in a mahogany box lined with satin. Red roses were thrown into the open grave, and snow flurries dotted the fresh dirt with white. A sad end for any life.

There was still someone out there who was responsible for putting Fiona in that grave, and it was our job to find him. Somewhere, in the secret life Fiona led, lay the key to bringing her justice.

FOURTEEN

Phyllis and her husband cleared out quickly, with barely a goodbye between them, and the rest of the mourners took the hint and went back to minding their own business.

Dickey and Vaughn waited for me and Jack at the end of the ceremony. I had to stay until the bitter end and make sure there was no funny business before Fiona was buried. I didn't want any stolen bodies on my watch.

It was always weird seeing Dickey and Vaughn standing so close together. They were a study in light and dark, complete opposites in every way, but still friends despite it all. Dickey was tall and golden, perpetual tennis tan and capped teeth. Blue eyes that I knew for a fact he enhanced by bright blue contacts and muscles he got honest by swimming every morning in the indoor pool he'd had installed when he and Candy had first married.

Vaughn was as dark as Dickey was light. Swarthy skin that had been passed down from some Mediterranean ancestor and black hair that he wore in a long ponytail. His goatee was always trimmed and neat and his eyes were black as pitch. He was just my height and wore diamond studs in both ears. Vaughn was just as in shape, if not better, than Jack or Dickey because he enjoyed rowing. He'd even had a shot at the Olympics a few years ago, but had turned it down because he said it had become too commercialized.

I thought it was interesting that Jack had more money than both of the other men combined, but he always managed to dress without having to make the latest fashion statement. That's probably why the two of us got along so well. Jack had money but chose not to flaunt it, and I had very little and just didn't care about making any kind of statement at all.

I usually didn't feel so self-conscious when Eddie was around because he was going soft around the middle, and I didn't have to pretend like I was using the gym membership they'd bought me for my last birthday. Only four men would buy a woman something as insulting as a gym membership for a special occasion.

"I've got to get back to the store," Vaughn said, leaning in to give me a kiss on the cheek goodbye. "I've got a couple coming to pick up a few things I bought for them at auction. But I so wish I could go to the bank with you guys. It sounds like fun." Vaughn always managed to make everything sound like a grand adventure. It was just part of his makeup.

"I'll make sure to give you the play-by-play later," I promised.

"Good. I also want to hear about the writer. I didn't think you'd ever get over that four-year drought. Though next time you should probably tone down the smile for the funeral."

Jack and Dickey burst out laughing and my face flamed. "If you're going to make fun of me I won't give you any details. And he took me to Dante's too," I said. Vaughn gasped in jealousy, and Jack and Dickey both *oohe*d and *ahhe*d appreciatively.

We said goodbye to Vaughn and turned toward our own vehicles.

"I'm not really supposed to open the bank on Sundays, but I can make an exception for this. It's not like I have anything better to do," Dickey said forlornly.

"Uh-oh," I said. "Trouble in paradise?"

Jack nudged me in the ribs in a subtle reminder to mind my own business, but I'd never been one to hold anything back.

"You could say that. Vanessa wants to have a baby."

Vanessa Hart was Dickey's secretary. NOT his wife. So I could understand why Dickey might be depressed about the situation. I was glad I wasn't in his shoes.

Jack broke his own rule and butted in. "So what are you going to do?"

"I don't know. I'd leave Candy in a heartbeat, but she'd skin me in the divorce. She doesn't care about Vanessa so much as long as she gets to be the *wife*. I've always loved Vanessa, but this is getting out of control."

"You're just now realizing this?" I asked.

"I've thought about breaking it off with Vanessa and finding someone new. Someone who has fewer demands and just wants sex, but I don't know if I can go through with it. The stress is really starting to get to me."

"Maybe you need a vacation," Jack suggested. Dickey really was looking frazzled and strung out.

"You're probably right. It's just that Candy would probably want to come with me. I just despise that woman. What in the world was I thinking when I married her?"

He'd probably been thinking he'd gotten her pregnant because that's what she'd told him, but it had turned out to be a false alarm. No one had ever accused Dickey of being the sharpest knife in the drawer.

"Sometimes when she starts yapping at me, I just want to grab her by the throat and start squeezing until her little nagging head pops right off."

"Whoa, buddy. Seriously. Take a vacation," Jack said. "I've got enough murders on my hands right now without having to arrest you too."

"Sorry," he said. "Let's head over to the bank. Being in the graveyard is depressing me more than I already was. Until now, I was pretty sure I'd already hit my lowest point. I think I'll try the new woman angle. It couldn't hurt."

Yeah, but it couldn't help either, I thought.

The drive was quiet to the bank. We followed closely behind Dickey's black Audi a block over to the parking lot of First National. "Do you really think Dickey would hurt Candy?" I asked Jack.

"I sure hope not," he said. "Even though I could understand the temptation. But he's got to get a grip before he has a heart attack or something. Juggling two women is hell on earth. That's why I stick with one at a time and never stick long."

I snorted out a laugh and got out of the car. Dickey was already unlocking the doors and keying in the alarm codes while Jack got his crime scene kit out of the trunk. It was nothing big, just a paper sack filled with surgical gloves and plastic baggies, all sizes, to put evidence in. The bank was silent as a tomb, and our steps echoed along the marbled floors. It smelled faintly of Pine-Sol and the desks were all polished and neat. Ferns hung from the ceiling and ficus trees sat in the corners. It was a cozy space. And Dickey had done a good job with it despite his hectic love life.

"Can you find out when Fiona was here last?" Jack asked Dickey.

"I can tell you that without looking it up," he said. "She was here just as Vanessa and I opened the doors Thursday morning. Eight o'clock on the dot. She went straight back to the safe-deposit boxes. Mrs. Mueller pulled in right behind her, so I was busy dealing with her in my office. The only time Mrs. Mueller comes in is when she has a complaint, so I didn't see Fiona leave."

The room that housed the safe-deposit boxes was the complete opposite of the front of the bank. It was cold and sterile. Long metal tables sat in rows and the boxes sat stacked on top of each other numbered from one to whatever.

"What's the number on the key?" Dickey asked.

"201," Jack said. The box was on an aisle right at mid-level. "Let's see what we've got."

The anticipation in the room was thick. Jack upended the box and all that floated out was a loose sheet of paper and a couple of thick brown envelopes. Everyone's disappointment was palpable.

"Bummer," I said. "I was hoping for stolen diamonds or random sex tapes."

"I was thinking maybe a severed hand or some other body part. I saw that in a movie once," Dickey said when Jack and I both gave him the *eww, gross* look.

"Why don't I just see what it says before the two of you come up with any more ideas," Jack said. He held up the loose sheet and I could just barely make out the words written in an elegant cursive script. Jack read the letter out loud.

. . .

Dear George,

I'm so sorry to have to leave you this way. I know you won't understand. That's why I couldn't tell you. You've done the best you can by me, but in the end it just wasn't enough.

I've found somebody new. Someone who can give me what I need without my having to tell him. I'm not faulting you, George. You must know this. I do love you, in my own way. And I'll never forget you.

I'm going to visit my sister for a couple of weeks and file for divorce. She's been missing me, and I figure I can appease her and get the divorce pushed through at the same time. You know how she's always disapproved of you.

I do have a surprise for you, George. I thought long and hard about what I could give you that you could remember me by. We grew up together and shared a marriage, so you'll always have those memories, but look in the envelope. I know you've been wanting to open a second shop over in Nottingham. Just think, you'll finally be a chain.

I'll miss you, my love. I hope you know I speak the truth, but my heart is telling me to take a different path.

Love always, Fiona

PS Could you mail the second envelope for me? I want to be out of town before it reaches its destination.

"Poor George," I said.

"Are you kidding me?" Dickey said. "This is George Murphy we're talking about isn't it? George the Terrible?"

"Yeah, I know," I said, coming back to my senses. "It's just that letter almost made him seem human there for a second."

Jack let out a low whistle that got both our attention. "That's a heck of a going-away present."

The first envelope was filled with money. "How much do you think is in there?" I asked.

"I'd say close to a quarter of a million just by looking. Maybe more," he said. "And you're never going to guess who the second envelope is addressed to."

"Who?" I asked.

"Dr. Henry Hides. 622 Covington Lane. Nottingham, Virginia."

"What? But I thought she'd be running away with Dr. Hides after everything we found out yesterday and him lying to us."

"Obviously not. Remember he was as surprised as we were that she was leaving town. I don't think he faked that reaction."

"Yeah, but now we don't have any clue as to who she was meeting."

"If she was earning this kind of money doing what we think she was doing, then she's got to have a record book somewhere."

"Why? It's not like she was paying taxes," I said.

"What do you think she was doing to make that kind of money?" Dickey asked.

"Nothing," Jack and I both said at the same time.

"Oookay," Dickey said, putting his hands up and backing away a few steps.

"She'd want to keep a log. Contact numbers, addresses, that sort of thing."

"They didn't find anything like that at her house," I said.

"No, but maybe she hid it somewhere else. We can assume by the letter that Fiona planned to leave the key with George before she left."

"Or maybe mail it to him," I added. "He said they were fighting when she left, or he was fighting in any case. Maybe she just forgot to give it to him."

"No, you're probably right about mailing it to him. She'd want to be on her way, have some distance from the uproar she was causing in a place like Bloody Mary."

"Well, be that as it may, all we can do is wait for this mysterious little black book to show up, and then we can see if our murderer's name is inside."

"If only it were that easy," Jack said. "Or maybe George knew Fiona planned to leave him and really did kill her."

"I hadn't thought about that," I said.

"That's why they pay me the big bucks," Jack said. "Let's get out of here. I have to get these logged into evidence, and then I need to get home. I'd like to get some sleep tonight. I'm running on empty."

I thought about home too and knew what waited for me there. Sleep was the last thing I wanted.

FIFTEEN

I groaned when I heard the phone ring.

"Good grief, can't a person sleep in around this place?" Brody asked next to me.

"It's your own fault," I said, grasping for the phone. "I'm used to going to bed earlier." I fumbled around the night-stand, bypassing a Kleenex box, torn condom packages, someone's underwear, and a ballpoint pen before I felt the cordless phone.

"Dr. Graves," I said. My voice was still husky with sleep and I closed my eyes and lay back down with the phone pressed to my ear.

"Wake up, sunshine," Jack said. "We've got another body."

That bit of information woke me up in a hurry. I sat straight up in bed and looked over at the glowing green numbers on my alarm clock. I was surprised to see it was after nine o'clock. I never slept that late. Must have been the company I kept.

"Where at?" I asked.

"The Hanover Hotel, fifth floor. Crime scene's just starting so you have time for a shower and a cup of coffee."

"I guess this eliminates George," I said.

"Yeah, that and the fact that I got a phone call from the lab in Richmond. The DNA's not a match, and neither is the mud Mooney pulled off the tire."

"Hell."

"I concur. George has already been released to go home. It looks like I went above and beyond the call of duty for nothing. Get here as soon as you can, Jaye. It's bad."

"I'll be there in thirty," I said, disconnecting. I hadn't asked who the victim was. I didn't want to know until I had to.

"What is it?" Brody asked.

"We've got another body. I've got to grab a shower and take my coffee to go," I said as I got out of bed. "I'm sorry I keep having to leave you here by yourself."

"It's no big deal. I'm a big boy. And besides, I've got plenty of work to keep me busy. Actually, if it's not too much of a problem I'd like to go to the crime scene with you. It might help me get a better picture if I can see firsthand what I'm writing about. A couple of books ago, I tagged along with a friend of mine who's the ME in Baltimore. Don't worry—I know how to stay out of the way at a crime scene."

"If you've observed the ME in Baltimore then I'm sure you're not going to be getting any extra knowledge from me."

"Not technical knowledge. But in Baltimore there were dozens of bodies going through the morgue a day. This is Bloody Mary, and only you can show me what it's like in a close-knit community. I want to know what everyone's reaction is, from the policemen working the scene to whatever stranger found the body, because more likely than not, everyone is going to know the victim."

"I'd have to clear it with Jack first."

"You do that and I'll get the coffee. We'll convene in the shower. How do you feel about multitasking?" he asked. The look he gave me was enough to get my blood moving and make funny things happen to my insides.

"I'm feeling very warm toward multitasking," I said.

Twenty-nine minutes later, we were on our way to the fifth floor of the Hanover Hotel. The sun was up and melting the snow by the time we'd left my house and the winter chill was already ebbing away. With any luck we wouldn't have a heavy snow again until the end of January or February.

Brody and I had both thrown on clothes as quickly as possible because I was sure we'd be late, and then Jack would have the right to make fun of me for an indeterminate amount of time. I checked my reflection in the mirrored wall of the elevator just to make sure all my buttons were done up correctly.

"You can't hide it. Everybody's going to know," Brody said, smirking. "You wear passion across your entire face. And you've got beard burn on your neck. Should've worn the turtleneck like I said."

"Great. Just great. I thought you were just trying to tell me how to dress." I pulled my collar up as high as it would go and wished I'd at least brought a scarf. I'd been lucky to remember my medical bag. "Be nice to Jack," I reminded Brody.

"Jack's jealous," he said. "He's not used to anyone getting to spend time with you but him."

This was true, but I felt disloyal saying so, so I kept my mouth shut. "He's just worried about me," I said instead. "He doesn't want me to get my heart broken."

"And what do you think?" Brody asked. "Do you think I'll break your heart?"

"I think it's a strong possibility you could," I said, not making eye contact.

Brody took my chin with his fingers and turned my face to look at him. And when he kissed me I felt all the passion we'd shared the past two nights. "I can honestly say that I've never felt for another woman what I feel for you. Is that enough for now? We've only known each other four days."

"It's enough," I said, giving him a quick hug before the doors opened. Actually it was more than I'd expected. I knew when I'd met Brody that he and Jack had more than just sarcasm and good looks in common. And it would be completely my fault if my heart were broken, because I should have known better than to get involved in the first place.

The elevator dinged to a stop and the doors opened slowly. Floyd Parker stood directly in front of me with his camera in my face. The flash was blinding.

"I knew it had to be you," Floyd said, camera still clicking. He was built like a linebacker, and he blocked my way as I tried to get off the elevator. His middle had thickened over the years so the red polo he wore couldn't quite stay tucked into his khakis, but his overpowering height was still the same. "Running a little late, aren't you, Doc? Did you get lost?" He eyed the beard burn on my neck and his eyes narrowed in speculation.

"Get out of the way, Floyd," I said, swatting his camera out of my face as the flash went off again. "You'll contaminate the crime scene, and you'd better hope Jack doesn't catch you up here."

He ignored me and turned his speculation to Brody. "You must be the writer," he said, snapping another picture. "You're front page news. Along with the murders, that is. We haven't had this much excitement in town since the Graveses killed themselves driving their car over that cliff. Death sells lots of papers." He chuckled and my blood boiled.

"They didn't drive over a cliff on purpose, Floyd," I said, standing on my toes and pointing my finger in his chest. "It was an accident."

"You can't prove that, Jaye. I heard from good sources that your parents were fighting like cats and dogs that day, and a witness said he swore he saw your dad speed up near the end of the cliff road."

"Yeah, except no one could confirm your sources. But that didn't stop you from printing the lies in your trashy paper."

He smirked because he knew the damage had already been done. Everyone in town believed my parents had killed themselves because of Floyd Parker. My hands shook, I was so angry. He changed the subject abruptly, leaving me flustered. I wasn't good with verbal sparring.

"I see you've found another man to screw to save you from your loneliness. It's really rather pathetic." He looked at Brody with sympathy. "She'll love you and leave you, just like she did to me. Though it wasn't all that great. Pretty terrible actually." He waggled his eyebrows and looked at my boobs. "But maybe she's gotten better with practice. Does she still make that little noise—"

Brody's elbow connected with Floyd's gut before he could finish and the air whooshed out of his mouth. The hallway teemed with police and the crime scene unit, and they'd all stopped working to listen to Floyd and me. I wasn't sure how long Jack had been standing there, but I found it difficult to look him in the eyes when he came up beside me.

"You're not supposed to be up here, Floyd," Jack said, hitting the elevator button and clamping a hand on Floyd's shoulder.

"Freedom of the press, Sheriff," he said with a sneer.

"Which doesn't mean a thing when I'm trying to catch a murderer," Jack said, getting right in his face. "You know, Floyd? You've been one of the first people on the scene of both murders. That seems pretty suspicious to me. Maybe you knew where the crime scenes were because you were the one to kill these women."

"Give me a break," Floyd said. "Or maybe I'm just better at getting information than your Keystone Kops. This rabble couldn't find their elbows if they had a mirror. Whoever's killing these women will get away with murder. Tough break, Jack. Maybe I should do an editorial on the sad state of our police force. How does that sound?" Floyd shoved a mini recorder in Jack's face.

Jack didn't even flinch. "Floyd Parker, where were you the night Fiona Murphy died?"

Floyd laughed until he saw Jack was dead serious. "Give me a break, Jack. How should I know?"

"Detective Nash," Jack said. "Escort Mr. Parker to the station. Maybe he can come up with an alibi."

"Are you kidding me?" Floyd yelled, shoving Jack in the chest and pushing him into the wall. "I'm going to own you and this whole town by the time I'm finished suing you."

Jack stood completely still, his fists balled down at his

sides. "Nash," he said again, "hold Mr. Parker on assault charges until I can question him." Jack's eyes never left Floyd's.

"My pleasure, sir," Nash said.

"If you go peacefully, Floyd, we'll do it without the restraints," Jack said.

The elevator doors opened, and Nash pushed Floyd inside. Floyd's face was red with anger and veins bulged in his forehead. If I were Jack, I wouldn't turn my back on Floyd anytime soon. Violence shimmered from every pore of Floyd's body, and he wasn't doing a very good job of controlling it. Men with that kind of explosive temper were capable of all types of things. I thought maybe Jack knew exactly what he'd been doing when he'd provoked Floyd.

The elevator doors closed, and the silence in the hallway was thick with emotion. Jack turned to me, but I still couldn't manage to look him in the face. I was embarrassed and angry. Sleeping with Floyd had been one of the lowest points of my life. Now everyone in town was going to know about it. And worse than the embarrassment, I was hurt. Mostly because there could have been a smidgen of truth to Floyd's story about my parents. I just didn't know.

I could feel Jack's stare boring into me and finally looked up. His eyes held a mixture of anger, sympathy, and something else. Disappointment? Or was I just projecting my own feelings?

"I don't want to hear about it, Jack. It was a long time ago."

"I wasn't going to say anything about your poor judgment. I'll save the potential blackmail information and use it later when I want something," he said, like he hadn't just been on the verge of a fight.

"Figures," I said.

"That's what friends are for." He started down the hall and Brody and I followed behind him. I slung the camera around my neck.

"Congratulations, by the way, on making it here on time," Jack said. "I figured you'd be at least an hour. Made me lose twenty bucks."

"Remind me to tell you about the wonders of multitasking sometime."

"If that means what I think it means, I'll pass. You should've worn a turtleneck," Jack said, eyeing my neck. He looked up and at least bothered to nod to Brody in acknowledgment, even if he didn't speak.

The door to room 508 stood open, and black fingerprint dust covered most of its surface and the doorknob. I took in the general atmosphere of the room before I went to look at the body. Jack and Brody stood still and quiet beside me. Out of respect or to gauge my reaction, I didn't know. Cops moved throughout the room slowly, some doing their jobs fiercely, others frozen in shock. Jeremy Mooney had tears tracking silently down his face.

"Who is it?" I finally asked.

"Amanda Wallace," Jack said.

I closed my eyes and let the news wash over and through me. Another Bloody Mary resident. I'd held a slight hope that the body would be from another town, so I wouldn't have to face the death of any more neighbors.

"Let's go look at the body," I said. "And then I want you to walk me through it. Kendra and Owen will be here shortly to transport the body."

Kendra Bloom and Owen Ferguson were pathology students at the Virginia Commonwealth University Medical College, and they came to see me on Mondays and

Wednesdays. Mostly I just helped them study since we hardly ever saw any action in Bloody Mary. It was part of their program since they were both first-year students, but next year they'd go off to a bigger lab and a more important doctor.

Amanda Wallace's nude body was lying naked and faceup on the king-size bed. Red rose petals were spread underneath her and a rope of pearls was wrapped around her neck so tight they were embedded in the skin.

I snapped a few pictures then opened my bag and pulled out a pair of surgical gloves. Amanda's hands were still grasping the pearls, freezing her last struggles before death. I motioned Brody to the other side of the bed so he could get a better idea of what I was doing.

"Cadaveric spasm is obvious by the way her hands are still locked at her throat," I told Brody. I realized Jack was just behind me as well and turned to talk to him as I went over the body.

"Usually it takes the body a couple of hours to settle into rigor, which always begins with the face and works its way down the body. But in a case where there was strenuous activity or struggle, something where the heart rate is accelerated, parts of the body can go into immediate rigor."

"Does that mean death was recent?" Jack asked.

"Not necessarily." I already had a pretty good estimate of time of death, but I checked her body temperature to confirm my thoughts.

She was pale, paler than the whitest marble, and I knew when we turned her the blood would be gathered at the lowest point of her body, mostly the buttocks and lower back. "She's got some skin under the nails," I said. I bagged her hands to keep the DNA from being contaminated.

"Do you think she got him?" Jack asked.

"I'd say it's probably her own. She's got scratches under her neck where she was trying to claw at the restriction, but we could get lucky."

"I need some luck," Jack said.

I checked the thermometer. "She's cold. I'd put time of death right around twenty-four hours," I said.

Jack sighed. I knew he was frustrated because twenty-four hours was a long time after a murder. A lot could happen in twenty-four hours.

"She's already at the beginning stages of algor mortis," I said. Algor mortis was what happened when a person came out of rigor. As rigor started with the face and worked its way down the body, coming out of it began the same way. Amanda's cheeks had already taken on a flaccid state, and the rest of her would follow over the next day or two. It was always a pain to have to massage a body out of the rigor state before I could embalm them. Fortunately, I had interns who could take care of that task for me.

"She's been sexually assaulted. I'll collect a sperm sample so you can compare it to the other," I said. I stood and gently turned her over. As I'd expected, her buttocks and lower back were a dark purple against the paleness of the rest of her skin. I looked for any similar blows like the one that was on the back of Fiona's head, but I couldn't see anything that would cause immediate distress.

"No blows or questionable bruising. A couple of contusions around the wrists, but that's the most of it," I said as I laid her back down and pulled off my gloves.

Kendra and Owen stood just inside the door, and I motioned for them to come take the body away. It was always best to think of them as *the body* instead of Amanda Wallace, married mother of two and treasurer for the Ladies of King George County.

"He was obviously able to overpower her without knocking her unconscious. What was she doing here?"

Jack ran his fingers through his dark hair. "Next of kin hasn't been notified yet," he said.

I was surprised to hear that. I figured as soon as the body of the councilman's wife had been discovered, Jack would have sent a policeman to let Harvey know. "Why not?"

"Because I need to ask Harvey some questions, and I need to have a clear theory to do it so he doesn't try to start an uprising against me. Why else would Amanda rent a hotel room when she lives less than twenty minutes away?"

Technically the Hanover Hotel was in King George instead of Bloody Mary because it sat on the east side of Queen Mary Road. "She was having an affair?"

"Looks like it to me," he said. "This room was rented under her own name for the whole weekend. She told the front desk manager she was going to make use of the spa for a relaxing couple of days and treat herself. So if you say she's been dead close to twenty-four hours, Saturday night was when her visitor came and stayed through to early morning by the looks of the breakfast trays.

"The *Do Not Disturb* sign was out, but she was supposed to check out at eight o'clock this morning. The floor maid was the one to find her when she came to clean the room. She's already been questioned and was sent home sedated."

I tried to look around the room through Jack's eyes. It was set for seduction—the rose petals, candle tapers burned so all was left was a puddle of wax, a sheer nightgown thrown over the chair.

"Maybe Harvey was her visitor."

"I don't think so. I don't see a woman pulling out the

stops like this when she makes it a point to tell people she's escaping for the weekend. Remember I told you Saturday night I had to go break up a fight at the lodge between Bob and Harvey. That was about one a.m. and both of them were piss-faced drunk. I gave them a warning and sent them both home to find their beds. I very seriously doubt Harvey had it in him to come here and make love to his wife all night."

"So Mrs. Wallace invites her lover to her hotel room, they make love all night, get up the next morning and order breakfast and then he decides to kill her? That doesn't play for me," I said.

"Me either," Jack said. "But what if the killer came after her lover had already gone? We tracked down the bellhop who delivered the room service, but he didn't see anyone in the room besides Mrs. Wallace."

"Wait. And she just lets him in?" Brody asked skeptically. He'd been so quiet I'd frankly forgotten that he was there.

"Let's say the lover leaves first thing Sunday morning," Jack said. "She kisses him goodbye and then decides to take a shower. After she showers, she does whatever it is women do to make themselves up in the mornings. There are enough cosmetics on the counter in there to fill up a department store."

Jack pointed to the silky peach robe lying on the floor close to where Amanda's body had been. "So she puts on a robe, and then she hears a knock at the door. She obviously opened the door for whoever was there, which leads me to believe she knew her killer."

"Geez, Jack. She's the wife of a councilman," I said. "She knows everyone in town."

"It makes sense that you're looking for one of your own," Brody said. "The killer is someone who knows both Fiona and Amanda—their habits and obviously their secrets. An outsider wouldn't be so specific."

"I know," Jack said. A look passed between him and Brody that I didn't understand, but the moment was broken when Jack continued with his timeline.

"So she lets the killer in and shuts the door behind him, and then he muscles her into doing what he wants instead of incapacitating her like he did Fiona. There's only one other couple booked on this floor at the far end of the hall, so chances are no one would have heard a scuffle or any screams. We're looking for a man with some strength. She fought him, but he still overpowered her. And when he was finished killing her, he planted one of Harvey Wallace's cuff links on the floor slightly under the bed."

Jack held up a plastic baggie with a black-and-gold cuff link that had the letter *W* printed on it. Everybody in town knew that was one of Harvey's favorite sets of cuff links. It had been a wedding gift from Amanda.

"That's handy," I said.

"Or maybe it really was Harvey. That would explain why she let him in. Maybe it all just boils down to an old-fashioned lovers' quarrel."

"So where do we start?" I asked.

"I'd think with the logical choice. The husband. In a community as small as this there's no telling how long it would be before he found out about the affair."

Ah, so that's why Jack hadn't sent anyone to break the news to the husband. He wanted to see his reaction first-hand. "The husband was the logical choice in Fiona's death too," I said. "That's where all the evidence pointed."

"Don't remind me," he said. "Foolproof evidence has been part of the problem to begin with. Meaning that I'm the one that looks like a fool."

"What about the lover?" Brody asked.

"He'll be next on my list. We just have to find him first. There aren't cameras on the floors, but there are a few in the lobby. We'll look at them and see if we can get an identity."

I went over to Brody and spoke softly. "I'm going to head over to the Wallaces' with Jack to break the news."

"That's not a conversation I'd want to be a part of," he said, shaking his head.

No kidding. I wasn't exactly thrilled at the prospect either.

"I'm going to head back over to the Bed and Breakfast for a while to get some work done," Brody said. "I wanted to let you know that I ate breakfast in the dining room here at the hotel yesterday morning to keep Mrs. Baker from asking me where I'd spent the night, so Jack will see me on the tape."

"I'll give him a heads-up," I said.

"Call me when you get finished and I'll pick up dinner."

"It could be late."

"I do my best work late at night," he said with a wink.

I gave him a quick kiss and then made my way back over to Jack, who was giving last-minute instructions to one of his officers.

"Are you done playing kissy-face?" he asked.

"Unless you want one too, big guy," I said.

He looked at his watch and sighed. "There just aren't enough hours in the day. I've got to wrap things up here, and I need to run by the station to check on Floyd's status. I'm going to make him sweat for as long as I can before I question him. That'll give you time to give Amanda's body a cursory glance to see if you find anything unusual. I'll pick you up at the funeral home in about an hour, and then we can go see if Harvey Wallace knew who his wife was having an affair with."

I blew out a breath and closed my eyes. "That'll be fun."

SIXTEEN

I was pretty sure Harvey Wallace had no idea about his wife's extramarital affair, considering he collapsed at my feet once Jack told him about the nature of his wife's death.

It had taken death threats and blackmail to keep the news of Amanda's murder from hitting the grapevine. Most of the threats were directed at Barbara Blanton in the dispatcher's office because she could never keep her big mouth shut.

"Geez, Jack. Maybe break the news a little easier next time," I said. Harvey was crumpled on the floor like a rag doll and lay pale and still as death. I bent down to make sure he was still breathing and gave Jack the thumbs-up sign when I saw his chest rise.

"I wasn't going to draw it out," Jack said, rolling his eyes. "That makes it worse for everyone. Bad news should be delivered quick and clean. Like a Band-Aid."

"So says the guy not lying in a heap on the floor. Help me get him to the sofa."

Jack lifted Harvey up without my help and moved him

to the sofa. *Someone had been working out,* I thought, eyeing the arm bulges appreciatively. I was still a woman, even if I was having regular sex now.

"Wow, Jack, that's impressive," I said.

"That's because you live on sugar and starch, whereas my body is a temple. Plus, the fact that I actually use my gym membership." He gave me a pointed look, one of those meant to instill guilt, but I looked up at the ceiling and started to whistle. I was a master evader of the guilt trip.

But Jack was right about one thing, there was no way I was going to give up powdered donuts to make my body a temple for anyone. Men liked a little softness to their women, right?

"Harvey," I finally said, putting my fingers at the pulse on his neck. It was rapid, but strong. "Harvey, can you hear me?"

Startled blue eyes opened, and I breathed a sigh of relief.

"Amanda?" he asked. He looked lost and old, fragile.

"I'm sorry about your wife, Harvey. Would you mind if we asked you a few questions?"

He sat up slowly and Jack and I sat in the dainty Queen Anne chairs across from him. Jack looked at Harvey with sympathy, and I knew this was harder for him than he let on. It was never easy dealing with grief, whether it was your own or someone else's.

"We need to do this by the book, Harvey," Jack said, "so we can find who did this to your wife."

"Yes. Do whatever you need to do," he said. His eyes were dilated and his voice shook slightly. "I understand the process and that I would logically be your number one suspect. But I assure you, I did not kill my wife."

"Can you tell us your whereabouts between seven and noon yesterday morning?" Jack asked.

"I was here," Harvey said. He touched the little lace doilies that sat on the coffee table, a telling nervous habit. He knew about the affair, I realized. But he didn't want to talk about it because then it would become real in his mind.

"You know I had too much to drink Saturday night, Jack. I was upset about things and wasn't thinking straight. And then Bob just compounded those problems by being Bob. Let me tell you, holidays have been hell the last twenty years when you have a father-in-law who would sooner serve you up on a platter instead of a turkey," he said with a rusty laugh.

"But what you said to me Saturday night brought some of my common sense back, and I realized I was making a fool of myself. So I came back home like you told me to and slept it off. I didn't wake up until after ten."

"Did you go out after you woke up?"

"No, I stayed here all day. I know it was my duty as a councilman to go to Fiona's funeral, but I just didn't feel up to it. I was feeling sorry for myself and the last thing I wanted was to go out in public."

"Were you and your wife having problems?" Jack asked softly.

Harvey nodded slowly; his eyes devastated but still dry. "It started just over a year ago. Look at me. I'm sixty-three years old, Jack, and she's a thirty-eight-year-old woman in the prime of her life. Bob should have shot me down for running off with his baby. But I loved her. Still love her. My youngest is eighteen now, just started college in the fall. I don't know what I'd do if a man old enough to know better came along and snatched her away from me."

"You fought over your age difference?" Jack asked.

I was completely surprised by this whole thing. I never would have guessed the Wallaces were having marital problems. They always seemed so happy together. It proved that no one really knew what went on behind closed doors.

"I asked her how she could still be attracted to me, still love the old man I've become. I'm not as good looking as I used to be. I have mirrors," he said, bitterly. "In my day, I could have had any woman I wanted. She told me I was being silly and she wanted to go see a marriage counselor."

Jack and I exchanged looks, remembering the therapist we'd already had one run-in with. But I also remembered that Dr. Hides had told us he wasn't a marriage counselor.

"Did you go?" I asked.

"No. I told her I wasn't going to see a shrink to tell me I should've married someone my own age. That made her cry because she didn't think I loved her anymore. I told her if it would make her feel better to see a shrink to go right ahead, but she could do it without me. She took me up on it too. Didn't speak to me for almost a week after that little fight."

"Do you have the contact information for her doctor?" Jack asked.

"It's probably in her Rolodex," he said. "I'll see if I can find it for you." He got up and headed to a back room where I assumed her office was located.

I took a minute to look around the room while he was gone. It was a cozy house in good repair. Amanda Wallace had obviously been very traditional in her decorating tastes. And expensive. If I wasn't mistaken, her dining room table and other various pieces were all Hepplewhite.

The sofa print was of large faded cabbage roses and a Persian rug was on the floor. I let my mind wander while looking over the room. Dr. Hides did seem to be in the middle of it all.

"I don't believe in coincidences, Jack."

"Me either, but let's see who the doctor is before we jump to conclusions."

Harvey came back with a business card and gave it to Jack with a shaking hand. He didn't bother to sit back down.

"She was with a lover, wasn't she?" Harvey asked Jack directly, his face blank of any emotion for the first time.

Jack looked at him with sympathy. "We believe so, yes. It's our number one priority to find out who the last person to see her alive was."

"I almost don't even want to know who it was. It's my own fault, you know? I didn't touch her in over a year. I just didn't see how she could want me. Sexually. I'd told myself I'd rather do without her than think she was pretending when she was in my bed."

There was nothing I could say or do to relieve Harvey Wallace of the grief and guilt he was feeling. Some things were set in motion long before people like me ever came to the scene.

"I wish I could tell you who he was, but I was just starting to suspect myself," he said, getting a grip on his thoughts. "I don't mean to rush you out, but I need to find a way to tell my children their mother is dead. We'll be in tomorrow, Dr. Graves, to discuss funeral preparations. Unless you need to see me sooner."

"Actually, it would be best if you can come in this afternoon and complete the paperwork. It'll take a couple of days before she'll be ready for the viewing because of the autopsy. You can always come back tomorrow with your children and make arrangements for the preparations." He was silent, just staring blankly at me as if my words hadn't yet penetrated. "I'm very sorry for your loss."

"Thank you," he said and shut the door behind us.

"Well?" I asked.

"Let's go pay a visit to Dr. Hides. I think he needs to have an ironclad alibi for yesterday morning or he's going to find himself under arrest."

"Before we start dragging people away in shackles, would you mind if we got something to eat? I'm starving."

"When aren't you starving?" Jack asked. "Where do you want to stop?"

"Martha's," I said automatically. "I need a burger with the works." Martha's was a burger institution in Bloody Mary. Martha herself had been behind the counter for the last sixty years serving breakfast, lunch, and dinner.

"The writer's not going to want to play kissy-face next time you see him if you get a burger with the works."

"The writer will want to play kissy-face at any opportunity he can find. The man is a machine."

"You serious about this guy?" Jack asked, pulling into the parking lot at Martha's Diner.

"I think I could be," I said. "I'm trying not to let myself."

"Why not?"

"He reminds me of you."

"Like hell," Jack said loud enough to have a couple of diners look in our direction.

"You'd be surprised," I said. "I don't know, Jack. I'm getting to that point in my life where I'm ready to settle down with someone. Maybe have a couple of kids. I'm not sure if Brody's anywhere near ready for that. I've got to prepare myself for when he moves on."

"Or he could decide to stay. He looked pretty serious about you when I saw you together earlier today."

"I think that was more of his effort to try and mark his territory while you were around."

We placed our orders and Martha made no secret about eavesdropping in on our conversation. It wasn't until Jack grabbed the bags to go that she decided to put in her two cents.

"You know, J.J., if you're wantin' to get pregnant so bad all you've gotta do is start pokin' holes in his rubbers. That's a sure-fire way to get knocked up in no time. That's how I ended up with my youngest."

"Thanks, Martha," I said. "I'll keep that in mind."

I wondered how long it would take for that bit of information to reach Brody's ears. I'd probably have to buy him an unopened box as a peace offering.

We took our burgers to go and ate them in the car. "How did things go with Floyd at the station?" I asked around a bite of burger. Grease dripped from the bottom and landed on the paper sack in my lap.

"He'd lawyered up by the time I got there, and his attorney advised him to cooperate. Floyd said he was home alone the night of Fiona's murder, and he claimed he was at the *Gazette* office during the time of Amanda Wallace's murder. He doesn't have anyone that can confirm his whereabouts for either."

"So what did you do with him?"

"In exchange for his cooperation I dropped the assault charges, and I told him not to leave town."

"That's it?" I asked incredulous. "The guy's the best suspect we have. He would have pounded you to a pulp in the hall if it hadn't been full of cops."

"Thanks so much for your faith in my physical prowess. We don't have any evidence to hold him. Floyd knows that and so did his attorney," he said, slamming his fist against the dashboard.

I knew from experience that the best course of action was to pretend I was invisible, so Jack and I finished our burgers in silence—his thoughts getting heavier the longer we sat there.

"Jaye," he said, "you're not going to like what I'm thinking."

"What is it?"

"You don't think Dickey could be Amanda Wallace's lover, do you?"

I started to say no automatically, just because it was Dickey. My friend Dickey. But then I stopped to think about the things he'd said to us at the bank. About him being tired of Candy and the baby pressures from Vanessa. And then I thought about what he said he'd like to do to his wife. Not good timing.

"I don't know, but maybe we'd better ask him," I said.

"Yeah, let's swing by the bank. This is sure to be pleasant." Jack started the car and pulled out of the parking lot.

"You don't really think Dickey could have anything to do with these murders?" I asked.

"No, I don't, but I wouldn't be doing my job if I didn't make sure. After all, I've been known to make mistakes on the job before."

"What happened in DC wasn't your fault," I said. "You were following orders. Maybe you should make an appointment with Dr. Hides to resolve this guilt you seem to be carrying around."

"Shut up," he snarled. "I'm not carrying around guilt."

"Whatever you say, Mr. Denial. But I'm here to listen if you ever need a sounding board."

"More like a concrete wall," he muttered, whipping the

car into a parking space in front of the bank. I slammed against the seat belt and muttered a curse as one of my onion rings fell to the floorboard.

"I'm sorry, what was that?" I asked.

"Nothing. Let's just get this done so we can get to Dr. Hides' place before something else happens."

"Hey, when it rains it pours, my friend. Take it from me. This is my life."

It felt good to step into the heated lobby of the bank. It looked much different than it had the day before. Every desk was occupied and the teller lines each ran three people deep. The smell of coffee was strong and fragrant, and I realized it had been a while since my last hit of caffeine. I'd had too little sleep and way too much stimulation to go for too much longer without falling over from exhaustion.

"Get it on the way out," Jack said. He always had the uncanny knack of knowing just what I was thinking. He took hold of my elbow in case I made any detours and headed toward Dickey's office.

Vanessa Hart sat at the cherrywood desk and guarded the gate to the inner sanctum like nobody's business. And she was not a happy woman. Her mink-colored hair practically sizzled with electricity, and she was filing the hell out of her nails. Red slashes of color tinged her cheeks and her normally friendly blue eyes shot sparks.

"We're here to see Dickey," Jack said cautiously.

She continued to file her nails and swing her crossed leg until I thought her shoe would fly off and hit some poor unsuspecting shmoe trying to withdraw from his checking account.

"I'm supposed to tell anyone who asks that Dickey is not available right now. He's engaged in extremely important banking business. I should also let you know that I'm only a secretary. Nobody important," Vanessa said with a choked sob.

We'd obviously come at a bad time. It was no doubt Dickey's fault. It's what he deserved for bringing his relationship into the workplace. Not to mention into his marriage.

"But you know what?" she asked, though I didn't think she really wanted an answer. "I'm through." She stood and grabbed her purse out of the bottom drawer of her desk. "I'm through with wasting my life on a man who doesn't care about anyone but himself. I'm through with this job and making this bank a well-oiled machine. I'm tired of standing in the shadows. I want things to go my way for once." She turned and yelled at Dickey's closed door. "I want someone who loves me, and I want children, dammit. I'm thirty years old, and I can feel my inside parts starting to shrivel up and die."

I knew where she was coming from. I'd started having crazy thoughts about marriage and children when I'd turned thirty too. I wasn't so sure about the insides drying up part though. That seemed a little irrational and I wasn't quite on the ledge looking down yet.

"You can go in if you want to," Vanessa said, smoothing her expression back to not so crazy. "He can find someone else to do his dirty work from now on. I quit." She stormed off with the rapid click of her heels beating steady against the marble floor and her coat slung over her shoulder. I was pretty sure her temper was hot enough that she wouldn't be needing the jacket for a while.

I looked at Jack and gave a little shrug. "You go in first," I said. "Just in case."

Jack rolled his eyes and knocked once before opening Dickey's office door. Dickey was chugging Pepto-Bismol straight out of the bottle. His tie was loose and twisted over his shoulder, his hair stuck up in spikes, and his eyes had bags underneath big enough to house orphans.

"What?" Dickey snarled. "Can't you see I'm having a crisis here?"

He went back to chugging the Pepto, and I pushed Jack forward slightly. I was pretty sure neither one of us had seen Dickey less than perfectly presentable. He was one of those people who could run five miles in the desert and go ten rounds with the champ and still have every hair in place.

"Well, I think things just got worse," Jack said, for some reason looking more cheerful than I'd seen him in days. He was enjoying Dickey's dilemmas. It was like watching a soap opera come to life. "Your secretary just quit."

"Perfect," Dickey said. "That's just perfect. What else could go wrong?"

"I wouldn't ask if I were you," I said. "It might speed up the process."

"What am I supposed to do? Didn't I tell Candy that I wanted a divorce?" He was sweating and turning an unhealthy shade of red.

I was surprised by this bit of news but worried about Dickey. "Calm down and take a few deep breaths, Dickey. You don't look so good. I only have a limited amount of space in my cooler, and I'd prefer to keep you from taking up residence there."

"Believe me, death would be a welcome relief," he said.

"What did Candy say when you asked for a divorce?" Jack asked. I winced because Dickey's color was starting to look normal.

"She laughed at me," he said, getting worked up again. "Can you believe she actually laughed? She said it would be a cold day in hell before I left her for another woman and she'd make sure I'd end up a pauper. She threatened to take the bank in the divorce. I don't even know if she can do something like that."

"If you asked for a divorce then why did Vanessa just quit?" I asked. It was my turn to be nosy.

"Because when I came in this morning I had to tell her it wasn't possible for me to leave Candy right now. I don't want to be a pauper," he said, perilously close to a whine. "I've never been one before, but I'm pretty sure I wouldn't like it."

I had to agree. Being poor sucked.

"But Candy has turned into one crazy cow. There's no way I'm going home tonight. I'd love to marry Vanessa and give her all the kids she wants, but I just don't see how I can."

"Maybe you should talk to an attorney," Jack suggested. "I'm sure there's a way to keep the bank in your possession. It's been in your family for generations."

"You think so?" Dickey asked, but he didn't look too sure.

"Or maybe you can find some dirt on Candy to help her loosen the reins a little bit." Dickey seemed to perk up at this idea. Nothing like a little blackmail to get the bloodstream moving.

"Okay, I'll do it," Dickey said. He looked so relieved that I didn't bother to remind him that he had a long uphill battle ahead with not one, but two women.

"Dickey, I hate to do this, but we didn't come here to solve your problems. I need to ask you a few questions. In an official capacity," Jack said.

"Why, what's happened?" he asked, nervous all of a sudden.

"Can you tell me your whereabouts Saturday night, from about eight o'clock on?" Jack asked.

Dickey licked his lips and leaned back in his chair. "Geez, Jack, do I need to call my attorney? What going on?"

"Just answer the question," Jack said, impatience flashing in his eyes. I could tell Dickey was working up a pretty serious mad, either because of the implication or because it was a good way to forget his own problems.

"I was at the River House," he said.

The River House was one of Dickey's vacation homes on the far side of King George and it overlooked the Potomac River. It was only one of the assets he was likely to lose in a divorce with Candy.

"Were you alone?" Jack pressed.

"No, I had a bottle of Jack Daniel's for company. Vanessa wasn't speaking to me and I didn't feel like going home to my wife, so I went to the River House. Alone."

"What about Sunday morning?" Jack asked. "Between seven and noon."

"I left to come back for Fiona's funeral around ten o'clock. I stopped by the house to change clothes. Candy wasn't home. She has tennis lessons on Sunday mornings and then brunch with her mother. I saw you at the funeral just like everyone else. Now will you please tell me what's going on?"

"In a minute," Jack answered. "What you said to us Sunday, about finding another woman? Did you succeed?"

"What?" Dickey asked.

"Yesterday you said you were tired of the whole thing. With your wife and with Vanessa. You said you were thinking about finding another woman. Did you have another woman?" Jack repeated.

"Are you kidding me? Isn't two enough? I've got enough

problems without adding any more into the mix. So to answer your question, no, I don't have another woman."

"Dickey," I said, trying to get him to divert his attention to me and lay off Jack a little. He was just doing his job. "Haven't you heard any news this morning? About what happened over at the hotel?"

He looked confused. "J.J., I walked in the bank at eight o'clock this morning and promptly had a huge blowout with the woman I love. In front of witnesses I might add. I haven't stepped foot out of this office for so much as a cup of coffee. Why? What happened?"

"Amanda Wallace was murdered in a room at the hotel yesterday morning," Jack answered. "It was similar to Fiona's death."

I could see Dickey was about to ask what that had to do with him when the lightbulb went on.

"You think I killed her," Dickey said, pushing his chair back so it hit the wall when he stood. "You think I could do that to a woman? Any woman?"

"Calm down, Dickey," Jack said. "The circumstances were questionable. I had to ask you about them."

"You mean Amanda Wallace was having an affair at the Hanover Hotel, and the only person you could think of who'd do something like that was me. Gee, thanks a lot. And then, not only would I sleep with her but then kill her when I was finished?"

I thought now would probably be a good time for us to go. Dickey had enough things on his plate at the moment. "Dickey, we never thought it was you, but Jack wouldn't be doing his job if he didn't explore every possibility."

"Yeah, right," he said bitterly. "Sorry I had to disappoint you. If you guys don't mind, I think I'm going to head out of here. I've had enough bad news for one day."

Dickey walked out without his coat, his appearance still disheveled and his office door wide open. Jack rubbed his eyes with his thumb and forefinger. "Sometimes I hate my job."

"Yeah, but the way I see it I'm not sure the day could get much worse. We already have a dead body and a pissed-off best friend. What else could there be?"

"Don't say that," Jack said. "Things can *always* get worse."

"Hey, I have an idea. If this thing with Brody doesn't work out, and since you don't want to get married for real, I was thinking the two of us could have a marriage of convenience. That way I wouldn't end up a spinster and I would have access to your bank account."

"So what you mean is that it'd be convenient for you," Jack said with a smile. I realized it had been a while since I'd seen a genuine grin on his face. He slung his arm around my shoulder and pulled me close.

"Well, yeah," I said. "That's how I prefer things."

"And what do I get out of it?" he asked, rubbing the tip of his finger down the side of my neck and sending tingles places that had no business getting tingles where Jack was concerned.

"W...well, come to think of it, I don't really have a lot of housewifely talents. I don't cook and I hate to do laundry and..."

"Honey," Jack interrupted. "You have the only talent I'd need if I was ever going to get married. You're female."

"Yeesh. Never mind," I said and pulled out of his grasp. My face heated and my skin turned clammy. Maybe Jack wasn't such a safe bet after all. Come to think of it, I probably wasn't such a good catch.

I froze. Why was I even thinking about Jack in that way?

"Get out, get out, get out," I said aloud, knocking my fist against my temple and squenching my eyes closed. When I opened them Jack was looking at me with a cocky grin and a raised eyebrow.

"Don't be ridiculous," I said, full of forced bravado. "I look okay now, but in fifty years I'm probably going to look just like my great-aunt Ruth."

Jack's smile faded and he looked at me with closer scrutiny. "You know, I think you're right," he said. "If I look real close I can see a few chin whiskers starting to sprout. If I remember right, Ruth had a full beard by the time she hit ninety. Facial hair on a woman is enough to keep any man from wanting to commit."

"I hate you," I said. But I felt under my chin for stray hairs just in case he'd been telling the truth.

We climbed back into the Suburban to go see Dr. Hides and had just turned off the county square into Nottingham when Jack's cell phone rang.

"Sheriff Lawson," he said. He was quiet for a few seconds, his attention still on the road. It wasn't until he said, "We'll be there," that I realized he was turning us around and heading back into Bloody Mary.

"Who was that?"

"That was Detective Colburn. He said he has some important information to tell me."

I could see the strain around Jack's eyes and the tension around his mouth. "Why does that worry you?" I asked.

"Because I think we may have just found Amanda Wallace's lover. I thought you said the day couldn't get much worse."

"I was just trying to keep a positive outlook."

"Well, if I'm right, it doesn't get much worse than one of my detectives being suspected for murder. I'm going to have to get a job at the 7-Eleven if I can't get this mess resolved."

"That might not be so bad," I said. "I hear they've got good benefits, you'd get free Slurpees for life, and you'd know what to do if there was ever a robbery."

Jack didn't appreciate my suggestions.

SEVENTEEN

Detective Marcus Colburn was a tall man, broad through the shoulders and thin through the hips. He was slightly graying at the temples, but attractive in a distinguished gentleman sort of way, and I'd guess his age to be around forty. I found myself thinking about what Jack said about the murderer being strong. Detective Colburn certainly fit the bill.

He'd decided to meet us at the park near Wooten's pond. Actually, he'd decided to meet Jack there. He was probably going to be surprised to see me. I knew him well enough to speak to him whenever I passed him in town, but not well enough to strike up a conversation at a party. He'd been on the force ten years more than Jack, but he'd actively supported him when he'd run for sheriff, so I'd always liked him for that.

"Detective Colburn," Jack said, shaking his hand. "Why don't we have a seat?"

I took my place unobtrusively on the other side of Jack and decided to let him handle this newest problem. After all, it was one of his men.

"Why don't you tell me everything you can, and then we'll decide what we need to do?"

"I want you to know I didn't find out about Amanda's death until right before I called you. I worked the night shift last night and I have it again tonight, so I was asleep until a couple of hours ago when the station called me to ask if I'd work overtime because of the murder." He stumbled over the word *murder* a little but quickly got himself under control.

Jack only nodded, and I guess that put Colburn at ease because he took a breath and pushed on. "I wanted to tell you that I was the one who met with Amanda Saturday night."

"What time did you leave her?" Jack asked, the friend replaced by the cop.

"Sunday morning, about seven thirty. We had an early breakfast because I had some things to take care of before I went on shift. Grocery shopping, that sort of thing. If I'd stayed longer she'd still be alive."

"You're as sure as you can be on the times?" Jack asked. "You know we'll check the videotapes at the hotel. It's best to be as up front as you can be."

"I'm sure," he said. "I'm not likely to ever forget."

"How long have you been involved with Mrs. Wallace?" Jack asked.

I saw Detective Colburn wince at the way Jack called her by her married name and wondered if he felt guilt over the fact that he'd been involved with a married woman.

"About six months. She was going to see her attorney this week to file for divorce. She said she wasn't going to stay in a marriage where she wasn't loved anymore. We were going to get married."

"Why'd she wait so long for the divorce?"

"She wanted to make sure her youngest was settled into college before making any drastic changes," he said. "I agreed with her."

"Do you know if she was seeing a therapist?" Jack asked.

"Sure. She's been seeing him for more than a year. She told me her husband wanted her to, and she said it was just nice to have someone to talk to that was completely impartial in the whole matter."

"Did she ever tell you anything about her sessions?"

"No, but she did say that he was the one who finally helped her settle on divorce. And he told her he thought it was good that she was entering back into a healthy relationship at this point in her life."

"Do you know what days she went to the therapist?"

"I think she usually went on Tuesday mornings, but she had to miss last week because she had an appointment with her regular doctor she couldn't miss. She made the session up on Saturday, though. He'd do that sometimes if she had to miss an appointment."

My hands clenched in my lap to keep me from blurting out what I was thinking. Amanda Wallace had been the Saturday appointment that Jack and I had to vacate the office for. Very interesting.

"What do I do now, Jack?" he asked.

My heart went out to the guy. He'd lost his lover and might even lose his job all in the same day.

"We're going to do this by the book, Marcus. It's not going to be easy, and you know there's no way it'll be kept quiet."

"I know. It doesn't seem to matter anymore."

"I'm going to call Stewart and have him handle this personally." Captain Stewart Smith was Jack's right hand at the station. He was also one of Martha's numerous sons.

One of the ones in the middle. "You'll need to go in and make an official statement. Volunteer to give a DNA sample and take a lie detector. You'll have to turn in your gun and badge until your name is cleared," he said.

I could tell by the look on Colburn's face that this was the biggest heartache of all next to the death of Amanda. To some men, there was no life without the badge. Jack was one of those, and apparently so was Colburn.

"I need you back at work soon, so get this done quick and get your name cleared."

"I don't know if I can come back," Colburn said, standing. He unholstered his weapon and handed it butt end to Jack. And then he unclipped the detective's shield he carried on his belt.

"Take as much time as you need, Marcus. The badge will be there for you when you're ready for it."

No one knew that little bit of wisdom better than Jack.

EIGHTEEN

"Why do I feel as if things are crumbling rapidly all around me?" Jack asked once we were back in the car and on our way to Nottingham to visit Dr. Hides.

"Don't feel bad," I said. "It feels that way to me too."

"You're no help whatsoever. I've changed my mind about Dr. Hides," he said.

"How's that?"

"I was going to question him at his office, then arrest him. I think I'm just going to arrest him first and let him stew in a cell for a while. Just think—if people were basically honest in nature instead of liars this thing would be solved by now. You know, I feel bad for Dr. Hides. Sometimes in small towns the paperwork can really get backed up and cause unnecessary delays."

"I've heard that," I said.

"And what's going on in this town? Isn't anyone faithful to their spouse anymore? It makes staying single a whole lot more appealing."

"People like you and me, Jack, we're so careful to let

anyone close, but when we do it's for life. Marriage will be like that when we're ready."

"Yeah, Lord knows if I ever do tie on the shackles, I'll be faithful. And you'll be faithful, but what if he's not?"

"Then I'll carve off his testicles with my scalpel and put them in formaldehyde so they can sit on my shelf forever and ever."

"You've obviously thought this through before. I have to say I'm starting to feel a little pity for Brody."

I decided to ignore him because we'd just turned onto Covington Lane. Dr. Hides' street looked the same as it had two days before. The same white car was parked two houses down and the red flag was up again on the mailbox in front of the attorney's side of the town house. This place gave me the creeps.

"You know what's missing?" Jack asked.

"The Stepford Wives?" I asked.

"No," he said, grinning. "Janette Taylor's car. She works Monday through Friday, isn't that what Dr. Hides said?"

"I can give her a call if you want."

"Yeah, why don't you do that? I'll try the door."

Janette picked up after the third ring, and if possible, she sounded worse than she had two days ago.

"Are you all right, Janette?" I asked.

"No, I'm not all right. I've got the cold from hell."

"Did you call Dr. Hides to let him know you weren't going to be in?" I asked.

"What are you, my mother? For your information he called me last night to let me know he'd come down with the same stuff. He cancelled all of his appointments for today. Now, please leave me alone to die in peace," she said and hung up.

"Well, that was pleasant," I said once I made my way back over to Jack.

"What's the story?"

"Both of them have the crud. They probably gave it to each other just by being nasty human beings."

"He's not answering the door," Jack said. "His car's parked at the back of the house."

"Janette did sound rather concerned about the doctor's health," I said, smiling. "Maybe he had a severe coughing fit and passed out. He could be lying in there now. What if he hit his head when he fell?"

"Good one, Dr. Graves. It'll help having you here to confirm that."

"Why?" I asked.

"So you can back me up when I say we had probable cause to enter. Look here, the door's wide open. I wouldn't be doing my civic duty if I didn't step inside to make sure there's not anything missing or out of place."

"You're pretty good yourself," I said as I followed him into the spacious foyer once again.

I smelled it before I saw the body. Death. The air was thick with the putrid smell of bladder and bowels and the coppery scent of blood, and no matter how much you tried to breathe through your mouth, that first whiff would be stuck in the back of your throat for hours, sometimes days. I'd gotten so used to the stench of death the past couple of days it almost seemed odd to go somewhere without it.

"I'd say Dr. Hides is definitely not feeling his best," Jack said.

I didn't think Dr. Hides was feeling anything. Dr. Hides was wearing a white bathrobe and hanging by a rope from the second-story balcony. It was odd; the downstairs was exactly as it had been a couple of days before—neat desk, stuffy furniture, long hallway, and straight staircase leading to the upper levels. You almost wouldn't even notice the body suspended above us if it wasn't for the smell, and the puddle of body fluids dripping on the floor. I was thinking Dr. Hides surely could have found a better way to deal with the common cold.

"I'm going to be right pissed if he offed himself because he was feeling guilty for murdering those two women. It couldn't possibly be enough justice."

"I've got my bag in the car," I said. "Why don't you call it in and we'll get started."

In the meantime, I hoped we didn't run into any more bodies. I only had room for one more in my cooler.

NINETEEN

The police were probably still a good fifteen minutes away since Jack had had to reassign officers to keep covering the crime scene at the hotel. He had everyone on duty until further notice, and I reminded him the council wasn't going to be happy about forking over the money for overtime. Let's just say that Jack's response to my comment was anatomically impossible.

I pulled on gloves and threw an extra pair to Jack, and I was careful not to touch anything until the scene could be documented. I took pictures from the bottom floor and then made my way upstairs to snap a couple of close-ups.

"He looks surprised," I said, looking at the dead doctor's face.

"Yeah, well who knows what was going through his mind in that last second. I haven't found a suicide note," he said.

"You know, that's a common misconception. Most suicides don't actually leave a note."

"I know, but Dr. Hides just seemed like the kind of guy

who would need to clear his conscience. I do have a small amount of good news," he said.

"What's that?"

"The warrant for the files came through first thing this morning. Apparently someone in the DA's office has a lake house on the Chesapeake Bay and the entire staff spent the weekend there. And Judge Andrews was out of town at a wedding. Fortunately, someone checked their voicemail and heard my frantic messages because it was waiting for me first thing."

"Then let's see what we can find." I watched Jack do something interesting to the locks on the file cabinet and the drawer popped open. "My, my, my," I said. "Somebody has hidden talents."

"I'm not the only one," Jack said. "Both files are gone."

It was then we heard the sound of sirens and feet clomping up the stairs outside. Officers I'd just left at one crime scene were coming into the door of another. They got to work, and I stood by Jack and waited for my turn to come up.

"You think he destroyed them so we wouldn't see what was going on in those sessions?" I asked.

"Maybe. Or maybe someone else got to them, and him, first."

"So what you're saying is that I should be looking for signs of homicide when I get up there."

"If you don't mind," Jack said dryly.

"Let's see if we can get a couple of your boys to lower him down. I can't really see myself hanging over the balcony to study a body."

"You never were the athletic type," Jack commented. "Lower him down, boys."

"I'll do it," Jeremy Mooney volunteered along with

another baby-faced officer. I was surprised that neither of them seemed bothered by such a gruesome death. They hadn't exactly had a lot of experience in such matters.

I got to work as soon as Dr. Hides was laid out in front of me. "That noose is very well done," I said, pointing to the thick shank of rope. "I wonder if the doctor was an avid boater."

"Maybe he was a Boy Scout," Jack added.

"Whatever he was, he's been dead less than two hours." His body was still warm, and his corneas hadn't yet clouded over. "He's got a broken neck. Instant death as soon as his weight reached the end of the length of rope."

I was feeling more than inadequate. I knew Jack wanted me to rule homicide, but it looked like a suicide. This was a moment where it would have been nice to have an actual medical examiner. Jack knelt down beside me.

"What is it?" he asked in a soft voice, so his men couldn't hear.

"I just don't know, Jack. It looks like a suicide to me. There's nothing I can tell you just by a visual examination here in the middle of the floor. I can smell alcohol on him, but that's not unusual in these cases. Now if something suspicious shows up in the tox screen, then you may have something. But right now..."

"Then let's do the tox screen," Jack said.

I put my hand on his arm before he could get up. "It might be more beneficial for you to send him to a medical examiner," I confessed. "I'm out of my league here, Jack, and I'm not afraid to admit it. One mistake on my end here could change the course of the entire investigation. If he hanged himself, that leaves probable cause that he was responsible for both murders and took his own life over guilt or some other reason. If someone else was responsible," I said, shrugging, "then we're far from through yet."

"I want you to do it, Jaye. You've seen the other murders. And if you take the time frame of when this happened, it's not so far out of the realm of possibility that someone else did this to him. My gut says the doctor is just another victim, which means the murderer knows the steps we're taking. He knew enough to know what time we found the body this morning and that we'd probably be headed here next."

When he put it like that I could see where all this suspicion was coming from.

"I've got a couple of officers looking through the trash and the shredder to see if they can find those missing files. But come on, Jaye, an outside medical examiner is not likely to see the big picture. I need you."

"Right, no pressure," I said. "I'll do it, but don't say I didn't warn you."

We bagged the body and left the cops to finish up the job. I had a long day and night ahead of me. I hoped Brody was a patient man.

I put Dr. Hides on ice as soon as I got back to the funeral parlor. I had Amanda Wallace to tend to before Harvey came in to view the body this afternoon, and she didn't look good. But before I began working, I had to do something for myself. Something selfish that had nothing to do with murders or police investigations.

So I left the basement, grabbed the emergency chocolate ice cream I kept in the cooler, and cried. Just cried—a pitiful, sorry-for-myself, good old-fashioned cry. I cried for

Fiona Murphy and Amanda Wallace. I cried for Dickey because he'd gotten himself in a mess. He was a dope, but he was still one of my closest friends. I even cried for Dr. Hides, and I didn't even really like him all that much. I cried for Janette Taylor and her miserable cold. I cried for the spouses who were left without partners because of senseless murders, and Jack because I could see the strain he was under and that these people mattered to him. I cried for Brody because, I might as well add that little twist of fate into the mixture. I rested my head on the table and let it all out in big gulping sobs.

The rattling of the screen door to the kitchen brought my head up with a start. I saw Brody through the glass in the door and motioned him in so I wouldn't have to move out of my comfort spot. I wasn't quite through feeling sorry for myself.

"Were you sleeping?" he asked.

"No way," I said, shaking my head. "I've got way too much to do to take time out to sleep."

"That's what I thought too, but you have the imprint of a spoon on the side of your face."

I reached up and felt the dents in my cheeks and shot Brody a dirty look. So maybe I fell asleep for a few minutes. Crying could wear on a girl. And it wasn't very gentlemanly of Brody to mention the creases.

"Tell me what's wrong, babe," he said, sitting across from me and then pulling me into his lap.

I snuggled up against him and breathed in his scent. I smelled my soap on his skin from our shower earlier. I couldn't think of anything more intimate. "Nothing really," I said. "Not anymore. I was just a little overwhelmed for a bit."

"I should have gotten here sooner, but I got caught up in

work. The book's going well. Something about this town really gets the process moving along."

"I'm glad things are working out," I said. In all honesty I didn't really care how it was going. I would have cared yesterday and I'd care tomorrow, but I was still in my all-about-me mode.

"I would have let you use my shoulder," he said in my ear and made me shiver. "And it looks like you've eaten lunch without me." He looked at my empty carton of ice cream and quirked an eyebrow at me. "I had grand plans for lunch."

"It was really more of a brunch," I clarified. "I haven't had lunch yet."

"Well. You're way past due," he said. "Why don't we go grab something? We can even go out of town if you want."

"How past due am I?" I screeched, jumping out of his lap to dig through my purse for my watch.

I always took my jewelry or anything else off that had the potential of coming loose while I was working on a body. I'd learned from experience that retrieval was not always easy. Or pleasant.

Brody beat me to it by looking at his own watch. I guess he didn't have to worry about it getting stuck in body parts while he was writing. "It's almost two," he said. "That must have been some nap you weren't taking."

"Oh, my gosh! It can't be that late. Mr. Wallace could be here at any time and his wife is *so* not ready for public viewing." I was practically shrieking, and I yelled the last bit as I ran down the basement stairs.

"I'll make you a deal," I said.

"Does it involve nudity?" Brody asked.

"Absolutely."

"Then I'll do it," he said.

"But you haven't even heard what I want," I said. "You could at least hear me out for formality's sake." I was busy pulling Mrs. Wallace out of the refrigeration unit, but I still saw him roll his eyes.

"Fine, what do you want me to do?"

"I'm running behind, so I'd like you to help me with the documentation and cleaning on Mrs. Wallace."

He was silent for a few seconds until I looked up at him. "Does it still involve nudity?" he asked.

"Yes, geez. And I'll even throw in dinner at Martha's."

"All right, but I want the sex first. I'm no dummy. And I brought my own condoms in case you decided to take Martha's advice to heart."

I knew it wouldn't take long for that bit of information to make its way around town.

Thankfully, Kendra and Owen had taken a couple of hours prep time off my work. They'd massaged out the rigor until Mrs. Wallace lay limp on my metal table with her hands down to her sides. They'd also taken the necessary blood and sperm samples, labeled them, and put them in the refrigerator so they could be sent out to Richmond.

I withdrew my own syringe.

"What are you doing?" Brody asked.

"The samples have already been gathered to go to the lab in Richmond, but I have small capabilities here to test for medications, illegal drugs, alcohol, or any irregularities in the system."

"You think she was drugged?" he asked.

"No, not if he's keeping with the same pattern he held with Fiona. But it never hurts to check."

Between the two of us, we were able to get her weighed and measured, all of her external injuries recorded, and her body cleaned minutes before I heard the buzzer ringing, signifying I had a guest in the lobby.

"He'll want to see her," Brody said.

"I know. He'll need it to be real to him. Right now all he has is our word that it's his wife who was the victim. I'd appreciate it if you'd wait in my office," I said. "He probably wouldn't be comfortable knowing you're here."

"Sure," he said, making his way toward my office door.

"And Brody," I said, waiting until he turned back to look at me. "Thanks for your help."

Mr. Wallace was not in good shape. And I'd learned something over the past year about being the bearer of bad news: I was always the one they blamed. It was obvious Mr. Wallace had gotten over the initial shock about his adulterous murdered wife and was now leaning toward other, stronger emotions. Anger being most prevalent.

"Have you found out anything to help the sheriff in his investigation?" Harvey asked as soon as I buzzed him in the front door. He stood rigid with his hands clamped tightly behind his back, his eyes hard and determined. I didn't bother to offer him a place to sit or something to drink. He was obviously on a mission. And all I was able to give him was the standard line.

"I can assure you this investigation is top priority, and I'll be able to help the sheriff more after I've finished my preliminary report." I didn't actually say the word *autopsy* because you'd be surprised how many people got upset that I was required to perform one, and I figured since Mr. Wallace was already upset it wouldn't help to remind him

I'd be cutting his wife open from bow to stern and removing all her organs.

"*Hmmph*. You think I don't know that the sheriff is up to his wazoo in this mess? I'd be surprised if the killer was ever brought to justice."

"What are you talking about? Jack is working practically around the clock to catch whoever did this."

"It might look that way to you, but we've had more death in this county in four days than we've had in the last fifty years, and all under his watch. You never saw us in a mess like this when Donald Drummond was sheriff."

It took a lot of willpower to keep from rolling my eyes. That Harvey would even consider comparing Jack and Donald Drummond was laughable. Sheriff Drummond never left the comfort of his desk chair and wouldn't know police procedure if it bit him in the behind. It was a darned good thing this hadn't happened while he was sheriff or we'd be in a real mess.

"You think because we're a small town we don't hear news from the big city. That mess he was involved in up in DC looks pretty suspicious to me, and don't think I'm not going to bring it up to the rest of the council at the special session I've called. He's going to have to answer some questions, like what he's going to do about the fact that he's got a murderer under his command, and how long he's known about it."

Ahh, so the news had spread about Detective Colburn and Mrs. Wallace. I knew it would only be a matter of time before it did, but I'd still hoped for maybe another day before the storm hit.

"Jack is a good sheriff and he will get the job done. I know this is a difficult time for you, but you need to be patient and let him do his job. We're all working around the clock on this, and Detective Colburn is on leave until the investigation is complete."

"Well as far as I'm concerned, Jack Lawson can work around the clock as an insurance salesman instead of the sheriff. And he will be by the time I've had my say."

In my job it was necessary that I have a compassionate nature and a sympathetic ear, but sometimes enough was enough. No one would talk about Jack that way to my face.

"Mr. Wallace, if I were you I'd be trying to help the police in their investigation by helping them instead of holding them up with false accusations. This county's police force is tired and ragged because the council refuses to hire more men, and if you really wanted to help you'd see to it that something was done about that instead of blaming Jack for nothing more than hiring a man that was intimate with your wife."

He inhaled quickly through his teeth, and I realized I'd taken it a step too far. Sometimes I did that when I was angry. *Oops.* I tried to soften the damage, but I knew it was too late. "I'm sorry for your loss, but I think you need to go home and be with your children right now, and let us all do our jobs."

He looked like he wanted to argue, and I had my fingers crossed he didn't want to go down and view the body. I didn't think he was quite ready for that particular step, and a part of me wished I hadn't rushed to get her body ready for viewing so I'd have a legitimate excuse to give him if he asked.

"It figures that you'd defend him," he hissed. "I've heard about the sick things the two of you do together down in that room of yours. You're perverts, both of you. I'm going to get in touch with John Luke Stranton. I want Amanda transferred to the Here and Gone Funeral Home."

I was so surprised about the pervert comment that it barely registered what he was saying about changing mortuaries. Were rumors really going around about Jack and me? You'd think I'd have caught wind of something like that. Or lost business. I'd have to ask.

I was mostly on autopilot when I told Mr. Wallace the body could be transferred after I'd finished my investigation. I needed to get to Jack and get to the bottom of this me being a pervert business. Everybody in town knew Jack was a pervert, but not in a too over-the-top, kinky way. Just in that he went through women like he did those little disposable Dixie cups you use when you brush your teeth.

But not me. I was as straight-laced as they came. Well, I guess technically in the last four days I'd been more open to things than usual, but it hardly counted. I wouldn't be able to survive another week going at my continuous rate, and I definitely didn't want to go to the hereafter in the throes of passion. How embarrassing. One of my first deaths after I'd taken over the funeral home was Buck Koch, and he'd died in a similar situation. Let's just say it was a close call for getting the casket closed. Buck hadn't died at half-mast.

I realized I'd been standing in the parlor, staring after Mr. Wallace long after he'd gone, and I remembered Brody was sitting in my office waiting to collect on nookie and dinner. I wasn't all that sure I was in the mood for either one after my conversation with Mr. Wallace. But I went back to my office anyway and found him sitting behind my desk with his feet propped on the corner.

"Don't get me wrong," he said. "I'm not going to welsh on our deal, but I don't think I can have sex without taking a shower first. I need some time to regroup after the whole dead body thing."

Made sense to me. Death was not an aphrodisiac. Well, maybe it was for some people, but I didn't really want to think about it because it grossed me out. We didn't have to deal with that nonsense in Bloody Mary. You had to go all the way to Richmond to find the real wackos.

There was a full-size bathroom that connected to my office, and we decided to get clean before we headed to Martha's. And it just so happened that once we were soaped up we felt like fooling around after all. Go figure.

"I'm starving," Brody said as he pulled on his clothes. "And I don't think my legs work anymore."

"I can't imagine why," I said, struggling to get my own clothes on. My brain wasn't sending the correct signals to all my extremities. Showers with Brody seemed to do that for me.

"We could always order pizza," I said. I was still thinking about what Harvey Wallace had said about me, and I knew every time I went out I'd be thinking people were talking about me behind my back and calling me Dr. Pervert.

"Unh-uh. You promised to take me out. I'm holding you to it."

"I don't think you've thought this through. We're going out to dinner at a place that will be jam-packed with people. Nosy people. And they won't bother to be subtle about it."

"Hey, don't I know it. I've been here four days. But I can handle myself. I'm a writer, for Pete's sake. I'll just lie like a dog and nobody will know the difference. Trust me. I'm a professional."

"Good thinking," I said, mentally shaking my head at

his naïvety. The people of Bloody Mary could give the CIA a run for their money when it came to ferreting out secrets.

We wrapped up in our coats—scarves and gloves because the temperature had dropped back to freezing once the sun had gone down. The melted snow would freeze overnight and leave the roads dangerous for the morning work traffic.

Thanks to my earlier nap, I was wide awake and my brain was ready to get things done. Brody was a very thorough lover, and I found myself in the strange predicament of having my mind well rested but my body turned completely wasted. The bad news was I still had a long night of work ahead of me and I needed all my extremities to work.

We took Brody's Escalade because it had the least amount of ice crusted on the windshield and headed into town. And for such a miserable night, Martha was doing a swift business.

"Looks like everyone in town had the same idea we did," Brody said.

"That's what I'm afraid of." If Brody meant that everyone in town had the same idea about coming into town to hear the latest gossip, that was. And we were walking right into the lion's den.

Heat cocooned me as soon as I walked through the doors, and the overpowering aroma of grilled onions and grease seeped into my clothes and hair. I knew from experience that I'd carry the smell of Martha's around with me for the rest of the night.

Conversations stopped when everyone saw that we were at the door, and all I could hear was the sizzle of burgers on the grill in the kitchen. As suddenly as it had stopped, voices whooshed into conversation while curious glances kept creeping in our direction. Martha herself came out from behind the counter to show us to a table.

"You're practically celebrities," Martha said as she raised her voice to a yell and led us to one of the many turquoise Formica tables that lined the edge of the room. There were little jukeboxes that sat on top, and the booths were torn and patched red vinyl. She plopped two greasy menus down in front of us and took our drink order.

It took less than thirty seconds for her to fill the order and get back to us. "I won't be able to hold 'em off for long," she said, "so be prepared to get some questions. Everybody's real curious about these murders. You'd think nobody ever watched the news or heard about all those killings that happen every day up in Fairfax or Richmond. Jack was in earlier to grab a couple of burgers to go, and I wasn't so sure he was going to make it back out again. These people are desperate. There's only so much you can do in this kind of weather, and in my experience you can only do that so long before you start to go a little crazy if you get my drift. Or get knocked up, whichever comes first."

Martha's "going crazy" comment concerned me a little. Most of the patrons in the room were old enough that too much "crazy" could be a health risk. It was probably wise for them to brave the elements and get out of the house so they could escape temptation.

"Did you take my advice about poking the you-know-what in the you-know-where?" Martha asked in a whisper. But Martha's whisper came out with the volume of a bull-horn, and everyone lowered their volume to hear my answer.

I kicked Brody under the table because he hadn't stopped laughing since he'd sat down. "Brody's just here doing research, Martha, but thanks anyway for thinking of me."

She gave an exaggerated wink and shifted her weight until one bony hip rested against the red vinyl booth. "Sure honey, your secret's safe with me. After all, you've got a reputation to protect and good standing in the community. But just between you and me, the Ladies Lodge is booked through March for showers and what not, so you might want to get your name in the pot before too long. With your mama not here, we feel responsible for you." She walked away without taking our order, probably just to make sure we stayed as long as possible to boost her business.

"Why is this town so desperate to see you with a man?" Brody asked.

I buried my face in the menu without reading the words just so I could avoid making eye contact while I answered. "Because this is fricking Bloody Mary, which means that a woman's goal in life is to graduate high school and go to college a semester or two to catch a man who's not completely worthless. And then once a suitable man is caught, the town will celebrate by throwing a shower of monstrous proportions and shoving you both down the aisle so you can get to the honeymoon and start procreating as soon as possible. It's one long, sick cycle, and I've been slipping through their grasps for years."

"So you're a challenge," Brody said, nodding his head like it all made perfect sense.

"In a nutshell. Mostly I'm just super picky and have no desire to throw my life away by learning how to make thirty-two different kinds of tablecloths or entering pies in the county fair. I'm told I take after my grandmother. She was a real rebel. She didn't marry my grandfather until she was in her mid-thirties. That was practically ancient in that time."

"So I'm just a diversion?" Brody asked.

"I'm not sure exactly what you are. You were a surprise. You kind of blindsided me."

"I'm good at that," he said with the smile that I'd learned meant good things would come to me later. "But get ready because people are starting to get shifty and head this direction."

"If we get into dangerous territory just stab me with a butter knife and get me to a hospital to escape the madness," I said desperately.

I was actually feeling pretty good despite everything on my plate and my confrontation with Mr. Wallace. Martha's words had had a lot to do with that. She wouldn't have mentioned my reputation or good standing in the community if there were a bunch of rumors going around about me being a pervert.

"Good evening, Dr. Graves," Ben Rooney said as he pulled a chair up backward and sat at our table, making himself comfortable.

Ben had been a farmer all his life, not a tobacco farmer like Jack's family, but an honest-to-God farmer with corn and wheat and pigs and cows. He always wore overalls and had a toothpick sticking out of his mouth. He'd never once gotten on to me, Jack, Dickey, Vaughn, and Eddie when we'd snuck into his fields at night, eaten corn right off the stalks, and told ghost stories.

Ben Rooney was a good man, and he and his wife had organized meals for me for a month after my parents died. Ben was one of the few people in town who actually knew my first name, so I was always especially friendly to those people so they had no reason to blackmail me later on. Besides, I didn't mind gossiping with people I liked. In fact,

I didn't really consider it gossip at all—just passing the time with a little colorful information.

Ben looked pointedly in Brody's direction, and I realized I was being rude. Just because everyone already knew who he was didn't mean they didn't want an official introduction.

"Brody, this is Ben Rooney. He and my dad were good friends." They shook hands, and Ben got down to business.

"I'm awful sorry to hear about Harvey Wallace moving Amanda over to Stranton's place. It just isn't right, them being members of St. Paul's and all. But the man is grieving and out of his mind, so you probably shouldn't hold it against him."

"No, of course not," I lied. As far as I was concerned, Mr. Wallace had known exactly what he was doing and just liked being a pain in the behind. And I'd hold it against him if I wanted. I had student loans to pay off, after all, and even though there seemed to be a crop of funerals right now, I sometimes went several weeks without having to prepare a burial.

"Well, it's good of you to be so understanding," he said. Several other people had moved in around us to hear better, not bothering to disguise the fact they were blatantly eavesdropping.

Martha had to fight through with the plates of food in her hand. It was a good thing I'd wanted a hamburger because that's what she'd brought for us to eat. I couldn't be so sure about Brody though. I winced in apology, but he only winked in response. He seemed to be enjoying himself.

"Comin' through," Martha yelled over the crowd. "I've got burgers with the works and fries." My mouth watered, but I knew I'd be popping Tums all night long. "These are on the house considering you haven't had a moment's peace since you've been here. Enjoy."

She was off again, doing a hundred things at once and keeping all her customers happy, which was why she'd been in business so long.

I heard someone else pipe up after Martha had gone in response to what Ben had said about Harvey Wallace. I groaned as I recognized the voice.

Hilda Martin. The same Hilda Martin who'd trapped her daughter in the basement with her handyman just to get her married off. The same woman who sat like a sentry behind the register at the grocery store so she could see what everyone was buying—like tampons or pregnancy tests—and then spread the news all over town. She was also giving Brody shifty looks, and I knew she was trying to figure out a way to trap him in her basement with her youngest daughter Cleo.

"I don't think you should make excuses for him, Ben," Hilda said. "He knows perfectly well that it's a direct insult to J.J. to move his business to another home when everybody knows she's got dibs at St. Paul's. It's not right."

There were a few head nods in agreement, and I had to keep myself from joining them. I kind of agreed with what she was saying. I did have dibs at St. Paul's.

"And the man can stick his head in the sand all he wants, but a blind man could tell that Amanda had a lover. Husbands just don't give a woman that same glow as a lover does. Look at J.J. here. She's shining so bright she's practically bursting with it. I don't think I've ever seen her looking so radiant."

Everyone turned from Hilda to stare at me and assess the damage. I did my best to ignore them by pretending they were all naked and their bodies were riddled with flaws. It didn't take away the embarrassment, but it made me feel better about myself.

"Roberta Clack over at the pharmacy said she couldn't blame Amanda one bit for going to another man, because she'd heard that Harvey has a problem with his you know what," Hilda said, pointing at her crotch, which I guess was her way of letting us know that he was impotent. Either that or maybe he could never get the tab in his zippers to lie down flat. Sometimes I had problems with that too. "And Roberta said he refused to do anything about the matter."

This was news to me. But obviously I wasn't as good at keeping up with the gossip as I'd thought, because I hadn't known about Amanda's lover either. I needed to get out more. I was missing all the good stuff.

"You people aren't getting the whole point," Carlton Fisk said. It was the first time he'd spoken aloud since we'd been there, but everyone quieted down to hear what he had to say since he was almost always right about everything.

"What you should be worrying about instead of who's sleeping with who is that there's a killer among us. All of us, even me, were sure that George was the guilty party after Fiona was killed. It just made sense," he said. "But with Amanda Wallace's death being so similar we have to look at our own."

"You really think the killer is living among us?" Jenny Negley asked. I was having a little bit of trouble looking at Jenny and not thinking of her dressed up as Catwoman and mewling at Jack. I was a little surprised she hadn't found some poor sap to try out her wardrobe on and take advantage of being snowed in.

"Well, what a thing to say, Carl," Hilda said. "If it wasn't so ridiculous it would be insulting."

"Who else could it be if it's not someone who knew that

George would be the first one blamed? What about those footprints and tire marks in the mud?"

Personally, I was thinking that Jack should hire Carlton on as a deputy. He seemed to have a pretty good handle on things.

"Well I heard that Harvey Wallace's cuff link was found in that hotel room that Amanda was murdered in," Stanley Lipinski said. "Maybe it's something in the water. Maybe men are just getting tired of their wives and getting rid of them."

"That's the stupidest thing I've ever heard, Stanley Lipinski, and it's no wonder you can't get Wanda to marry you with that kind of nonsense coming out of your mouth."

I could tell things were going downhill fast, and I was trying to figure out a way to escape without having to have Brody stab me with a butter knife.

The sound of Brody's voice had my mouth dropping open in surprise.

"Why don't you all try and think of strangers you've seen in and out of town the last few days? It could be someone just passing through," Brody said. "Or maybe someone from one of the other towns?"

"You mean like you?" Stanley asked. "I saw you over at the Diamond Shamrock station in Nottingham earlier this morning, and you were driving around in King George a couple of days ago."

Wow, Stanley got around town. I guessed that's what people did when they were retired—snoop on other people.

"I've been everywhere in this county," Brody said patiently. "I've been doing research and interviewing residents. It's just part of my job."

"You should be ashamed of yourself, Stanley. Don't talk to him that way," Hilda said. "This is Brody Collins, and he's a real mystery writer. You can even get his books in the checkout line at my store." She said it like having his books in her store was the pinnacle of Brody's success, and he couldn't expect to go any higher than that.

Hilda's little round face pinkened, and I could practically see a lightbulb go off above her head. "I know," she said. "I have the perfect solution. I think we should get Brody to find the murderer. Wouldn't that be great? And then he could put all of us in his book when he was through. It would only be fair on account of us helping him solve the crime. Not that Jack's not doing a good job," she said, looking at me apologetically, "but Brody here is an expert on these things." She turned back to Brody with glee in her eyes. "I've read all your books, you know. So has my daughter Cleo. Maybe you could stop by her place and sign all her copies before you leave town."

So that's how she was going to do it, I thought. Not nearly as clever as throwing him in the basement, but it wasn't too shabby as far as husband-snagging plans went.

"Your sheriff is doing a good job and I don't want to step on his territory," Brody said, shaking his head in apology. "It's a professional courtesy."

There were several *hmm*s of understanding, but most people looked like they didn't care one way or the other about professional courtesy as long as it fed the gossip mill and kept them in dinner conversations for the next week. I gave Brody a *you're on your own; you started this* look, and kept my mouth shut.

The restaurant was so quiet you could hear a pin drop, and Brody looked a little pale under his collar. "Well," he started, "I don't know the people in this town as well as you guys do, but it seems to me we're looking for someone who obviously has issues with women. Both victims were killed in the same manner, and there was rape involved. In the case of the first murder, it was my understanding as well that the husband was most likely responsible, but the DNA test came back negative, so I'd say just by that information that more than likely we can cross out the husband as the main suspect in the second murder as well."

Brody cleared his throat and looked at me with panic-stricken eyes, as if he'd just realized the downward spiral he'd begun. But he forged ahead. "Obviously the killer is trying to throw the police off by implicating other people, but he's not worried about being caught or he wouldn't care about his DNA being left behind."

"So who do you think it could be?" Jenny asked.

"I don't know, but from my experiences with other police departments and profilers, I'd say the killer is probably a white male, probably no older than forty and in good shape because he killed them both in such a physical manner. He seems well organized, so he's probably done this before."

"We should make a list," Harry Breuer said from one of the barstools. "We should make a list of every white male in Bloody Mary under forty and see who hates women the most."

There was a surge in volume from the crowd, and I closed my eyes and prayed I was dreaming.

"I bet there's a lot of those," Stanley said. "What about you?" he asked Brody. "Do you hate women?"

"I love women," Brody said, taking my hand in his and giving it a squeeze. I heard a few titters in the background and knew I'd pay him back later for bringing me into this after I'd tried so hard to be wallpaper.

"I heard Dickey Harlowe's having woman problems right now," someone else said. "I heard his wife's about to skin him good in a divorce. And I heard his secretary left on his boat with all the petty cash from his office. I bet he hates all women right now. We should go find out."

There were several more men mentioned, including Jack, several other cops, a councilman, Lanny Wilcox because he'd apparently caught an STD from a hooker over in Fairfax, Ian Rutledge because he'd given Hilda Martin a dirty look when she'd stolen his parking place last week, and Vaughn because he was gay, and apparently that meant he hated all women. I tried to mention that Vaughn didn't hate me, but Hilda was quick to point out that no one really thought of me as a girl most of the time and probably Vaughn didn't either. I wasn't really sure if I should be insulted or not.

"You need to do something," I whispered to Brody. "They're getting all excited, and pretty soon they're going to be knocking down doors and stringing people up. This is an action-first, talk-later kind of group. And we are south of the Mason–Dixon line, which means to us things like the police and law and order are more guidelines than things you actually have to obey. When it comes down to it, everybody in this room will take matters into their own hands just on sheer principle. And Jack is going to be pissed if he gets word of this."

"You mean *when* he gets word of this," Brody said, shaking his head. "I swear I didn't know it would end up this way. I was only trying to give them enough to back off for a little while."

"They'll never back off," I hissed. "They're like rabid dogs after the same bone. And when the bone's gone, they'll turn on each other."

"Right," he said. "I'll fix this." Brody stood on the vinyl booth seat and waved his hands in the air to get silence. The crowd quieted, but there were a few rumbles in the group, and I could have sworn I heard somebody pump a shotgun. Bloody Mary was all about the right to bear arms.

"Excuse me, folks," he said, soft enough to where they had to stop talking and listen close. Neat trick. "No matter what my opinions are, I want you to remember that they're only that. Opinions. You have trained police to see to this matter and I wouldn't want an innocent person getting hurt because you took matters into your own hands." He made eye contact with several men who looked like they were planning to do just that. "Bloody Mary is a small town, a safe town, and you've already had too many deaths. Let's let Sheriff Lawson do his job by staying out of his way and answering whatever questions he asks. Cooperation is the best way all of us can help.

"I've only been here a short time, but I've come to know most of you at least in passing, and I'd hate to see something bad happen to anyone else, to your friends or family. This is a good town with good people. And I'd like to help you take care of it.

"I think the women need to make sure they're not out alone, and I think you all need to watch out for your neigh-bors. Can I count on you to keep Bloody Mary safe?" he asked the room in general. There were several head nods and more "you bets" coming from the same group that was hostile only moments ago.

Brody was a miracle worker in my opinion, and when he grabbed my hand and pulled me through the crowd and back out into the cold, I realized watching him work had made me a little hot as well.

"Man, you should run for office," I said, trapping him against the side of his car and then kissing the daylights out of him. "We could play loyal constituent when we get back to my place." I wiggled my eyebrows suggestively.

"Hah, very funny." He kissed me back with lots of heat and even more tongue. "Okay, you've convinced me," he said, shoving me inside the car. "But I'd rather play crooked congressman than loyal constituent. Everybody knows that crooked congressmen conduct their liaisons in the back seats of their cars."

It sounded good to me. As far as I was concerned the sooner the better.

TWENTY

BRODY WASN'T REALLY PAYING ATTENTION TO THE ROAD when we stopped in front of the funeral home. The Escalade skidded on a patch of ice and somehow ended up parked on the front lawn.

I laughed and Brody cursed and somehow through it all I ended up with my shirt off and Brody's pants unzipped.

"We could go to jail for this," Brody said on a strangled gasp. "But it might be worth it."

"Don't worry, I have an in with the police. Maybe they'll let us share a cell." I looked up just to check and make sure there wasn't anyone peeping in the windows, but they were properly fogged over. No one could see in and we couldn't see out. Perfect.

Things were rocking along nicely when flashes of light started appearing behind my closed eyes and the *whoop, whoop, whoop* of a police siren intruded on my copulatory bliss.

"Jaye, I swear to God that'd better not be you in there," Jack called out. I could see his flashlight muted through the outside of the fogged windows.

"Crap," I said, clambering over the seat to pull my clothes back on. Brody was in a completely indecent state and currently laughing his head off. "Shut up and get dressed. This is no laughing matter."

"You're right," he said, failing to hide his smile. "But this is totally going into my book."

"You wouldn't dare," I whispered, trying to keep Jack from hearing what was going on inside the car. "Not unless you want to find out what it feels like to be embalmed while you're still alive."

"Oooh, vicious. I can tell you're a real tough guy with your shirt on inside out like that."

"Jaye, I'm giving you two minutes to get inside with your clothes on so I can ask you and your boyfriend some questions," Jack said.

"Oh man, he's pissed," I said as I listened to him walk over the frozen grass with crunching steps and slam the side door that led into the kitchen.

I did one more clothes evaluation on both of us and decided not to push on the two-minute threat. I didn't want to see what would happen if I was late. I also wasn't sure this was going to be the most comfortable meeting Jack and I had ever had, but I did the admirable thing and went in the door first to face the music instead of throwing Brody under the bus. Or in this case, in front of Jack's fist.

I didn't find Jack in the kitchen as I had expected or in my office. I was starting to think that maybe I dreamed the whole embarrassing scene, but I saw Jack's coat thrown over the stair rail.

We finally found him in one of the small viewing parlors. The one I called the blue room because of the pale blue printed wallpaper and dark navy indoor/outdoor carpet. It looked like any ladies' parlor, I guess, with a couple of settees and chairs bunched together around a coffee table. The only difference was the platform at the back of the room where a coffin would sit.

Jack was lying flat out on one of the settees. His feet hung over the end and a bag of ice was draped across his eyes. I felt guilty because Jack had obviously been working himself to the bone while I was romping in the back seat of an SUV.

Brody pushed me forward because I was stuck in the doorway, and I dragged myself over to one of the chairs across from Jack. I was kind of wishing I had a bag of ice too. My head was starting to pound from all the blood that was rushing to my face.

"Umm, Jack?" I said because he still hadn't moved to acknowledge I was there. Nope, it didn't look like he was going to make this easy. I probably deserved it. I cleared my throat and Jack took the ice off his eyes and gave me a look that had my chin coming up in defiance.

"Sometimes you push friendship right over the boundaries, Jaye. Like when we were in the eighth grade and you talked the rest of us into spying on Walter Duberry through his windows because you were convinced he was a drug dealer."

"Yeah," I said. "But that ended up okay because it turned out he liked to sneak home in the afternoons and watch porn before his wife got home."

"Yeah, except that it was homemade porn between him and a couple of the cheerleaders at the high school, and my dad had to fire him from working the fields once Walter had been arrested. I couldn't sit for a week after he'd gotten word of what we'd been doing."

I twitched in my own seat because mention of it

reminded me how sore my own behind had been. After we'd all been congratulated for catching Walter in the act, we'd gotten a blistering lecture about invading people's privacy with drugstore binoculars. Probably they were worried about the other things we'd seen around town and wanted to nip this new hobby of ours in the bud.

"This isn't the point, Jaye. I can name a million instances just like it." His eyes shifted to Brody, and if looks could kill Brody would be dead meat. "I'm going to pretend I didn't just catch you doing something completely illegal, not to mention idiotic, and then go home and use Clorox on my eyes."

I figured telling Jack I appreciated it wouldn't get me any brownie points, so I didn't say anything. I watched Jack pull his recorder out of his pocket and set it on the table in front of him like he did whenever he questioned witnesses or suspects, and I got a little tingle along my spine.

"I have some questions for Mr. Collins, Jaye, and I expect you to sit there with your mouth shut until I'm finished." He didn't give me a chance to respond but turned the recorder on. He was really pissed.

Brody was slouched back in his chair, and I had to look closely to make sure he was even awake, he was so relaxed.

"Can you state your full name, age, and where you're from for the record?" Jack asked.

"Brody Collins. Thirty-five. I'm originally from Boston, but I currently live in Richmond, Virginia."

I decided staying silent was to my advantage. This was information that I didn't know, and I had to admit I was curious, not to mention slightly embarrassed. I knew nothing about Brody Collins except that I liked his books and he knew his way around the female anatomy.

"Can you tell me what you were doing at the Hanover Hotel on Sunday morning?" Jack asked.

I knew I'd forgotten something. I sat up in response to Jack's question, but Jack gave me another look before I could say anything and come to Brody's defense.

"I was having breakfast," Brody said.

I could practically hear Jack grinding his teeth.

"Was there any reason you didn't volunteer this information at the crime scene earlier this morning?"

"I guess I just wasn't thinking about it," he said. I applauded his chivalry at trying to protect me from being the screwup, but I didn't think this was the best time to go heroic and mess with Jack.

"Did you eat alone? See anyone you know?"

"Yes, I ate alone. I also saw several people I've had occasion to meet since I've been in town."

"For someone who's been in town such a short time you sure have seemed to shoehorn your way into the community," Jack said.

My eyes widened in surprise. He'd already heard about what had happened at Martha's. And then I caught the look he was giving me and knew he was talking about something else entirely. He was talking about Brody finding his way into my bed. Not that it was any of his business. The recorder was still going, so I held in what I felt like saying.

"Getting to know people in the community is part of my job. I do it everywhere I go," Brody said. "It's become a habit."

"And how much longer are you planning to grace Bloody Mary with your presence?" Jack asked.

I was still in the chair beside Brody and thought I might hate Jack at that moment for asking a question I didn't want to know the answer to.

There was a pause pregnant with meaning between the two men before Brody answered. "I'll be gone as soon as the book's finished, maybe before if I don't have any follow-up questions on any of my research."

Well, I guess I'd known that deep down inside, but it didn't make me feel any better hearing it out loud. Jack turned off the recorder, and I could tell by the smug look on his face he'd done this whole thing just to make a point. I was so angry I was practically vibrating in my chair. Angry at both of them.

"I suggest that next time you have information you need to give me, you do so before I'm blindsided by seeing you on tape and then have to waste valuable time tracking you down to ask questions," Jack said.

They just sat back and faced each other, doing the whole macho thing with me standing outside looking in. Well, enough was enough.

"What is this, Jack? You haven't interrogated enough friends today?" I asked. He went pale at that, and I wished I could take the words back, but it was too late. "This whole thing was my fault because I was supposed to let you know he was on the tape. He told me this morning at the hotel."

"Geez, Jaye, you seem to be slipping in all your responsibilities."

I knew he was referring to the two bodies I had downstairs. But when I really thought about it, I didn't think that was a fair accusation. They'd both been on ice less than twelve hours. Not even I was a miracle worker, and he wouldn't make me feel guilty for not being one.

I didn't have a snappy comeback I could say without crying, so I sat there rigid and tried to breathe out of my mouth slowly so steam wouldn't come out of my ears. Brody tried to take my hand, I guess for comfort, but I moved out of reach. I might as well start distancing myself now instead of getting my heart broken later.

"I'll need your report first thing in the morning," Jack said. "Bring the samples with you so we can get them sent off."

"I'm sure you'll be making the trip personally," I said in my snottiest voice, remembering his last trip to see the lab tech.

"No, I'll send a deputy. I've got too many things to see to here to take time out for fun and games."

Another score for Jack, I thought. Apparently, I had too *much* time for fun and games.

"I got the word back on Fiona's financials," Jack said, ignoring the daggers I was shooting his way. "She's got bank accounts all over the place, and they're all filled with more money than we could imagine. We also found a town house registered under her maiden name. I had a couple of my detectives check it out and they found the Lexus in the garage. It looks like we were right about her running her business out of her other house. We'll just say that the décor definitely ran to a specific clientele, especially with all the restraints bolted into the walls and the wide selection of whips she had on display.

"I'm still waiting on a phone call from George to see if they had a will, joint or otherwise. I don't have a clue as to who she was running off with, but I've got to focus on other things right now."

I felt the heat of embarrassment and anger form in the pit of my stomach and spread outward. Tears escaped out of the corners of my eyes, and I brushed them away viciously, daring either one of them to make a comment.

"My buddy at the FBI, the same one who dug out Fiona's financials for me, is running like-crimes through

VICAP, the Violent Criminals Apprehension Program. I'm going to owe him a hell of a favor because if I had any sense at all, I'd be asking for the FBI to take over the investigation so this thing could be solved. He's going to keep this under his hat a couple of days because he thinks I'll get more out of the people that live here than a stranger would. I should hear something from him soon as far as like-crimes."

Jack stood, shoved his recorder in his pocket, and tossed the ice bag in the trash can in the corner. I'd have to fish it out later because no doubt it'd leak everywhere, and I'd have something else to deal with.

I was still pretty much glued to my chair, strenuously coping with the crap that was my life. I couldn't decide if I should consume more ice cream and cry more or get to work. Probably I should get to work and not think about anything that had to do with the two men in my life. Actually, neither one of them seemed to want to be a part of my life right now, so maybe I shouldn't even worry about it. Yeah, good luck with that one.

"See you in the morning, Dr. Graves," Jack said and left.

I got up from the chair slowly, feeling a decade older than my thirty years, maybe two decades, and walked into the kitchen to start the coffee I'd need to keep moving for the rest of the night. My body was stiff with anger and something else along the lines of despair.

Brody followed behind me, and I could tell he was searching for something to say that would make everything better and let us end up like we'd been in the car less than an hour before. But I just couldn't do it anymore, and nothing he said was going to change my mind.

"I think we have some things to talk about, Jaye."

Huh, so this is what it takes to get him to use my name.

"I'm pretty sure I don't want to talk about anything right now. I've got to get to work."

"You have to admit things are happening pretty fast between us," he said, moving so I didn't have any choice but to look at him. "I'd like them to keep happening, but I can't just leave my home and move here. I'd be willing to try for long distance if you are. You just never know about these things. What we feel is more than likely temporary. I'm not sure I believe in forever."

I could have said a lot of things. I could have said that yeah, all my relationships that have been temporary have made me feel like my heart's being ripped out of my chest and stomped to smithereens. I could have told him what I really felt and scared him so far away that he'd have to move to another state just to be comfortable. But I didn't say anything. It was obvious Brody wanted to keep things up long distance just so he'd have a handy sex partner. I wasn't up for handy sex. I was up for relationship sex. The forever kind.

"I think we should just end it while it's easy, Brody."

Easy? Who was I kidding?

"That way nobody gets hurt," I continued. "Now really, I need to get to work, so I'd appreciate it if you'd leave now." My voice was even though my hands shook a little as I took a mug from the cupboard.

"I care about you. No one has ever meant as much to me as you do. And I'm not afraid to admit it scares me a little."

"This is pointless. I'm giving you an easy out. Why won't you take it? Are you waiting for me to give up all the dignity I have left and tell you I love you?"

He went pale at my declaration but chose to ignore it. "I'm worried about you, Jaye." He put his hand on my arm and turned me around so I'd have to look him in the eye.

"What? Why? Because I'm not falling at your feet and agreeing to your ridiculous deal for quick sex with no commitment? Why on earth would you possibly be worried about me?"

He took a deep breath and looked me straight in the eyes. "Because I think Jack killed those women."

TWENTY-ONE

"Have you absolutely lost your mind?" I asked quietly. I had my body under rigid control so I wouldn't do anything stupid.

"I know you don't want to hear this, but I want you to listen to me. And I want you to use your head. I know he's your friend, but Jack has the potential for the kind of violence that it took to commit these crimes inside him. Couldn't you see it in his eyes when he was sitting in front of you a few minutes ago?"

I shook my head, more to keep the words from penetrating my brain than to deny that I had noticed.

"He's got a reputation with women. He uses them and tosses them aside. I'd say that's a type of abuse right there."

"Are you sure you want to go casting that stone?" I asked more calmly than I felt.

"It's different between us, and you know it. I've heard things about what happened with Jack in DC that don't appear in any official reports. And they aren't good. He knew enough about the victims to know what kind of home life they had. He knew about Fiona's abusive husband and could have planted the necessary items to implicate George. And his own detective was having an affair with the second victim. Do you honestly believe he had no idea about that when it was happening right under his nose?" he asked, shaking me a little. "And then what about Dr. Hides?"

"This is the most ridiculous thing I've ever heard. Jack's my best friend. I'd know if he'd done something like that."

Wouldn't I?

"What about Dr. Hides?"

"I didn't want to tell you this, but I saw Jack in Nottingham early this morning while I was getting gas at the Diamond Shamrock. It was after we were finished at the crime scene, and you weren't with him. Dr. Hides hadn't been dead long when you'd gotten to him. And Jack knew exactly where to go and what he had to do to get rid of those files."

I remembered that Jack had asked for an hour to get things in order before we went to see Harvey Wallace. My stomach felt heavy, like I'd swallowed a ball of lead, and I had to ask myself if Jack could have taken that hour to kill Dr. Hides. Was a man I'd known my entire life capable of such a thing? There was no doubt that Jack was capable of violence. You could always see it just under the surface, and his temper had gotten him in trouble when he was younger. But he'd learned to keep it under control as he'd gotten older. And one of Jack's best traits was his sense of honor. He had a strict moral code that made him one of the best men I'd ever known, but that didn't mean he didn't bend the line every now and then to get what he wanted.

"And I bet if you ask him, he won't have a solid alibi for the time of either murder," Brody pressed on.

I tried to think back frantically through the last four days. I wanted to say that I could give Jack an alibi, but I couldn't. He'd been off duty the night before Fiona's murder. He'd told me he had a date, but I didn't know who with. I'd seen Jack Sunday morning before Fiona was buried, and I remembered he'd looked tired and worse than I'd seen him in years. Had he come straight to me after killing Amanda Wallace?

I did know one thing, Jack had been the one to call me and tell me the news of both murders. And now I didn't know what to think, or who to trust.

"You need to leave," I said dry mouthed, pointing toward the door.

"Just promise me you'll be careful, Jaye. I don't like leaving you here with all of this going on."

"I'll lock up behind you. Just go. Please," I begged.

"All right. But I want to tell you that I hope it's not Jack for your sake. You may not believe it, but the last thing I want is for you to be hurt. In the meantime, I'll keep digging and maybe I'll find out something that will point to someone else."

I stayed silent and flinched when I heard the sound of the screen door slam behind him. I couldn't watch Brody drive away. I was too busy trying to keep myself upright. What he said couldn't be true. Jack would never do those things. But the doubt was there, planted firmly, and I knew it would only grow over time until the issue was resolved.

I lost the battle to keep my dinner down and barely made it to the bathroom before I was violently ill. When my stomach was empty I dunked my head under the faucet and came up sputtering. I couldn't think of these things now. I had Amanda Wallace and Dr. Hides waiting for me.

I couldn't keep my personal world from crumbling around me, but I could always help the dead.

TWENTY-TWO

"HOLY CRAP," I SAID FOR THE SECOND TIME IN LESS than a minute. It was five o'clock in the morning, and the night had been filled with one surprise after another. I was revved on coffee and no sleep, and I had a decision to make. I had to decide whether or not I could trust Jack.

I'd known Jack my whole life and couldn't imagine him not continuing to be a part of it. Jack was more to me than a best friend, and I realized I didn't care what Brody thought. I could trust Jack with my life. I knew this deep down inside. But I was going to have to confront him with it anyway just to get the thoughts out of my head.

I could never tell when Jack was lying to me, probably because I was so bad at that particular skill myself, but I felt that if I asked him directly I'd somehow instinctively know the truth.

I gathered my completed files, shoved them in my briefcase and grabbed another cup of coffee to go in one of the insulated mugs I bought by the case. I would have to contact John Luke Stranton to come retrieve Amanda Wallace as soon as the Here and Gone opened, but that was still several hours away.

I headed toward my Suburban and noticed the only lights on the entire street were coming from my windows. It was too cold for me to head back inside to shut them all off to save on the electricity, and I was much too tired to make the extra effort.

I'd been wearing the same clothes for almost twenty-four hours, I had no idea what my hair looked like, and I hadn't had anything in my stomach but coffee since I'd purged my dinner the night before. But boy did I have some news.

The streets were dead, as I'd expected them to be at this time of the morning, and there were only two cars parked in the lot in front of the police station. One of them was Jack's cruiser.

I took a deep breath and was glad I'd decided against putting food in my stomach. I wasn't feeling all that hot again, and I was starting to have second thoughts about confronting Jack.

I looked through the big, glass-front windows that ran the length of the station and walked inside. It was Jeremy Mooney's turn to work the night shift obviously since he was sitting behind the desk reading *Field and Stream* and eating a Snickers bar.

It was sweltering inside, probably the heater was broken again, and it smelled a little like boiled cabbage and Pine-Sol. The floor was industrial tile and all the desks were lined in rows, all stacked with piles of papers and no sense of order whatsoever. The phones were quiet at this time of night, giving the place an eerie quality.

"Quiet night?" I asked, scaring the daylights out of

Mooney, causing him to drop his Snickers and reach for his gun.

"Don't shoot," I said, throwing up my hands.

"Geez, J.J. You scared the hell out of me," he said, pressing a hand over his heart.

"You were pretty absorbed in the wonders of *Field and Stream*. I came to see Jack. Is he in his office?"

"Yeah, I'm pretty sure he hasn't been home since yesterday morning. I told him about three a.m. to throw in the towel. I think he's finally sleeping."

"I hate to wake him, but I've got some important information. You might as well stay here and keep reading. There's no need for him to be mad at both of us," I said and headed back to Jack's office.

Jack's office was a box that was glassed in on three sides. The back wall was covered in wood paneling and a cheap door led to a small private room. A small bathroom with a stand-up shower connected next to it. Jack kept a trundle bed made up just in case he needed a place to crash and clean clothes in a chest of drawers. It was his private space but hardly what you'd call a home away from home.

I shut the door to his office and was grateful he habitually kept the blinds to all the windows closed. I didn't want Jeremy being a witness to what I was about to do.

The door that led to Jack's one-room sleeping quarters was locked. I put my ear next to the door but couldn't hear anything. Jack wasn't a snorer so I couldn't tell if he was actually asleep or not. I grabbed the Polaroid camera that was sitting on his desk, checked it for film and then dug around in his bottom drawer to look for the spare key to the door.

"Here goes nothing," I whispered.

The key turned in the lock soundlessly, and I pushed

the door open and slipped inside. And there was Jack, just as I'd known he would be. Jack hadn't slept with clothes on since he was five years old, and some things never changed.

But it was obvious some things *had* changed. *Holy cow!* I hadn't seen Jack naked since he was twelve. What a difference those puberty years could make.

I moved closer and got the camera ready. I mentally counted down from five in my head and then snapped the picture. I figured the noise and flash would have woken him, but he was still breathing deep, so I snapped a couple of more and then did some looking of my own.

"I can't imagine what you're doing," he finally said, startling me enough to where I let out a squeak. "If you keep staring, you're going to make me blush."

I had no idea how long I'd been standing there ogling Jack. I must have been out of my mind, but I was caught now and had to bluster my way through.

"I'm blackmailing you," I said, holding up the pictures of him naked.

"You think there's a woman in this county that hasn't seen me naked?" he asked.

"No, probably not. But my roommate from college is a graphic designer, and I can get her to superimpose your picture, let's say, with another man," I said, waving the pictures over his head. "Desperate times call for desperate measures."

"Give me those," he growled, moving as fast as lightning and rolling with me to the floor. This was not a position I'd ever been in before, and I had to say it wasn't completely unpleasant. One hundred and eighty pounds of naked Jack Lawson was pinning me to the floor, and all I could think about was what Brody had said about him killing those women. I needed serious help.

Stupid, stupid, stupid, I thought, banging my head against the floor. Jack had gotten hold of the photographs, but he hadn't bothered to get off of me. I opened my eyes, and he was looking at me closely. I could feel every inch of him pressed against me. I mean every inch, and I had no idea what I should be feeling. Lust? Definitely. Where had that come from? It was a first for me. Fear? Even more definitely. That was the kicker.

"Why are you trying to blackmail me?" he said. His mouth was only an inch away from mine, and all I'd have to do was move just a little for our lips to touch. But instead I opened my mouth to speak. Usually a bad idea with me.

"I wanted something to blackmail you with so you'd tell me the truth on whether or not you killed those women," I said, all of a sudden feeling stupid, foolish, and like a traitor for even saying it. I knew better. Deep in my gut I knew better. Dammit.

"What did you say?" Jack asked, raising himself up slightly, but still holding me down.

"Never mind. It was a stupid thing to say. I recant. You don't have to answer the question."

"Like hell I don't," he yelled, getting off of me and walking over to the chest of drawers to pull clean clothes out. "Why would you ever think something like that about me?"

I didn't say anything, but he already knew the answer by looking at my face.

"Ah-ha, let me guess, your new boyfriend told you I could have been the one to do it. I'm sure he made it pretty convincing since he sees me as competition. Is that it?"

"He's not my boyfriend," I said. That's the only denial I could make because Brody *had* made me think those things about Jack. And I wasn't going to touch what Jack said about him being Brody's competition. I loved Brody, more than I'd ever let myself love anyone in that way, the lousy, spineless commitment-phobe.

Or maybe it wasn't love. How was I supposed to know? Maybe I didn't have the capability to love someone in that way. Or maybe I was one of those people who made it hard for other people to love me in return. But I knew one thing for certain. I did love Jack. He was the only family I had left. We had something special. We had a history. And friendship. I was an idiot.

"I'm sorry, Jack. I didn't mean it. I swear. It's been a hard twenty-four hours for me. Please, Jack," I begged. "I'm sorry."

"I'm going to take a shower," he said, walking into the bathroom and shutting the door with a finality that scared me.

The phone on Jack's desk warbled and broke the silence he'd left in his wake. I was still on my knees in the middle of a room that was barely the size of my closet, feeling like my whole world had just shattered.

"Get that, will you," he yelled through the door.

It was on its fourth ring by the time I answered. "Sheriff Lawson's office," I said.

"Is Jack in?" a deep voice asked on the other line.

"He's unavailable right now. Can I take a message?"

"This is Agent Carver. That punk had better not be sleeping, especially since I've been up all night working on this mess for him. He's going to owe me a big one after this."

"Oh, Agent Carver, this is Dr. Graves. I'm the coroner who's been working with Jack on these cases. He told me you'd be calling soon."

"Ah, so this is the infamous J.J. Graves," he said. I could

tell he was smiling by the tone of his voice. "Jack's told me all about you. You seem like a handful."

"He says that occasionally," I said through gritted teeth.

"Well, I'm glad I caught you because now I can give you all the information instead of having to wait for a return phone call. I'm ready to hit the sack."

"You've found a match for like-crimes?" I asked.

"I've found something interesting, that's for sure. I can't begin to tell you how many unsolved sexual assaults we have in the system, or even unsolved sexual assaults that resulted in homicide. But I've found a pattern I thought was interesting. I've got unsolved cases in Atlanta, New York, Baltimore, Portland, and Trenton.

"In Atlanta, the perp used a knife. All vics were women. He slit their throats ear to ear after he raped them. There were four bodies total, and then the murders stopped after a couple of weeks and no one's heard from him since. Crimes unsolved.

"In New York, we had four more victims, all women, sexually assaulted, and all four killed with a single gunshot to the right temple. He staged them all to look like suicides. All four of those also remain unsolved.

"In Baltimore, we've got three victims. If there was a fourth, they never found her body. These women were all buried alive in different parks throughout the city."

"Rape?" I asked, already knowing the answer.

"Yep. In Portland, the victims were beaten to death, and in Trenton more variations with a knife, only a lot messier than the first time around."

"Were any of the victims men?" I asked, curious to see if my suspicions rang true.

"Actually, yes," he said. "How'd you know? The fourth victim in the Portland murders and the third victim in

Trenton were both men. And they were both sodomized. Tell me what you've got."

"The same," I said. "Third victim was a doctor, older man, purported suicide by hanging at first glance, but when I got him on the table I realized he'd been raped as well. He wasn't found nude, so I didn't even suspect a rape. Our guy doesn't care about leaving his DNA lying around."

I heard papers shuffling across the phone line and knew Agent Carver was checking for the same. "I'm not seeing it here," he said. "He didn't leave anything behind with these victims."

"I guess maybe that's why he feels like he can with the victims here in Bloody Mary."

"I'm going to fax everything I've got to Jack's office," Carver said. "I want you to call me if you need help. He's gotten three, but in all the cases except the one where he buried them alive, there were four victims. And I think that's just because they never found the fourth body."

"We'll call if we need you," I assured him and disconnected.

My brain was tired, and I was seeing double. I heard the fax machine ring and start to whine out sheets of paper. I lay down on the floor to wait for them to finish. Jack was still in the shower, and it wouldn't hurt to rest my eyes for a few minutes. And if a few tears fell, it was only because I was too tired to control them.

TWENTY-THREE

I woke disoriented and, weirdly enough, floating, but it turned out it was only Jack, picking me up off the floor and sitting down with me cradled in his lap. I rested my head on his shoulder and breathed in his familiarity and comfort. He wiped the traces of tears off my cheeks with his thumb and kissed the top of my head, then my cheeks, my chin, my lips.

My breath hitched painfully, and varying emotions bombarded me. Confusion, love, anger, sorrow, and not the least of which was attraction. Not good. As if my life wasn't complicated enough.

"I'm so sorry," I whispered.

"Shh... It's okay. Me too," he said. And we sat there for a while, each lost in our own thoughts, but it was only so long before the real world intruded again. I awkwardly dislodged myself from Jack's lap and moved to the chair on the other side of his desk.

Jack's office was spartan to say the least. He'd once told me he'd work out of the back of his car and not have an office at all if it would let him hire one more cop. The blinds on the windows were bent and only attached to the window frame by years of dust. The gray carpet was worn and threadbare in places, and his desk was metal and dented on every side like it had been dropped down a couple of flights of stairs. There were no plants or photos anywhere around, nothing personal to try and cheer the place up a little.

"Was that Carver on the phone?" Jack asked.

"Yeah, he's faxing a few open cases he thought would pique your interest. He's got similarities in several different states that could be our guy. The only difference is that he didn't leave any DNA at the previous crime scenes, so you might not be able to tie him to our murders without a confession."

"And it might not be our guy at all."

"Possibly. But this feels right, especially after what I found out during the autopsies. Dr. Hides was raped," I said. This news got Jack's attention, and he had his cop face back in place, ready to absorb the details. "Carver told me there were two male victims who had also been raped in two separate cases."

Jack got up and then walked to the fax machine. He picked up the pages and flipped through until he found the pages he wanted. "What did you find on the tox screen?"

"He had way over the legal limit in his system punched up with a couple of painkillers. I found that he did show signs of early cold symptoms, so him calling Janette Taylor and cancelling his appointments was probably legitimate. There wasn't anything in his stomach other than the liquid he'd consumed before he died," I said. "Hey, while you're over there, make me a copy of those pages."

He did as I asked and brought them back to me. "Seems early to start out the day that way. Do you think he was planning on killing himself anyway? Booze and pills?"

"Could be, but he didn't have enough in his system to do anything but knock himself out for a few hours, and I don't remember seeing the pill bottle lying around anywhere."

"There wasn't one gathered into evidence," Jack said, confirming my suspicion.

"Which means that Dr. Hides was given the drugs by the killer and he took the rest of them with him when he left. What he had in his system is not normally a fast-acting drug. It usually takes twenty to thirty minutes to seep into the system, but the alcohol probably helped speed up the process, slowing his reflexes and bringing on extreme lethargy in about ten minutes."

"He didn't have to drug the women to overpower them," Jack said. "Why'd he change his pattern?"

"Maybe he didn't want to take any chances with a man. Hides wasn't a big man, but he was bigger than the women. And maybe in a neighborhood like that, where the houses are practically on top of each other, he was afraid to make too much commotion in case there were any neighbors within hearing distance."

"The deputies who canvassed door to door didn't come up with anything useful. Everyone they talked to said they didn't notice any cars up or down the street besides ours when we pulled up, and no one noticed any strangers walking around."

I gave this a couple of minutes' thought and drew a few conclusions, but I wanted to see what Jack thought so I let him continue before I voiced my own opinions.

"So let's say that the killer parks his vehicle a couple of blocks away and walks the distance to Dr. Hides' residence. There are several businesses with crowded parking lots close enough to get there quickly and back without anyone noticing. He cuts up the side of the house and goes right to the front door like his patients do.

"There was a back door leading in through the kitchen, but I'd think it would be unlikely for him to enter that way because the backyard is fenced with a padlock. We didn't see any signs of disturbance in the backyard. There was still a little snow on the ground and everything was pristine. And if this guy were wrapped up in a coat and scarf, no one would be able to distinguish any features if they did happen to catch a glimpse of him.

"There were signs that Dr. Hides had been holed up in his office working. There were a couple of patient files on his desk, a box of Kleenex, some juice, and cough drops. He's busy trying to concentrate on work and ignore the cold when he hears the doorbell. He's irritated at the interruption, maybe thinking one of his patients showed up anyway even though he cancelled. He gets up to answer the door, leaving everything as it was on the desk, and opens the door to the killer, who probably made his way inside the house by threatening the doctor with a weapon of some kind.

"There were no signs of struggle, so the doctor must have followed directions, thinking he'd be fine as long as he did what the man said. Suppose the killer enters the house with the doctor at gunpoint, and they head upstairs to the second floor because he doesn't want to have to haul the doctor up the stairs himself. Too much work. He tells Hides to take the pills and drink the alcohol to keep him from struggling, and as soon as they take effect he rapes him. We found the doctor only wearing his robe, but there were some pajamas found inside the laundry hamper."

"So he takes Dr. Hides' pajamas off, rapes him, puts the robe back on him while he's still disoriented and groggy from the drugs, puts the noose around his neck, and throws him off the second-story balcony."

"Yeah, that sounds good. It's better than anything else we've got at this point."

"He was taking a chance being in there so long," I said. "At the minimum, he would have been there between forty-five minutes to an hour between walking to and from the house, the rape, and then searching for the files."

"Dr. Hides' keys were found on the desk. After he was through throwing the doctor off the balcony, he put the pajamas in the dirty clothes hamper, grabbed the keys, and took the two files. He locked the file cabinets back up and put the keys back where he found them. Cleaned up after himself to make it look more like initial suicide. He's well organized, and he's had a well-thought-out plan with every murder. I'd say it took him no more than half an hour inside the house."

"Seems like a lot of trouble to go to when he didn't bother to disguise the other victims with apparent suicide. Why'd he change this time around?"

"Not a clue," Jack said, shrugging. "What about Amanda Wallace? Did you find anything similar in her system?"

"I didn't find alcohol if that's what you're asking," I said. My brain was fuzzy and tired and my heart hurt just a little, so I laid my head on Jack's desk and looked at my feet. "She was eight weeks pregnant, Jack."

"What more could happen during this case? Do you think Colburn knows?"

"No, he would have said something when we met with him yesterday. But she knew. I'll have to check to make sure, but I'd bet anything that she had an appointment with her

OB the morning she cancelled her regular appointment with Dr. Hides."

"This is a mess. I'm going to have to tell Colburn the news," Jack said, rubbing his face. "He's got a right to know about the baby. All we have to worry about now is the riot between Harvey Wallace and Colburn when this news makes its way around town. I'm hoping to God her funeral doesn't end up like a battleground. Sorry to hear about Harvey moving Amanda to the Here and Gone, by the way."

"It happens," I said. At this point I was ready to shut down the funeral home for a few weeks and hibernate with a dozen or so books and a bottle of gin. "I think you should tell Colburn about the baby, but why don't we keep the news just between the three of us? The Wallaces are going to have a hard enough time dealing with the way Amanda died. Knowing about the baby will just bring them more pain. Her children deserve to keep as many good memories as possible of their mother."

"Fine by me," Jack said. "I'd prefer not to have to open that can of worms anyway. Why don't you go home and get some sleep, Jaye? You look terrible." He pulled me up out of the chair and gave me a hug, rubbing the back of my neck in slow circles. It felt so good to lean on someone for a minute that I rested my head against his chest and could have fallen asleep where I stood.

"If I wasn't so tired I'd hurt you for saying that. But it's probably true, so I'll let it pass this once." I took a shaky breath and knew I needed to get it all out. "I'm sorry if I let you down yesterday. I was wrong. About everything."

I hoped he knew I was talking about Brody because I didn't want to have to go into detail. It was still too raw for me to think about, much less speak about. It's never good to find out that someone doesn't want you or love you enough.

"I wasn't thinking straight," I said. "But I've got things under control now. I'll do better next time."

"Ah, Jaye. You have never once let me down since I've known you. I was a jerk for doing things that way, and I should be the one apologizing. But that doesn't mean I'm not glad that you've come to your senses about other matters."

He ran his hand over the back of my hair and pushed stray pieces behind my ears.

"I've got to head back over the Alexandretta Boutique in a couple of hours. Marie called and told me one of her other employees saw a man in a black SUV drop Fiona Murphy in front of the store one day. I'm going to see if I can get a description. I tried to stop by and talk to her yesterday morning before I picked you up to go see Harvey Wallace, but it turned out she called in sick, so it was a bust."

I felt like an idiot. Jack had had a perfectly legitimate excuse for being in Nottingham yesterday morning, and I felt lower than slime for even considering that he'd had anything to do with murder.

"I'll let you know what I find out," he said.

I pulled out of his grasp and then reached for my bag, shoving the papers Jack had copied inside. I had to concentrate to put one foot in front of the other without falling over from exhaustion.

"Oh, and Jaye," he said, stopping me before I made it out the door. "I think you and I have some things to sit down and talk about when all this is over. It's time, don't you think, to get things out in the open?"

I wanted to pretend like I didn't know what he was

talking about. I was all too afraid the dynamics had changed between us and exactly what that would mean to our friendship. I was thinking after this was over I should probably take a vacation to some tropical island for a month or two. Or maybe I'd join a convent and never look at a man again. If I'd had more energy I would have run like crazy from the look in Jack's eyes. It wasn't one I'd seen before, and it wasn't one I was sure I wanted to see.

Hmm... Something to think about.

TWENTY-FOUR

Jumbled pieces of information were rearranging themselves in my brain to make a coherent thought. There had been something pricking at my memory ever since I'd talked to Agent Carver, but I couldn't bring it to the surface. I'd have to put it on hold until after I'd been horizontal for a few hours.

I looked at my house as a stranger would. It seemed like I hadn't been there in days, or felt the softness of my own bed. But it had only been a day—only a day since I'd woken with Brody, made love with Brody. And only a day since it had all come crashing down around my ears. Pretty crappy day all in all, if I say so myself.

I barely remembered to pull the keys out of the ignition before I stumbled out of the car and through the front door. I left clothes in a trail behind me, left the red light flashing on the answering machine, and fell face-first onto the bed. The last thing I thought before I drifted off was that the pillow still smelled like Brody.

I sat up in bed with the air trapped in my lungs and my body covered in sweat from the nightmare. Sunlight streamed through the blinds in my bedroom and reflected off dust motes in the air.

"No, no, no," I sobbed, pulling on the first clean T-shirt and shorts I found in my drawer. The nightmare was still fresh in my mind, and I wanted it to be gone. I wanted to be wrong. I should have seen the similarities sooner. If I hadn't been so tired, so overwhelmed with what had been happening in my small town and my life, I would have.

My feet hit hard against the wood of the stairs and echoed through the empty house. My bag was still on the kitchen table, and I rummaged around until I had the open case files of the other murders in my hand.

"Oh, Brody."

Brody had been here at the start of it all. He'd been at every scene. Stanley Lipinski had placed Brody in Nottingham the morning of Dr. Hides' murder. I tried to think back to the morning of Fiona's murder. He'd shown up around town early that morning looking for me and not trying to hide it. He'd said he'd found out about the murder from inside sources. And he'd admittedly been at the hotel the morning Amanda Wallace was killed. Breakfast was an easy way to cover what he'd really been up to. And he was certainly strong enough to come out the victor in any physical battle. He definitely didn't have the physique of a man who sat behind a desk all day.

I was an idiot. Why hadn't I seen it sooner? I hadn't wanted to see, that's why. I'd been blinded by my emotions. I dumped the papers on the floor as I scrambled to get to the phone on the desk. To call Jack.

"What are you doing, Jaye?" Brody asked from the doorway.

I froze with the receiver in my hand, panic clutching my chest. Goose bumps whispered over my chilled skin and my breathing was labored. "Stay away from me," I said. "I know you did it."

"What are you talking about?" he asked, seemingly confused. His voice was calm and soothing, as if he were dealing with an irrational child. "You think I killed all those people? How could you think that? Why would you think that?"

My finger still hovered over the numbers on the phone, ready to dial if he stepped any closer. "I was finally able to put it together after getting more than a couple of hours of sleep. Amazing how the mind shuts down when a body is sleep deprived."

"I believe the sleep deprivation was a mutual decision on both our parts," Brody said. "It's been pure luck that I've gotten any work at all done. Come on, Jaye. Put the phone down and let's talk this out."

"You can't change what you've done," I said. "You were here from the beginning. It almost seemed too easy that you'd show up on my doorstep just a couple of hours after the first murder. I probably made it easier for you each time. What better way to research your book than to create the crimes in real life? Is this what you do for all your books?"

"Jaye, you've got to listen to me. I've never killed anyone. I swear that to you. And I need to tell you something else. Something I should have said from the first moment I sat across from you in candlelight. I love you."

"Don't tell me that!" I screamed. "You never loved me. You used me and probably laughed at how easy I was."

"That's not true. I do love you, and I've had a lot of time to think about things between last night and now. I thought about us mostly, but I thought about the murders too. I know who the killer is, Jaye."

"Yeah, you already shared that information. And it's not Jack by the way."

"I know that," he said. "I was jealous."

"What?" Confused didn't begin to describe what I was feeling at that moment. "Well, if Jack's not the killer and you say you're not the killer, then who did it?"

Brody didn't get a chance to answer. The gunshot sounded like a cannon inside the house. My ears rang and the stench of cordite burned my nostrils. It seemed like everything happened in slow motion. I watched the front of Brody's chest expand and open as the bullet exited. Wood from the wall splintered behind me, and I screamed as the red bloom of blood covered his shirt and splattered on the carpet and the desk that I was still standing behind.

Brody dropped to his knees, the look of surprise still on his face, and fell forward. I rushed around the desk to get to him, only thinking that I had to save him. He loved me. I'd almost forgotten about the gunman in the doorway.

"I hate to say it, but your boyfriend was right," the man said. "He wasn't the killer."

TWENTY-FIVE

Jeremy Mooney smiled a smile so familiar it hurt to look at it. His eyes held the look of someone who wasn't altogether there, and his skin was sallow and slicked with sweat. He was still in uniform and his police issue revolver was in his hand.

"Cat got your tongue, Dr. Graves? I've never known you to be speechless. Aren't you going to say anything?" he asked.

"I think you're finally starting to grow a little facial hair," I said. "Congratulations." My voice was steady and calm. I ignored the gun pointed at me and kept going to Brody's still form. I was in the place inside my head that I'd had to create when I was doing ER rounds at Augusta General. I had one goal and one purpose—to save a life— even though in my mind I already knew it was too late.

"Leave him be," Jeremy said. "He's already dead. There's nothing you can do."

I choked on a sob and kept going, kneeling beside Brody's still form just so I'd have the proof I needed. Jeremy was right. Brody's pulse had already stopped. Was it my curse to lose everyone I loved, or worse yet to lose the people that loved me in return? I was frozen in shock, but the cold steel of the gun against my head brought me back to reality.

"I'm so sorry about your loss," he said, laughing. He nudged me to stand up, and I did so slowly. Brody's blood was thick and sticky on my fingers.

"I'm going to put away the gun for now," he said. "I don't want to use it on you. But don't get any ideas. I'm stronger than I look. I have to use my hands on you for this to be perfect. I've wanted to use my hands on you for a long time."

I frantically tried to think of a way I could get out of the house and find help, but there was no way I could move fast enough. I might have a chance if I could get to the basement and lock myself inside, but I didn't particularly want to get a bullet in the back.

"You know, Jaye," he said. "You were the start of all of this, going back before I had to start punishing Bloody Mary's fine, upstanding citizens. Practice makes perfect. But you're the reason so many people have died. How does it feel to know you're responsible for so many deaths?"

I felt sick. Could I really be at fault?

"I've always been fascinated by your ability to face death with such cold indifference. You love death—the blood, the last breath. The power." He looked at me like we shared a bond that no one else could understand. "You know, when I was younger, I loved watching your reactions as the people closest to you were buried in the ground. But you never shed a tear."

"I don't like to cry in front of people," I said softly,

trying to imagine how my pride looked to others. Did they think I was cold and uncaring? I wasn't sure I had any feelings left at all. The grief in my life had been so overwhelming all I felt was numb.

"You and I, Jaye," he said, motioning at me with his hand. "You don't mind if I call you by your first name, do you?" He didn't wait for me to answer. "We're alike in so many ways. I don't feel anything but a cold void when I take someone's life. You and I were meant to be together. But it didn't matter what I did to get your attention. You never noticed me."

"That's not true, Jeremy. I've known you my whole life. How could I not notice you?" I tasted the coppery tang of blood in my mouth and realized I'd been biting my lip to keep from screaming.

"But you didn't want *me*," he said.

"How was I to know you felt that way? You were so young. You're still young."

"I'm a man! A flesh-and-blood man," he screamed.

"You're right, Jeremy. I'm sorry," I said, my self-preservation instincts kicking in. It was never a good idea to antagonize a sociopath.

"That's right. Show a little respect," he said with a smile that sent chills down my spine. "You know, it was because of you I became a cop. Everybody knows how much you love Jack. How could I not want to get close to him to get closer to you? But it didn't work out that way, so I had to find other ways of getting your attention. A murder here, a murder there. Different places. Different people."

He shrugged over the lives he'd destroyed as if they were meaningless. "It was all just practice for this one moment," he said. "You'll be my finest work."

He inched closer to me, his sweaty palm reaching toward my face but not touching me. I couldn't help but shrink back with the fear that seized me.

"Don't be afraid, Jaye. Not yet," he said. His damp finger slid down my cheek and bile rose in the back of my throat.

"Don't touch me," I said. The calm I'd managed earlier had deserted me and my voice shook.

"I apologize," he said, his smile almost gentle—his eyes crazy. "It seems I owe you more than one apology. The saying is true. The past does always come back to haunt you. Your parents' death was very tragic, but it was quite the stroke of good luck for me. I couldn't figure out a way to get you to come back to Bloody Mary, and then it was like my prayers were answered when your parents died.

"You're crazy," I said, but he just smiled, his eyes empty.

"It was important for you to be alone—really alone—so you could realize how badly you needed someone to take care of you. But even then, you never saw me." Jeremy's crazed eyes turned thoughtful and he giggled. "But it doesn't matter now. I got what I wanted. You packed up from the city and moved back to Bloody Mary, and here you are."

I remembered the pain and loneliness after my parents' deaths. Jeremy was right. I had been truly alone. I'd questioned everything, and had trusted no one. And during my darkest times, Jeremy had be rejoicing in my misery as only the insane could.

"You know, Brody showing up in Bloody Mary couldn't have been more perfect," Jeremy said. "His curiosity made my job easier. Actually, everybody in this town made my job easier. Being a cop who people underestimate has its advantages. I was able to travel all over the county, choosing my prey carefully—watching—waiting. I watched you, Dr. Graves."

Sweat glistened at his temples and slid in rivulets down the side of his face. He ran his fingers through his damp hair, causing it to stick up in little spikes. "Aren't you going to ask me why I picked the victims I did? Why I picked you?"

"Wh...why did you pick them?" I asked, afraid I already knew the answer.

"I met Fiona Murphy at a private club in DC one weekend. You could say it was a special club for people who enjoyed certain things when it came to sex. I'm not afraid to say that it scared me when she recognized me."

I remembered what kind of things Fiona had enjoyed, and couldn't imagine the Jeremy Mooney I'd thought I'd known doing those things.

"It was our little secret," he continued. "And you could say that Fiona and I had each other by the short hairs. Everyone in town thought George was an abusive husband, but I knew that it was Fiona who liked the abuse. She told me how she was planning to leave him because he wasn't as harsh as he used to be. He was getting soft. And this idea started to form in my head." He looked at me and smiled again.

I was trying to listen to what he was saying and think at the same time, but I wasn't having much luck.

"Anyway, I began seeing Fiona pretty regularly."

"You were the one she was going to run off with?"

"Yeah, she played right into my hands. I already knew about George, and what kind of person he was, so the scene wasn't difficult to stage. It just took patience and timing.

Fiona had a secret that no one in town knew about except for me and her husband—to an extent—but even he didn't know what she really liked. She was an interesting woman. It was pretty slick police work by Jack to find the house in Nottingham. I tried to delay the results as long as possible, but Colburn was looking over my shoulder the whole time, afraid I was too stupid to understand the information I had."

I knew the only chance for survival I had was to keep him talking. Since he'd put the gun away, I was slowly putting distance between us inching my way toward the door. Surely Jack or someone would check on me at some point. Amanda Wallace still needed to be transferred to the other funeral home. Maybe Harvey Wallace, beating down my door in anger, would be the one to save me.

"What about Amanda Wallace?" I asked.

"That's an easy one. It didn't take very much digging to find out she was having an affair."

"But she was pregnant!" I shouted, anger finally starting to replace fear.

"I know," he said. "That was her secret. I almost left her alone when I realized half the town already knew she was having an affair, but then I followed her to her doctor's appointment. She drove all the way to Caroline County to see her doctor just so she wouldn't run into anyone she knew. She thought her secret was safe.

"She met with her lover several times a week, and when I followed her to the hotel, I knew the time was right. I went up one of the fire escapes and avoided the cameras. I had photographs of her and Colburn, and I threatened to send them to her husband. I told her I'd find a way to let him know about the baby. She let me right in the door, offering me anything I wanted to keep quiet. She really wasn't as satisfying as I thought she'd be. She didn't struggle nearly as much as Fiona did. Fiona had a lot more fight in her."

"How did you find out about their connection with Dr. Hides?"

"Actually, both of them seeing him was just a coincidence, but once I started seeing Fiona I worried that she'd tell him about me. And it turns out I was right to be worried, which is why I took the file. Dr. Hides held the secrets to a lot of people's lives in that locked cabinet of his. I took Amanda Wallace's file because I wanted you to be surprised about the baby. Surprises are good. Don't you think, Dr. Graves?"

"I think you're bonkers. You've killed God knows how many people for years just because you had some pathetic schoolboy crush on me and wanted me to notice you. Well, I have news for you. I would have never noticed you that way. I'm only interested in men."

I expected the crack of his hand across my cheek and braced for it, but that didn't make the pain any less. He'd been right when he'd said he was stronger than he looked. My head whipped to the side and blood filled my mouth.

Jeremy took a few deep breaths until the rage left his face. "Naughty, naughty, Jaye. You're not going to make me angry by taunting me. You should know by now that I have exquisite control." He moved closer to me, and I automatically backed up, but the wall loomed behind me. I was out of room.

"And of course Dr. Hides was a liability because he knew all about me, so he had to go. Did you know he was blackmailing Fiona? For a little over a million dollars and her services for free just to keep her secret. He wasn't able to get as much from Amanda Wallace, but he was blackmailing her too. That put an interesting twist to things, I think. I know you and Jack thought that it was him all along. I was watching you when you found him. I enjoyed the expression on your face. I've watched you a lot, Dr. Graves. Bet you didn't know that."

"No, I didn't."

When the phone rang, I think it surprised both of us. We stared at each other to see who was going to make the first move.

"I think we'll just let it ring. If I had to guess I would say that's Jack. That woman from the boutique got a good look at me when I was with Fiona. Who knew? I would've had to take care of her eventually, but I would've made it look like an accident. Jack's probably just now gotten a description of me from the woman, but he won't make it all the way from Nottingham in time to save you. He does so want to be your hero." Jeremy sighed dramatically. "Ahh, young love. Of course, I'll have to kill him too because he's found out *my* secret."

The phone stopped ringing, and I wanted to shout in frustration and beg for my life all at the same time.

"Now I think it's important that we talk about *your* secret, Dr. Graves. You're a fascinating creature. It's really no wonder that I wanted you." His smile was admiring and sinister both at the same time. "I wonder what the people of Bloody Mary would say if they found out you'd killed a man."

Up until he'd said it out loud, I'd thought he'd been bluffing about knowing my darkest secret. It wasn't one I'd want anyone to find out, even if I wasn't around to know they were talking about it.

"You know the evidence against me was inconclusive," I said calmly. "That's why it was in a sealed file and I was able to keep my job at the hospital."

"Just because they couldn't prove you did it doesn't mean they don't know you did. Dr. Givens would have loved to see you rot in jail. Did you tell yourself it was a mercy killing? To end that man's life because he was suffering and begging at the end? Did you cry for him?" he asked. "Did you?"

"Yes. Yes, I cried for him," I screamed. I was crying now, wishing for things that couldn't be and a life I'd never really lived. "But I would do it again because he thanked me as he went to sleep that final time. He was finally at peace after so many months of unbearable pain. He was my friend."

"Do you kill all your friends? Is that why you have so few?"

"No, but I wouldn't mind killing you right now."

"Tsk, tsk. Don't forget your Hippocratic Oath. Again," he said. "I'm afraid we're going to have to hurry this along. I'd like for you to be good and dead when Jack gets here, so it has more of an impact. He loves you. Did you know that? I'm a trained observer. He's loved you for years, but you're oblivious to anyone's feelings but your own. As usual."

"Jack's never been interested in me that way. We're just friends."

"Don't kid yourself, sweetheart. Just because he would screw any woman in the state of Virginia doesn't mean he doesn't want you. But he'll keep screwing those other women because he knows if it's ever you it's going to matter, and then his tomcat days will be over. It's a shame neither one of you will get to figure it out. Now," he said, all business. "How should we do this?"

"How about you leave and get a head start, because Jack is going to tear you apart when he finds you."

"It's good to see you can keep your sense of humor at a

time like this. You could at least make this interesting. I'll even give you a handicap."

I stood there looking at him, not sure what he wanted me to do.

"Run, dammit!" he said, slapping me again across the same cheek as he had the last time. I didn't take time to feel the pain. I just ran. I sprinted out of the study to the front of the house. All I needed was to reach the door.

I heard his footsteps behind me and knew I'd never make it. He took me down with a tackle around my knees, and I wrenched my shoulder as I hit the floor. The faces of Fiona Murphy and Amanda Wallace went through my mind, frozen forever in death, and I remembered what he'd done to them.

I screamed—guttural, animal sounds produced from true fear—and fought with everything I had left inside me. My nails clawed the side of his face and my knee desperately tried to find a clear shot to the groin, but he was strong. He rapped my head hard against the floor and addled my senses long enough to pin me down so I couldn't move at all. My left eye was almost completely swollen shut, but the other one widened in horror as he pressed his full weight against me.

He laughed close to my face so spittle rained down and covered my blood-soaked skin. "Don't worry, Dr. Graves. There's just not enough time for what you're thinking. Dirty girl. Though you have no idea how often I've thought of the two of us together that way."

I reduced myself to begging when I saw the void he'd spoken of enter his eyes. He put his hands around my neck and began to squeeze. My air was cut off immediately and my lungs burned. Dark spots danced across my vision, and my legs jerked in reflex. My attempts to remove his hands were easily dodged and only made him squeeze harder.

I knew it was over for me—would have known it even without seeing the look of triumph on his face. But I had one final moment of satisfaction before I died—when I heard the sound of Jack's voice and saw the red splatter of blood across Jeremy's chest and neck. The warmth of his blood on my face was the last thing I felt before darkness claimed me.

TWENTY-SIX

It was the irritating beeps that rang frantically in my ears that told me I wasn't dead. Or wasn't dead anymore, at least. I'd been there, seen what the other side had to offer before life was so cruelly forced back into my body. At least *there* I'd been at peace, with no pain. *Here* there was unspeakable pain.

Brody was gone. And the anguish from that memory was worse than any ache in my body. But somehow I was still here. Was it my fault Brody was dead? Because I hadn't trusted him enough? Because I hadn't let myself love him enough? Those weren't questions I was ready to answer just yet.

It was Jack's voice I finally heard that made the beeps slow to an easy rhythm. It was his hand holding mine and his voice that was choked with emotion.

"You gave me a scare, Jaye. I thought you weren't going to make it," he said.

I opened one eye slowly, but things were still fuzzy. And I knew before I tried that speaking would be pointless. Jack's eyes were bloodshot and his smile strained. Several days of beard growth on his face made me wonder how long I'd been in the hospital.

"You're not going to be able to speak for quite some time," he said. "He crushed your windpipe, and there was some bleeding on the brain. So no singing or autopsies for you anytime soon. Maybe all that time they spent on you in surgery will help that tone-deaf problem you have."

I smiled as best I could and squeezed his hand just because it felt good to be alive, even if there was unspeakable pain and a long road ahead of me. The morphine started to work, and I slowly went back under. The last thing I heard him say was enough to let me rest in peace.

"I got him for you, Jaye. I got the bastard who did this to you. You can rest easy now, and I'll be right here when you wake up. I'm going to be here from now on."

EXCERPT OF A DIRTY SHAME

Continue the J.J. Graves series with <u>A DIRTY SHAME</u>, available at all retailers.

There was something about the dark.

The way it surrounded completely—a gentle embrace that comforted with a soft sigh and a delicate touch. The way it could intimidate and threaten, so the blackness was almost debilitating.

The dark wielded power.

But to me, the darkness was a place to hide—a place to bury my face when it was covered with tears, and a place to huddle protectively when the nightmares came lurking. And they always lurked.

My name is J.J. Graves, and the darkness had become my friend over the past months. So it seemed fitting that I wait until that blackest time of the night to slink my way back home—to the home that had left a bitter taste in my mouth and sweat coating the palms of my hands. To sneak back into the town that had raised me and gossiped about me with equal fervor.

I jerked at the wheel of the old Suburban and pulled to the side of the road on the outskirts of Bloody Mary, Virginia. I lowered my head to the steering wheel and took a few desperate breaths that did nothing to relieve the tightness in my chest. The windows steamed slightly and the sound of harsh breathing echoed in my ears. I tried to ignore the pounding inside my skull and the way the heater couldn't quite chase away the chills that racked my body, but it was no use.

"Come on, Jaye. You can do this."

My voice was still hoarse and low, though the pain had been gone for several weeks. The doctors said to be patient. That things would return to normal the more I let myself heal. But I wondered how anything would ever be normal again when all I could think about was the blood coating the floors of my childhood home—violent splatters that gleamed like the black center of a Burmese ruby as death tried to claim me. In my dreams I still heard the deafening sound of the gunshot and felt the blood that rained down on my skin like scalding tears. It was easy to forget how hot fresh blood was. It was always cold by the time I had my hands in a body on my table.

Jeremy Mooney had taken something from me that day, when he'd had his hands wrapped around my throat. I couldn't say exactly what it was he'd taken. I only knew I was different now. I'd watched him murder a man I'd been intimate with—a man I'd told myself I could love if I only allowed it. Guilt and self-loathing ate at me because I hadn't known if I could really be in love with Brody, while feelings I couldn't put into words were forming for Jack—the man I called my best friend. The guilt still ate at me. And I'd been avoiding Jack because of it.

I didn't love easy, and honestly, I wasn't even sure I

knew what love was. I'd thought my parents had loved me. But I'd been wrong there too.

Terror had crippled me after my brush with death. And I hated that about myself. I'd never been a coward. Had never been one to hide from a scandal or the terrible things life seemed hell-bent on throwing in my path. Lord knows I'd faced enough of them in my thirty years. But I guess everyone has a breaking point, and I'd finally met mine.

I was broken. And I had no idea how to fix myself.

I took another deep breath and slowly straightened my spine, wiping the inside of the windshield with the back of my sleeve to clear away the steam. I put the car in drive and checked my mirror for any traffic before I pulled back onto the road. It was habit. There would never be any traffic on these back roads at this time of night.

Bloody Mary, Virginia, was like a throwback to another century. It was one of the four towns within King George County and it was full of just shy of three thousand of the most contrary people I'd ever met. My mother always said it was because there was nothing to do in town except drink or procreate. My mother, come to find out, had been a consummate liar, but I was pretty sure she was right about that one thing.

It was a postcard of a town—towering trees and clapboard houses with American flags flying from the porches. The main roads were bricked and the sidewalks were cracked. It was a town that boasted family values and the American Dream. The shops closed before dark and everything shut down on Sundays. People got up early and worked hard, and they went home to their families and home-cooked meals.

King George wasn't a rich county, for the most part. There were pockets where the wealthy lived, of course, because the scenery lent itself well to the monstrous homes those with money tended to own. But most people in King George County were solid, blue-collar working class. It was a good place to raise a family and settle down to a comfortable life.

Maybe that was the reason driving back home made me feel out of place. A family and a comfortable life didn't seem to be in the cards for me. I was fourth-generation mortician. First-generation law-abiding citizen. And I was all that was left of the Graves family legacy. By all accounts, I should have been buried next to my parents in the Bloody Mary Cemetery. But for some inexplicable reason, I was still breathing. The blood was still pumping through my body and causing my heart to pound erratically. I had no idea why God had chosen to spare me. It was just another thing to feel guilty for, wondering if He'd made the right decision.

My headlights slashed across the old playground equipment on the opposite side of the country road—rusted seesaws and metal slides that would blister the backs of some poor kids' legs in the heat of the summer. There were patches of dirt where grass should have been and scarred picnic tables strategically placed under the towering oaks. It was a park well-tended, but in an area that couldn't afford anything better.

The crunch of gravel beneath my tires seemed unusually loud over the whirr of the car heater, and I turned my head in surprise when a gust of wind had the seesaw moving up and down on its own, giving a ride to what I imagined to be the ghosts of two invisible children. My skin chilled and my flesh pebbled as I got the sense I wasn't alone.

But it wasn't ghosts I had to worry about. It was flesh

and blood. Human. At least what was left of him. His skin was pale in the glare of my headlights, and now that I'd seen him I wondered how I ever could have missed him.

"Oh, God."

I made a hard left with the wheel and drove onto the playground, so the bright yellow of my headlights gave center stage to the man chained to the tree. His naked body was mangled and so bloody I couldn't pinpoint the mortal wound. Heavy chains wrapped around his chest—I got the impression they were there to hold him up instead of restraining him. His dark hair hung down and his hands were limp at his sides, though from the looks of his misshapen fingers, they would have been useless anyway.

I felt the initial rush of fear even as my training kicked in.

In a former life that seemed like an eternity ago, I'd been a medical doctor doing rounds in the ER at Augusta General. After my parents had died amidst lies and scandal, I'd had no choice but to pack up and move back to Bloody Mary and take over the family mortuary business. Mostly because it was damned hard to do rounds while the FBI was trying to question me about my parents' illegal activities. It didn't put patients at ease when they found out my parents had been using their funeral home to hide and transport smuggled goods. Sins of the fathers, and all that. Go figure.

Once I'd moved back home and taken over the business (or what was left of it), I'd somehow gotten roped into acting as coroner for the whole county. Fortunately, we didn't get a lot of suspicious deaths in this part of the country, unless you counted the serial killer who'd murdered three people last winter. Almost four.

I took a long look around the area and shoved my cell phone in my pocket before flinging the door of the

Suburban open and stepping to the ground. The piercing cold of a March wind slapped at my face and sliced through my long wool coat, past the threadbare lining and straight to my bones. I didn't bother with gloves. I stuck my hand inside my coat pocket and pulled out the small Beretta that had become like an appendage since my incident.

The wind blew the door of the Suburban shut almost before I could get out, and I looked around slowly, trying to see beyond the thick copse of trees and past the shadows that resembled grotesque pictures of my darkest nightmares.

Guilt was a vicious and cruel emotion. In the past I would have rushed straight to the victim, searching for that one last hope that he might have a chance for survival. But I'd learned the hard way that survival is something you have to fight for, and sometimes you have to be selfish when it comes down to your life or a stranger's.

I breathed out slowly and put the Beretta back in my pocket, focusing my full attention on the man. If I'd had my wits about me sooner, I would have realized at first glance that hope for his survival had run out a long time ago.

Whoever had done this to the man had made a mess out of him. It looked like his hands and feet had both been crushed, as well as his knees. There were small wounds all over his body, but most of the blood loss came from the area of his genitals. Someone had decided to castrate the victim and remove all signs of his manhood. Blood loss and shock would have been enough to kill him.

I fought the urge to start an examination. I didn't have my kit or any gloves, and technically I wasn't coroner since I'd taken leave after my own brush with death.

But something stirred inside me that I hadn't felt over the last few months. A spark of life. Of purpose. Lying in a hospital bed gave a person too much time to think—to question how much worth one really had. And I wanted this case. I wanted to keep my mind and my hands busy so I wouldn't think of other things.

I needed to call into the station and report the scene, but even the thought had my breath hitching and sweat trickling down my spine in cold rivulets. I wasn't sure I was ready to face them all. My friends. My acquaintances. My enemies. Being back in town would almost be as big news as the body. But mostly I wasn't ready to face Jack.

There wasn't a choice. The universe had decided it wasn't through with me yet, even though I'd started to wonder. I'd have to face everyone sooner or later, so I pulled the phone from my pocket and dialed before I could second-guess myself. "Dispatch," a woman answered.

"This is Dr. Graves. I've got a body."

CHAPTER TWO

I moved the Suburban and parked a little farther down the lane to let the official vehicles get through, and I sat there in the dark with my coat wrapped around me until the first squad car arrived on the scene. I'd only had to wait about fifteen minutes. That had given him long enough to roll out of bed, throw on some clothes, and make the drive across town. Not bad.

The eerie yellow of headlights cast shadows around the sharp bends in the road as the black-and-white came to a stop in front of me. He hadn't bothered with flashing lights or blaring sirens. It wasn't Jack's way. He was a good cop. Too good of a cop to be stuck in Bloody Mary writing traffic tickets and settling petty disputes. But he had his own demons to deal with, and I knew better than anyone that sometimes you just needed a refuge. Maybe

I'd never really understood the demons he faced until now.

My lungs started to burn and I realized I was holding my breath. It had been twelve weeks and four days since I'd last seen him, and I hadn't even been able to say goodbye or tell him I was running away for a while. I couldn't face him. Not after everything we'd been through.

He'd have understood my reasons for leaving, and he would have helped me pack and make the arrangements with more ease than I'd managed on my own, but things were off between us. Jack Lawson was the best friend I'd ever had. He was still the best friend I'd ever had. But something had changed in those days before my near death, and we looked at each other differently now. Or maybe it was just me looking at the world differently, and it wasn't him at all. That would almost be worse somehow.

Jack's deputies wouldn't be far behind him, and part of me wanted to stay hidden inside the Suburban until there was a crowd surrounding us. That cowardice was the exact reason I pushed open the door and put my shaky legs on the ground. I left my headlights on and leaned against the hood of the car, trying to look casual, and then I watched as he reached into his cruiser and grabbed two silver travel mugs of steaming coffee and a high-powered flashlight.

I tried to look at him as a stranger would. We'd been in and out of each other's pockets our whole lives, and it was easy to take someone for granted when they'd always just been there. I'd forgotten how big he was—six feet five inches of solid muscle—broad shoulders and lean hips. He'd been SWAT in DC before he'd taken the job of sheriff here, and he still kept the same rigorous exercise regimen.

His dark hair was cropped close to his head and a five o'clock shadow peppered with the occasional hint of silver covered his face, though he was only a couple years over thirty. His buckskin-colored shearling coat was unzipped so I caught a glimpse of his green flannel shirt and shoulder holster as he walked with easy strides toward me. He was backlit by the glare of his own headlights, and even in the shadows, he made an impressive picture. He'd always been too handsome for his own good, but I'd never thought of him as such until recently. He'd just been Jack.

"Your hair's longer," he said, handing me one of the mugs.

I tried not to flinch at his nearness. I'd had a little trouble with people being close enough to touch me after my incident. He pretended not to notice when I scooted over a little, and he leaned against the hood next to me as we sipped our coffee in silence for a few minutes.

I'd never been one to think on my appearance overly much. I'd spent too many years in med school and living on an hour's worth of sleep to have time to care. But part of me wondered what exactly Jack saw when he looked at me. I hardly ever wore makeup, but I had good skin, nice gray eyes, and high cheekbones I'd inherited from someone. I was mostly average in every way—average height, average weight, average breasts. Not like the women he was normally attracted to. And I knew, because I'd seen legions on his arm over the years.

"I wasn't expecting you until sometime tomorrow," he said, breaking the silence.

I looked up sharply so my gaze rested on his chin. I didn't quite have the courage to look him in the eye yet. I hadn't told anyone of my plans to leave my parents' cabin in the Poconos. I hadn't even decided I was leaving myself until twelve hours ago. Some of the things I'd found out about my parents while staying there hadn't made it a place of rest. And the FBI had managed to find me there as well. Almost two years after their drive over a cliff and there were still unanswered questions. I knew some of the answers now. But I wished I didn't.

Jack's fingers barely touched my chin and he tilted my face up until our eyes met. I tried not to jerk out of his grasp, but it was difficult. The only thing that kept me still was the fact that I knew he'd be hurt if he knew I no longer liked to be touched. Even by him.

"You didn't think you were staying up there all alone without someone keeping tabs on you, did you? What if you'd gotten into trouble or had a relapse?" He raised a brow in question and I could see the censure in his gaze, letting me know without words that he'd been hurt I'd left without saying goodbye.

I could have gotten angry at his overprotective nature, but I just didn't have it in me. I think somewhere inside, I'd known he wouldn't just let me go away on my own. He'd probably alerted every cop in the area to keep an eye out for me. I turned my head away, and he dropped his hand so it curled back around his cup.

"Backup will be here soon," I said to change the subject.

"We've got a few minutes. I told them to take their time."

"Why would you tell them that?"

He dug into his coat pocket and pulled out a pair of thin latex gloves. He held them up in front of my face so I had no choice but to stare at them.

"Because I thought I'd need the extra time talking you into coming back," he said, smiling sheepishly. "But I can tell by the gleam in your eye I might have overestimated my time frame a bit. I've got a job opening for a new coroner.

What do you say, Dr. Graves? The hours are lousy and the pay is even worse."

He could have said a million different things on this first meeting after being separated for so long. He could have asked how I was doing or feeling. He could have pulled me into his arms and tried to rekindle that brief moment before my incident where the sparks between us had almost turned to flame. But he just stood beside me like he had my whole life—solid and undemanding—and gave me the one thing he knew I needed more than anything else.

Tears clouded my eyes and I blinked them away rapidly before I made both of us more uncomfortable than we already were.

"It just so happens I'm between jobs at the moment," I said, taking the gloves.

Our hands met briefly and I jerked, but I felt the heat of his touch all the way to my toes. I pushed the feeling away and busied myself with putting on the gloves so I wouldn't have to look at him and see that he hadn't felt it the same as I had.

"Show me the body," he said, putting on his own gloves and turning on the flashlight. "Walk me through it."

I discarded my long coat and tossed it back in the Suburban, forcing myself to deal with the cold. I couldn't afford to ruin a perfectly good coat with blood and other unmentionable things that no dry cleaner would ever be able to get out. My finances were in dire straits at the moment, and a new coat wasn't on the list of necessities.

"I'd pulled over to the side of the road just there," I said, pointing to the skid marks my tires had made when I'd slammed on the brakes after my brief panic attack. Jack didn't say anything, but I noticed the corners of his mouth tighten as he looked at the evidence of my loss of control.

"I didn't see the body until I pulled back out onto the road and my headlights glanced off him. Scared the hell out of me," I admitted. "Playgrounds are creepy at night."

"I've always thought so," he agreed. "Worse than a graveyard."

We walked up to the tree where the victim was chained, and I felt my strength slowly seep back into my bones. My thoughts were sharper now and the cold had been forgotten. Only the victim existed for me now.

"I don't recognize him right off," Jack said, positioning the flashlight on the ground so it acted as a spotlight.

"Me either, but I'm not sure his own mother would recognize him at this point."

A couple of squad cars pulled in behind us, and the deputies were quiet as they got their equipment out of the car. Jack had managed to amass a competent police force over the few years he'd been sheriff, drawing in men who'd served in larger cities and who had specialized in different areas. I recognized Marcus Colburn immediately. The same man who'd tried to kill me had murdered Colburn's pregnant lover. I was actually surprised to see he'd stuck around, especially since his lover had still been married to one of Bloody Mary's council members during their affair. The situation had been messy at best.

I was willing to bet Jack had gone to bat for him. Colburn had worked as a cop in Bloody Mary for ten years, but before that he'd worked violent crimes in Arlington, so his experience was invaluable to a small force like ours. He helped train the younger cops when something like this came up. Jack nodded to his detectives and we took a couple of steps back so they could start documenting and securing the scene.

"Let's get spotlights set up," Jack called out. "It's too

dark for Dr. Graves to examine the body. I want everything, no matter how inconsequential, tagged and documented."

A smattering of yes sirs filled the air, and everyone got to work. Lights flashed from the cameras, but I hardly noticed as I tried to take in everything I could with a quick visual examination.

"He's been tortured," I said, thinking aloud. "All his fingers are broken. Toes too. Not just broken, but crushed to pulp, as if a hammer had been taken to them. I don't suppose the Mob has infiltrated King George County."

"Not unless you mean the mob that hit the Piggly Wiggly during that snowstorm in January. I had to arrest three women fighting over the last package of toilet paper."

"The fun never stops," I said dryly. "I'll be able to give you more specifics once I get him on the table. It looks like he's been out here a little while. Or at least dead a while. He's already out of the stages of rigor, so I'd put death between thirty to forty-eight hours ago."

"I'll check and see if we've had any missing persons reports," Jack said, using his cell phone to call into the station and make the request to whoever had drawn the short straw to stay behind.

"Someone was supremely pissed at this guy," I said once he'd hung up. "His kneecaps are shattered. The blood on the lower half of his body makes it too difficult to see his other wounds, but he was definitely alive when they relieved him of his genitalia. There's too much blood for it to be otherwise."

Jack winced. "Would that be the cause of death?"

"Most likely. If they didn't clamp the arteries and stop the blood loss, he would have gone into shock and eventually bled out. They knew what they were doing with the torture. Nothing was so severe it would have killed him."

"What about that?" Jack asked, pointing to the black spot just below the hipbone that was crusted with dried blood.

I leaned in closer to get a better look, and I hissed out a breath between my teeth. It didn't matter. The smell of charred flesh burned the inside of my nose, and I knew I'd be smelling it in my nightmares.

"He was branded," I said almost to myself, following the unusual pattern with the tip of my gloved finger. I looked up at Jack and saw the anger smoldering behind his dark eyes. "I'll take an imprint of it once I get back to the lab so we have a better picture, but it looks like someone left us a calling card."

"That'll certainly make them easier to find," he said.

"I need a camera and a recorder," I said. "I'll need to collect some samples here because of the shape the body is in. I don't want to pick up anything extra or leave something important behind."

Jack walked back to his cruiser and he popped the trunk, producing both items.

"Record for me," I said, snapping a few close-ups of each area of the body. "The victim is male, between the age of twenty-five and forty-five. Brown hair, brown eyes. Small scar on chin not congruent with current wounds. Probably sustained from childhood. He's a big son of a bitch. Probably your height, Jack. But he's got a little more weight on him. Ligature marks are visible around ankles and wrist. Slight abrasions around the neck and a few rope fibers. Bones in the hands and feet are crushed. So is the patella and surrounding bones in the knees. Blood loss looks like COD as there are no other mortal wounds that I can see. Unless he had a heart attack from the stress first."

I took a step back and looked at what was left of what

had been a man. There was pity inside of me, but also anger. I knew what real cruelty was, but it never ceased to amaze me that there were those who found joy in inflicting it.

I scrubbed my hands over my face and felt the tightness in my chest. "This can't be real. What are we dealing with here?"

He held up a finger as his phone signaled a text message. "I don't know what we're dealing with, but maybe I know who. Reverend Thomas called into the station last night and said he thought Reverend Oglesby was missing—he's the new priest the church brought in a few months ago," he explained when he saw my blank look. "But the officer who took the call didn't put much credence in it because Oglesby was supposed to be on vacation for a week visiting his father.'"

I looked at the man strapped to the tree. A man who could have been someone chosen by the church to do no harm and help whomever he could. A man who was supposed to be gentle and kind.

"He deserves better than this," I said.

"Everyone deserves better than this. Let's cut the chains and get him the hell down from there."

CHAPTER THREE

An audible gasp could be heard from a few of the younger cops as the victim was lowered to the ground onto the clean plastic tarp I'd spread out. I didn't see any new faces in the crowd. Everyone on scene had been through the horrors of seeing death up close. But this death was something more. It was more personal. More violent.

"Go ahead and leave him facedown and get the shots of

his back," I said to Colburn. I took my own pictures, documenting each laceration.

"You got it, Doc." He didn't spare me a look, but he said, "It's good to have you back."

I nodded and realized that was as good of a homecoming as any.

"Is the perimeter up?" Jack asked Colburn.

"It's up. I've got Lewis and Martinez following the trail with flashlights, but we'll wait until daylight before we start combing the area. Nothing but woods and dead leaves around here," Colburn said, looking around. "We'll be lucky to find anything more than beer cans and used condoms. The teenagers like to come out here to party."

"Yeah, well, at least they're using condoms," Jack said. "We've only got another hour until sunrise. Call in and get whatever you need for the search. Let's use three-man teams to keep the traffic down and switch them out every two hours so eyes can stay fresh. I don't want any screw-ups on our end."

"You got it, boss." Colburn moved off to give instructions to the others.

"Colburn seems to be doing okay," I said quietly. We both kneeled down next to the body, and I looked at the flayed skin on the victim's back.

"He's doing better," Jack said. "I thought I was going to lose him there for a while. He wanted to quit. Started drinking a bit. But he straightened himself out pretty quick. Colburn's a fighter. After I convinced him to stay on, the city council decided they needed to get involved and boot him out of town. They wanted to make a law keeping known fornicators from representing the city."

I felt a laugh bubble up at the absurdity, but held it back in deference to the body in front of me. It was easy to forget that not everyone around us had seen as much death as Jack and I had in our lifetimes. Relieving stress and tension through laughter in the face of violence was commonplace with cops and morticians. But these guys were young and unseasoned, and they just wouldn't understand. They'd go home and make love to their wives or girlfriends in a frenzy of lust, or they'd find their tempers flare throughout the day while that adrenaline from fear and the thankfulness for just being alive tried to surface.

I scratched at my cheek with the back of my hand so no one could see me smile. "Did you tell them half of the city employees would have to resign? Including their sheriff?" I asked.

He turned to look at me, and I hadn't realized how close we were. Close enough that our whispers could only be heard by each other. Close enough that I could see how the black of his pupil melded into the dark brown of his iris. My lungs burned and I reminded myself to breathe. In and out. Inhale and exhale. Conscious breathing had become a habit over the past months. I knew all too well what it felt like when the air stopped. When the oxygen didn't fill the lungs, no matter how hard you tried.

"You're going to hurt my feelings, Jaye. Haven't you heard? I'm a changed man." His smile was pure sin. A little apologetic and a lot determined as he seemed to stare straight through me—to the part of me that was scared down to my toes to examine what it was he was trying to say—to the part of me that wanted him to touch me even though the thought of contact with anyone made me physically ill.

I cleared my throat and broke eye contact, not knowing what was going to come out of my mouth until the words formed. "You can tell the victim's been flogged with something other than a belt or regular whip. The jagged tears in the flesh indicate some kind of metal might have been sewn into the device." The words were stiff, as if I'd been giving a lecture instead of talking to the one person in the world who knew me best.

I felt more than heard Jack's sigh. His soft exhalation of breath fluttered the hair around my face, but I tucked the loose strands ruthlessly behind my ear, pretending to be completely absorbed in my analysis. It was a lie. My brain had stopped functioning the moment those dark eyes had dared to show me something a little more than I was ready for.

Maybe I'd come back home too soon after all.

Jack didn't wait for me to get it together. He asked the obvious question. "What the hell is that white stuff?"

I shook free of wherever it was I'd mentally travelled and saw what he was talking about. Little white granules, no bigger than grains of sand, coated the edges of the ragged flesh.

"Salt," I said hoarsely. "Whoever did this poured salt in his wounds."

Jack pulled a small black case from the inside of his coat pocket, no larger than one of those useless evening bags women were forever carrying around, and opened it to reveal an assortment of useful tools. I had one just like it, but I'd tossed it in a box to be given away to Salvation Army before I'd left town.

"Nice tools," I said, recognizing the set as my own.

"A recent acquisition. I probably even know where you could get a set for yourself."

"That could be useful, considering my new job."

He pulled out what looked like a dentist's pick and handed it to me. I scraped gently at the salt until I had enough to put in one of the plastic Ziploc bags rolled up inside the case. I passed the tool back and grabbed the tweezers so I could get the rope fibers I'd seen around his neck.

"Where are his clothes?" I asked. "Where's his car?"

"I've got a uniform checking out Reverend Oglesby's house, but he lives over in King George Proper, so it'll be a while before he reports in."

"Hand over a couple of the larger bags," I said. "Most of his fingernails have been removed, but he still has the thumbnail. Maybe he's got some skin under there."

I bagged both of the victim's hands, though the task was more unpleasant than I remembered. It might've had to do with his hands feeling like sacks of uncooked rice floating in gelatin instead of skin and bones.

"Do you want to turn him?" Jack asked.

"No. I've got everything I need for now. I can do more at the lab. There's not much more for me to do here."

Jack nodded and called out to a couple of his men. "Let's get him loaded up."

My lab was in the basement of Graves Funeral Home, and it had all the necessary equipment for preparing the flesh for burial or making serious Y-cuts for autopsies. It hadn't been used in a while, and I was nervous about seeing it after being gone for so long. Would the smell of embalming fluid and antiseptic have dissipated over time, or would that lingering scent of death still hover in the air?

I stood and let a couple of the uniforms maneuver the victim into a body bag. An ambulance had arrived on scene at some point and one of the EMTs had wheeled over a gurney. The back of my Suburban was stacked high with suitcases and a few boxes of my parents' belongings I'd found in a closet at the cabin. Once I got rid of the boxes and burned everything inside of them, I'd have a lot more room for bodies in the back. Until then, I had to make do with the ambulance.

"I hope you're not expecting a fast turnaround on this, Jack. That guy has so many wounds I'm not even sure where to start. And—" I took a shaky breath before I could finish. "I just don't know how long it will take me."

I braced myself for his touch. He watched me closely as the weight of his hand landed softly on my shoulder. The longer we stood there like that—after I reminded myself to keep breathing—the more I started to relax. The tension crept out of my body and I kept my eyes steady on his. The strength and support of his touch never wavered. I could trust Jack with my life. I already had.

"Just take it one step at a time. I'll be with you every step of the way on this one. At least until you get settled back in."

I'd normally be annoyed at having someone underfoot while I was working. Especially Jack. He'd never been comfortable watching the things I had to do down in the funeral home basement, and I didn't need to lose focus if I was going to do this job well. But I was grateful he'd taken the choice away from me. The last thing I wanted was to be alone with a John Doe and my own thoughts.

I'd never been truly comfortable with the dead. Or at least I'd never been before. Maybe things would be different now that I'd almost been one of them.

"We need to verify ID so I can notify next of kin. I'll get his prints and make a comparison from inside his house."

We walked back to our cars and I pulled off the latex gloves with a snap before shoving them in the back pocket of my jeans. I opened the door of the Suburban and propped my foot on the sideboard before turning back to Jack. The sun was just beginning to lighten the sky to a pearl gray. Colburn and the other cops would be starting a search of the area before too much longer, and I'd be back on familiar ground, keeping company with the dead and wondering why I wasn't one of them.

Life was a funny thing. A finite thing. And you never realized how finite until you'd crossed that line from life to death and then back again.

"Jaye?" Jack asked. By the look on his face, it was obvious he'd tried to get my attention more than once.

"Sorry." I scrubbed a hand over my face and then massaged the back of my neck. "I guess I'm just tired. It's been a long night."

"You should grab a couple of hours' sleep before you start on the body. He'll keep until we verify the ID. Where are you staying?"

I turned my head and watched the light spread through the trees as the sun rose. I didn't want to face the question Jack was really asking. Whether or not I'd be able to stay alone in the house I'd almost died in.

"I'll stay at the funeral home for now. I've decided to put the house on the market."

It was the first time I'd said it out loud, but immediately I felt as if a giant weight had been lifted off my chest. I was selling the home that I'd grown up in. A crumbling legacy I was supposed to pass on to my nonexistent children. And I was okay with it.

"You know I've always got an extra room if you need it," Jack said, tucking my hair behind my ear. "And I'll even promise not to sneak in and take pictures while you're in the shower and sell them for a quarter in the lunchroom."

I narrowed my eyes, remembering the moment well. Third grade hadn't started off well for me. My dating life had pretty much been ruined by the time I was eight. "You still owe me eleven dollars for that stunt."

"You can send me the bill. Or I can buy you a cheeseburger."

"That's a damned expensive cheeseburger. I think a cheeseburger and a beer will cover the tab."

He smiled—a flash of white teeth and just the hint of one dimple that had driven one of his high school girlfriends to rhapsodize over it in haiku on the bathroom wall of the stadium.

"Works for me," he said. "It's a date."

Jack was already inside his cruiser by the time I got my mouth closed. I had a feeling I'd just been manipulated by a master.

"Dead body," I reminded myself. "Priorities." I slammed the car door shut and started the engine. Inhale and exhale. Breathing gave me something to think about the whole way back to the funeral home. I was alive. That was the only thing that mattered. Everything else could wait.

Continue the Story: BUY NOW
A Dirty Shame

ABOUT THE AUTHOR

Liliana Hart is a *New York Times*, *USA Today*, and Publisher's Weekly bestselling author of more than eighty titles. After starting her first novel her freshman year of college, she immediately became addicted to writing and knew she'd found what she was meant to do with her life. She has no idea why she majored in music.

Since publishing in June 2011, Liliana has sold more than ten-million books. All three of her series have made multiple appearances on the New York Times list.

Liliana can almost always be found at her computer writing, hauling five kids to various activities, or spending time with her husband. She calls Texas home.

If you enjoyed reading this book, I would appreciate it if you would help others enjoy this book too.

Recommend it. Please help other readers find this book by recommending it to friends, readers' groups and discussion boards.

Review it. Please tell other readers why you liked this book by reviewing.

Connect with me online:
www.lilianahart.com

JJ Graves Mystery Series

Dirty Little Secrets

A Dirty Shame

Dirty Rotten Scoundrel

Down and Dirty

Dirty Deeds

Dirty Laundry

Dirty Money

A Dirty Job

Dirty Devil

Playing Dirty

Dirty Martini

Dirty Dozen

Dirty Minds

Dirty Weekend

Dirty Looks

Dirty Liars

Dirty Valentine

Addison Holmes Mystery Series

Whiskey Rebellion

Whiskey Sour

Whiskey For Breakfast

Whiskey, You're The Devil

Whiskey on the Rocks

Whiskey Tango Foxtrot

Whiskey and Gunpowder

Whiskey Lullaby

The Scarlet Chronicles

Bouncing Betty

Hand Grenade Helen

Front Line Francis

The Harley and Davidson Mystery Series

The Farmer's Slaughter

A Tisket a Casket

I Saw Mommy Killing Santa Claus

Get Your Murder Running

Deceased and Desist

Malice in Wonderland

Tequila Mockingbird

Gone With the Sin

Grime and Punishment

Blazing Rattles

A Salt and Battery

Curl Up and Dye

First Comes Death Then Comes Marriage

Box Set 1

Box Set 2

Box Set 3

The Gravediggers

The Darkest Corner

Gone to Dust

Say No More

Laurel Valley

Tribulation Pass

Redemption Road

Midnight Clear

Forgiveness River

Atonement Trail